Robert B. Parker's

The
Bitterest Pill

THE SPENSER NOVELS

Robert B. Parker's Old Black Magic
  (by Ace Atkins)

Robert B. Parker's Little White Lies
  (by Ace Atkins)

Robert B. Parker's Slow Burn
  (by Ace Atkins)

Robert B. Parker's Kickback
  (by Ace Atkins)

Robert B. Parker's Cheap Shot
  (by Ace Atkins)

Silent Night
  (with Helen Brann)

Robert B. Parker's Wonderland
  (by Ace Atkins)

Robert B. Parker's Lullaby
  (by Ace Atkins)

Sixkill

Painted Ladies

The Professional

Rough Weather

Now & Then

Hundred-Dollar Baby

School Days

Cold Service

Bad Business

Back Story

Widow's Walk

Potshot

Hugger Mugger

Hush Money

Sudden Mischief

Small Vices

Chance

Thin Air

Walking Shadow

Paper Doll

Double Deuce

Pastime

Stardust

Playmates

Crimson Joy

Pale Kings and Princes

Taming a Sea-Horse

A Catskill Eagle

Valediction

The Widening Gyre

Ceremony

A Savage Place

Early Autumn

Looking for Rachel Wallace

The Judas Goat

Promised Land

Mortal Stakes

God Save the Child

The Godwulf Manuscript

THE JESSE STONE NOVELS

Robert B. Parker's Colorblind
  (by Reed Farrel Coleman)

Robert B. Parker's The Hangman's
  Sonnet
  (by Reed Farrel Coleman)

Robert B. Parker's Debt to Pay
  (by Reed Farrel Coleman)

Robert B. Parker's The Devil Wins
  (by Reed Farrel Coleman)

Robert B. Parker's Blind Spot
  (by Reed Farrel Coleman)

Robert B. Parker's Damned If You Do
  (by Michael Brandman)

The Bitterest Pill

A JESSE STONE NOVEL

Reed Farrel Coleman

G. P. PUTNAM'S SONS   New York

PUTNAM
— EST. 1838 —

G. P. PUTNAM'S SONS
Publishers Since 1838
An imprint of Penguin Random House LLC
penguinrandomhouse.com

Library of Congress Cataloging-in-Publication Data

Names: Coleman, Reed Farrel, author.
Title: Robert B. Parker's The bitterest pill / Reed Farrel Coleman.
Description: New York : G. P. Putnam's Sons, 2019. |
Series: A Jesse Stone novel; 18
Identifiers: LCCN 2019011107 | ISBN 9780399574979 (hardcover) |
ISBN 9780399574986 (epub)
Subjects: LCSH: Stone, Jesse (Fictitious character)—Fiction. |
Police chiefs—Fiction. | BISAC: FICTION /
Mystery & Detective / General. |
FICTION / Suspense. | GSAFD: Suspense fiction. | Mystery fiction.
Classification: LCC PS3553.O47445 R638 2019 | DDC 813/.54—dc23
LC record available at https://lccn.loc.gov/2019011107
p.   cm.

Printed in the United States of America
1   3   5   7   9   10   8   6   4   2

BOOK DESIGN BY KATY RIEGEL

IN MEMORY OF PHILIP KERR

Fifty years and a trillion dollars after we declared the war on drugs, drugs are now more prevalent, cheaper, and more potent than ever before. If this is victory, I'd hate to see defeat.

Don Winslow

Robert B. Parker's

The
Bitterest Pill

One

The world had changed. Paradise had changed. Most significantly for Jesse Stone, his life had been turned upside down. He was a man wise enough to know that life comes with only one guarantee—that it would someday end. As a Robbery Homicide detective for the LAPD and as the longtime chief of the Paradise PD he had seen ample proof of that solitary guarantee written in blood, in wrecked bodies, and in grief. It wasn't that long ago that his fiancée's murder had given Jesse all the proof he would ever need. He remembered an old Hebrew proverb about how people's planning for their futures was God's favorite joke. Still, at an age when most men were steeped in haunting regrets of what could have been and what they might have done, Jesse had been given the most unexpected gift a loner like him could receive. Cole Slayton, Jesse's son, had arrived in town just as Paradise was shedding its old skin and transforming itself into the place Jesse was currently seeing through the night-darkened windows of his latest Ford Explorer.

This end-of-shift drive through the streets had long been a ritual of his. A way to make sure things were intact and that the citizenry could rest well. Still, Jesse didn't fool easily, and he was especially keen not to fool himself. He understood that Paradise was a different place than the village he'd come to all those years ago as a man looking for a fresh start. In those days, Boston, less than twenty miles south, seemed a million miles away, a world apart. Nowadays, Paradise, though not yet quite a suburb of Boston, felt much closer than ever before. As the big city's influence crept north, it brought a new vibe to town that not all the natives of Paradise appreciated. Jesse had mixed feelings about the shift. Although he had long ago settled into the seaside rhythms of the town, Jesse enjoyed the new urban vitality, the pace and diversity Boston's encroachment brought with it. But as Vinnie Morris had once warned him, as Boston would come toward Paradise, so, too, would come its sins. Vinnie had phrased it less artfully.

Jesse had already seen some evidence of that. Nothing dramatic. No crime wave, per se. Yet there was an increase in urban gang activity in Paradise and the surrounding towns. Graffiti and vandalism had been on the rise, as had auto theft. Drug arrests had also ticked up and the local cops now carried naloxone with them. None of the crime particularly scared Jesse. He didn't overreact, as the mayor and town selectmen had, nor had he turned a blind eye. He had prepared his cops as best he could. He had joined with the chiefs of the nearby towns and the state police to work out strategies to deal with the changes in the criminal landscape.

At the moment, though, it was Paradise's recent past and hatred, humanity's most ancient foible, that occupied Jesse's thoughts. He was driving by the empty lot where the old meetinghouse once stood. Several months ago, a white supremacist group had come to town with mad dreams of sparking a national race war. They hadn't achieved their twisted goals but had left a trail of destruction in their wake. One of the casualties was the old meetinghouse, a building that had once been used as a safe haven for runaway slaves along the route of the Underground Railroad. It had been blown to bits by a powerful bomb blast. Jesse shook his head because more than the old building had been lost. Paradise had been shaken to its core. Families had been terrorized, several people were dead, and he'd been forced to fire Alisha, his best young cop. There was a big debate going on about whether to faithfully reconstruct the old place, create some sort of memorial, or let the past go altogether and sell the lot for new construction. Those were decisions above Jesse's paygrade, and he was glad of it. What concerned Jesse was the notion that the destruction might be an omen of things to come, that the world's ills, not only Boston's, were headed for Paradise's doorstep. He turned the corner, leaving the ghost of the old meetinghouse in his rearview mirror.

These ritual drives through Paradise had once been a prelude to a different and more personal ritual—drinking. Even now, remembering the steps of the ritual, he got a jolt. Throwing off his blue PPD hat and jacket as he entered his house, tossing the mail down on the counter, approaching the bar, twisting the cap off the smooth, rectangular bottle of Johnny Walker Black Label, pouring the beautiful amber fluid over ice, the gentle snap and crackle as the room-temperature scotch hit the ice, the clinking of the ice as he swirled the glass, sniffing the perfectly blended grace notes from the charred oak barrel in which it had aged, lifting the glass to toast Ozzie Smith, and then, finally, the first magic sip. He could almost feel it, the warmth at the back of his throat, spreading down to his belly, through his body, and reaching his fingertips. But Jesse hadn't had a drink in many months because his new nightly ritual involved sharing a room with fellow alcoholics who gave one another the strength they needed to stay sober.

At first he had driven to meetings down in Boston at an old Episcopal church. That's where he'd met Bill, his sponsor. But making that trek several times a week had become unwieldly and impractical. Besides, Jesse's drinking hadn't ever been much of a secret to begin with. The only people in Paradise who didn't know about Jesse's struggles with the bottle were transplants from Boston and children under ten years of age. So he'd recently begun attending AA meetings in and around Paradise. He was headed to a meeting in Salem when the phone rang. The Explorer's display showed the call was from the Paradise Police Department. He pressed the button on the steering wheel.

"What?"

It was Molly working the desk. "There's trouble, Jesse."

"There's always trouble. What kind?"

"The worst kind."

"Tell me."

"Patricia Mackey just found her daughter . . . unresponsive. She's dead, Jesse."

"Jeez, no." Jesse pulled over. "Where? How?"

"In her bedroom. And, Jesse . . ."

"Uh-huh."

"Suit's there now. He found drug paraphernalia."

"On my way."

Jesse had been a cop for too long to think anything connected with drugs was an anomaly. And suddenly Vinnie Morris's warning rang loud as cathedral chimes in Jesse's ears.

Two

A thousand things went through Jesse's mind as he pulled up to the Mackey place, and not a single damn one of them was any good. He didn't need to be a parent to know that a mother and father should never have to put a kid in the ground before them. Not ever, not for any reason. Drugs, disease, a careless accident, what did that matter? And now that Jesse *was* a father, Heather Mackey's death cut even deeper than it had during all the previous cases he had worked involving the death of a child. He hadn't been there to watch Cole grow up, hadn't known the boy existed until a few months ago, but that was beside the point. The bond he felt couldn't have been stronger had he been in the delivery room to hear Cole cry or to watch him open his eyes for the first time.

Suit Simpson greeted Jesse at the curb.

"Hey, Jesse. Molly told me you were on your way."

"I see the ME's men are here." Jesse pointed at the van. "ME inside?"

Suit nodded. "Peter, too. He's working the scene."

"Did you use the naloxone?"

Suit shook his head. "Too late. She was already gone. Such a waste. She was a pretty girl."

"Death doesn't care about pretty or ugly. Only we do."

"I guess."

"Is Selectman Mackey home yet?" Jesse asked.

Suit shook his head. "He's down in Boston, lobbying for highway funds. Mrs. Mackey was having trouble getting him on the phone until a few minutes ago."

"Talk to me, Suit."

"The kid's in her bed—" Something caught in Suit's throat. He might've been an ex–football star and a man to have on your side in a fight, but he was a gentle soul. That used to concern Jesse. Not anymore. He had taken a bullet in a gun battle with Mr. Peepers, and when the shit hit the fan at the old meetinghouse, Suit had walked back into the building to lead the people inside to safety. He'd done it knowing there was a good chance he would die in the process.

"It's okay, Suit." Jesse patted him on the shoulder. "I'll see for myself."

The Mackey house was at the foot of the Bluffs. It was a new-to-look-old Cape Cod–style home with a detached two-car garage and vinyl siding meant to look like overlapping cedar shingles. There was a bluestone path leading up to two granite steps and a welcoming red door. The red door didn't feel very welcoming just then. Jesse let himself in, Suit trailing behind. The second he entered, he heard Patti Mackey's robotic, disembodied voice. Jesse stopped to listen.

Sue, yes, it's about Heather . . . No, she's not in some kind of trouble. She's dead . . . You heard me right . . . I'm numb, Sue. I shouldn't be, but I'm numb. Is something wrong with me?

In Jesse's experience, Patti's denial and distance weren't unusual.

She was in a kind of self-protective shock, but it would wear off, and when it did . . . He had seen that dam break too many times for his liking. Once was too many. And there was no getting used to it. It was difficult to witness, so much so that he had always been glad not to be a parent. Now that layer of insulation had been stripped away. He followed Patti's voice into the kitchen. Jesse had known the family for a long time and thought he should talk to Patti before going to see to Heather. It was a sad fact of his job that Heather was beyond his help.

Patti was a gray-eyed beauty with fair, freckled skin and long auburn hair. She could have passed as Heather's much older sister. She was placing the phone back in its cradle when Jesse reached the kitchen. She turned to him—eyes empty, face blank. The moment she saw him the walls came down and she crumbled into Jesse's arms. The tears came in a rush, soaking Jesse's uniform shirt. Her body clenched and every part of her shook. But it was the sobbing that haunted him. The shrieks coming out of her were feral, primeval. He knew it was moot to try and say something soothing, so he stroked her hair and waited for the first wave to subside. When it did, Jesse sat her down at the kitchen table and held her hand.

"What happened, Patti?"

But it was too soon. She couldn't even form words.

"Officer Simpson," Jesse called for Suit.

When Suit stepped into the kitchen, Jesse told him to sit with Patti and to get her anything she needed. As he left the kitchen he leaned over and whispered in Suit's ear, "Just keep her out of the bedroom."

The ME was to the side of the bed, jotting notes down on a pad. Peter Perkins stopped what he was doing and held up a plastic evidence bag containing a syringe.

"Found it at the side of the bed."

Jesse nodded, distracted. He was focused on the dead girl on the bed, dressed in a too-big Red Sox T-shirt. If not for the two other men present and the odors in the air that came with sudden death, Jesse might have been able to fool himself that the girl was simply in a deep sleep. He supposed she was, really, in the deepest of sleeps.

The ME stopped his scribbling and turned to Jesse.

"She's been dead about two hours. No obvious signs of foul play. We'll have to wait for the tox screen," he said, "but it's a heroin OD. I'd make book on it."

Jesse asked, "Was she a heavy user."

"I don't think so. No track marks. Only one fresh puncture wound that I can see." The ME took the girl's left arm, turned it up, and pointed to the inner fold of her forearm. "See it?" He didn't wait for Jesse to answer. "I'll know more when I get her on the table. I'm done with her, if you want to have a look. I'll send my crew in to bag her." He looked back at the girl. "A shame."

Three

A *shame.* Sometimes all it took were a few syllables to sum things up. But those two simple syllables were also woefully inadequate, because while they summed things up, they would also leave a thousand questions in their wake. The questions for Jesse and his department would be the easy ones: When did the girl start using? Who was her supplier? Could they catch him or her? Could they make a case against him or her? The questions for Heather's parents would be the harder ones: How could we not have known? What didn't we see? How had we failed her? And some of those questions, maybe all of them, would go forever unanswered. Jesse liked the Mackeys and hoped the questions wouldn't tear Patti and Steve apart, but Jesse had seen the scenario play out a hundred times before. The parents would need someone to blame and, short on answers or with answers they didn't like, they tended to blame each other.

If there was anything that experience had taught Jesse about drug cases, it was that they didn't happen in a vacuum. Where there was one case there would be others. It wasn't a matter of if, but a matter of how many, how severe, and when. The tough thing was that to limit the damage, Jesse was going to have to ask some of those hard questions of the Mackeys, and he was going to have to do it sooner rather than later. Sooner being now.

He found Patti Mackey in the kitchen, Suit standing silent guard over her. Jesse was glad for Suit being on hand. One of Suit Simpson's remarkable qualities was that in spite of his size, he was almost always a comforting presence. People just felt at ease around him. The same could not be said of Jesse. He supposed he was a little softer around the edges these days, now that he was a father and he was no longer drinking, but there was something about his self-containment that didn't allow people to feel the kind of comfort around him that they felt around Molly or Suit. He was okay with that. Those qualities helped make him good at his job. Still, there were times, especially times like these, when he wished he had the knack.

Patti was no longer wailing. No, she sat at the kitchen table nearly as still as her daughter had been. Jesse had seen it before; the stages of initial shock play out in only a very few minutes. First the disbelief, then the flood of pain that came with the realization that your child was lost to you forever and that there would never be another unblemished day for the rest of your life, then the momentary self-imposed numbness. It wouldn't last long. Her zombielike state certainly wouldn't survive the ME's guys toting the body bag down the stairs.

"Patti," Jesse said, "I've got to ask you some questions."

"What?" Her answer seemed to come from somewhere very far away. Her red-rimmed eyes unblinking. Her expression excruciatingly blank.

Suit made to leave the room, but Jesse waved for him to stay, to sit at the table beside Patti Mackey. When Suit had taken a seat, Jesse began again.

"Have you noticed anything strange about Heather's behavior lately?"

Patti blinked, fighting herself. "Different? No, not different. She just seemed a little more tired lately. Her stomach was giving her trouble, but she's a—was a junior and, you know, looking at colleges and taking tests and all. Now, I don't—"

Jesse knew it was unkind, but he had to keep Patti in the moment and not let her drift into the dark place just yet.

"Patti, Patti, come on. I need you to focus. So she was a little depressed and tense with all the junior-year stuff. Anything else? Was she keeping new company? Any new boyfriends? Girlfriends?"

But it was no good. Patti still wasn't ready. The strength she was using to hold it together was blocking her ability to think deeply or to feel anything. And then, when the front door opened and the ME's men came in, one holding a folded body bag under his arm, Patti exploded out of her chair and charged at them, clawing. "No! No! You leave her be. That's her room. This is her house. You don't touch her. You don't touch her!"

By then Suit had caught up to her and was holding her back, clamping his arms around her. She put up a hell of a struggle, and Jesse could see that Suit needed to exert some strength to hold Patti back. Even as Suit held her, Patti screamed and kicked at the air.

"You leave my daughter be. You leave her be! You're not going to put her in a plastic bag, not my girl, not my beautiful little girl."

But that was exactly what those men were going to do. They were going to place the body of Heather Mackey, cheerleader, popular high school junior, in a liquid-proof bag and pull a zipper up over her cooling, lifeless face. Then they were going to carry her down the stairs and out the front door, place her remains in the back of a van, and drive her to the morgue.

Jesse nodded for Suit to take Patti Mackey into the living room.

"You keep her there no matter what," he said.

Jesse watched the sad procession. The ME first, his men behind him, and Peter Perkins in the rear.

"Chief," the ME said as he passed, head down. "I will have the results for you as soon as I can, but the tox screen is going to take a while."

"Do what you can, Doc."

Peter Perkins stopped and stood in front of Jesse.

"What is it, Peter?"

"I heard an author interviewed on TV last week. He said we declared the war on drugs fifty years ago. We've spent a trillion dollars fighting it, but that drugs were cheaper, more available, and more potent now than ever before. Said that if that was victory, he'd hate to see defeat."

Jesse didn't say anything to that. What was there to say?

Four

Jesse's son, Cole, was sitting on the sofa, watching TV and drinking a beer. Cole and Jesse weren't yet at the hugging, *I-love-you-Dad-I-love-you-Son* stage. It was unclear if they would ever get there. Still, there were moments when Jesse found himself staring at his son in awe. They didn't look much alike, though Cole was tall, athletic, and sturdily built. Cole's looks, as they say in the South, favored his mother. They shared more in terms of personality. Tonight it wasn't awe in Jesse's eyes, but fear. Fear, not for himself. It was the kind of fear he only ever experienced over people he cared for.

"Hey," Cole said, not turning away from the screen.

"Hey, yourself."

"It's kind of late for you to be coming back from a meeting. Did you go down to Boston?"

"No meeting tonight. Work."

Cole finally looked away from the screen and at the face of the father he had known for only the last several months. Regardless of the short time, Cole had learned to read Jesse's grudging expressions. He recognized some of them from the mirror.

"Something bad, huh?"

"Seventeen-year-old girl ODed."

Cole shook his head, sipped his beer. "Heroin?"

"Yeah. What made you say that?"

"Say what?"

"Heroin."

Cole shrugged. "I don't know. Was she a junkie?"

Jesse shook his head. "The ME doesn't think so. Why?"

"Back home—I mean, before I left L.A.—there was a lot of that. Inexperienced users ODing. The cartels are cutting their shit with—"

"Fentanyl," Jesse said, finishing his son's sentence.

"Why do you do that, ask me a question you know the answer to?" Cole asked, angry.

Angry was Cole's default setting. He'd shown up in Paradise while Jesse was still in rehab, and everyone who'd crossed paths with him, before or since, couldn't miss the massive chip on his shoulder. Although Cole had accepted the truth of what had happened between his mother, Celine, and Jesse all those years ago in L.A., he hadn't been able to shed the resentment and sense of abandonment he'd harbored against his father. Given his struggles with alcohol, Jesse understood how that worked. As Dix said, "Recognition is the easy part. Just because you know the truth of things, it's impossible to snap your fingers and make patterns of behavior disappear. Logic and reason are woeful in the face of deeply ingrained feelings."

"Sorry," Jesse said. "I was thinking aloud."

"No problem." Cole went back to the TV.

Jesse stared at the beer in his son's hand. Most nights, it didn't bother Jesse. He had been sober for months now, and drinking had never been a social activity for him anyway. Oh, he drank socially.

Drunks didn't need much prompting. For Jesse, though, it was his drinking alone that did him in in the end. He had been around a lot of drinkers and lots of drinks since returning from rehab. It was hard at first, but easier all the time. And when sobriety got challenging, he'd just call Bill, his sponsor, and Bill would talk him down. Tonight, though, that beer looked pretty damn appealing.

Cole noticed Jesse staring at the beer.

"Sorry."

Before Jesse could stop him, Cole clicked off the TV, went into the kitchen, and poured the beer down the sink. They might not have worked everything out and they still tiptoed around each other, but Cole didn't want Jesse to go back down the rabbit hole. He wasn't sure what he wanted from Jesse. He wasn't sure when he came to town and he wasn't sure now. At least he had a better idea of what he didn't want. He hadn't come all the way across the country to watch alcohol destroy his father the same way cancer had destroyed his mother. Although Cole still lugged that chip around on his shoulder, he was smart enough to know that parent issues were more easily resolved with a living parent than with a dead one.

Cole poured the rest of the six-pack down the sink as well.

Jesse said, "Thanks."

"Whatever. I'm going to bed. Daisy's got me in early tomorrow doing some prep work in the kitchen."

"You going to work there for the rest of your life?"

Cole laughed, but it wasn't a happy laugh. "You got me the job there. You embarrassed?"

"Never."

Cole tried not to smile at that, but failed. "No, I'm not going to work there the rest of my life. Who knows, maybe I'll become a cop."

Jesse knew Cole was trying to get a rise out of him. "Uh-huh" was all Jesse said to that. "Good night."

The beer might have been down the drain, but the smell of it hung in the air. Jesse filled the kitchen sink up with soap and water, then let it drain out. When that was done, he dialed Bill's number and talked about why it was better to be sober. As they talked, Jesse kept picturing Heather Mackey's lifeless body in her bed surrounded by her little-girl stuffed animals.

Five

Jesse's first stop the next morning was at the high
school, and his first stop at the school was the office of
Principal Virginia Wester. His initial instinct had been to go back
to Heather's family to see if Selectman Mackey had anything to
add to whatever little his wife had said the night before. But since
the case wasn't murder, at least not in the way he understood it, or
an apparent suicide, Jesse figured to circle back to them in a day
or two. Right now they would be caught in the throes of grief and
in the midst of doing something no parent ever wants to do, let
alone think of. People sometimes plan for their own deaths—buy
plots, draw up wills, sign DNRs, choose readings, etc.—but he
had never known anyone who planned for the death of a child. No,
he would leave the Mackeys alone for the moment.

Freda Bellows had been a fixture at Paradise High School for
nearly forty years. In her time as a secretary to the principal, she'd
seen five principals come and go. Freda, a thin, jovial woman,
loved being around the kids and was the unofficial institutional
memory of the school. A few years beyond retirement age, she had
been granted special dispensation by the Board of Selectmen,

allowing her to stay on until she decided she'd had enough. That was one of the things Jesse liked about small-town life. In L.A. or Boston, exceptions were frowned upon. *If you do it for one, you'll have to do it for all, and you know how much that will cost.* In a place like Paradise, exceptions weren't seen as calamities but as kindnesses. Freda usually had a smile for everyone. Not today. Today she greeted Jesse with red eyes and choked-back sobs.

"Oh my God, Jesse," she said, a mascaraed tear running down her wrinkled cheek. "I can't believe it. Heather was such a wonderful girl. Was it an overdose? They're saying it was heroin. I can't believe it. Was it heroin?"

He put a hand on her shoulder. "I can't talk about it, Freda."

"I'm sorry, Jesse. I understand. Would you like to see Principal Wester?"

"I would."

"Go on in."

Virginia Wester was the new principal at Paradise High. Ten years Jesse's junior, she was a handsome woman with dark blond hair, worn-penny eyes, and a perpetually stern look on her face. Smiles seemed to come at a premium for her. That was fine with Jesse. He wasn't exactly a backslapping good-time Charlie himself. They had never exchanged much more than perfunctory hellos at town functions, but that was about to change.

"Chief Stone," Wester said, extending her hand as she came around the desk to greet him. "Sad day. Terrible day."

He shook her hand. "Jesse."

"Excuse me." She was confused.

"Please call me Jesse."

She didn't know what to do with that. Should she smile and make a similar gesture or tell him that such informality made her uncomfortable. She opted for saying "Please, sit."

He sat.

"Obviously, we've heard the news," she said. "We would like to help any way we can, but unless I know what we're—"

"I usually can't comment on an ongoing investigation, but if it will help you to help me . . . It looks like a heroin overdose. We don't have the tox screen back yet, but we're pretty sure."

Wester leaned forward, a strained expression on her face. "Was it—I mean, did she—"

He understood. "It doesn't appear to be a suicide, no. There was no note, but there isn't always a note. I suppose one of the reasons I'm here is to find out if I'm misreading the situation. How was she doing in school?"

Wester tapped a key on her keyboard. "I thought someone from the police would be here today, so I already had her records for you to look at." She turned the screen to face Jesse. "As you can see, Heather's grades had been gradually slumping over the last several marking periods. It began midyear last year and continued. She'd gone from an A-plus student to a B-minus kid, on her way to C."

"Did you intercede? Were her parents aware?"

Wester gathered herself, her whole body seeming to clench. "Even in a relatively small town, a principal can't afford to know every student's progress or—"

Jesse understood her defensiveness. "I'm sorry. I didn't mean that to sound like an accusation or criticism. I'm just trying to get a picture of Heather. I didn't want to bother her parents today. I'm sure you understand."

"No need to apologize, Chief Stone. I overreacted. Heather's death, any student's death, is very upsetting. It has me on edge and causes a ripple effect among the students. Kids think they know how to handle these things, but they don't. We'll have grief counselors in, but most of the kids won't seek their help. As far as

Heather goes, I think you would have more luck speaking with her individual teachers. I've had Freda print out a list of her teachers from this term and the last term of her sophomore year. She will also supply you with their schedules."

Jesse stood, shook her hand again, and turned to go.

"Chief Stone . . . Jesse."

He looked back. "Yeah."

"Anything else I can do . . ."

"Of course." He shook his head.

As Jesse walked out to speak to Freda and get the things Wester had promised, he reminded himself how he was far more familiar with premature death, in all its forms, than most people would ever be or want to be. Death, even when it's expected, even when it comes as a relief, shakes people up. The death of someone so young really does a number on people because it reminds them of just how vulnerable and fragile all life is.

Six

Fifty-five, balding, and seemingly reticent, Harvey Spiegel had been Heather Mackey's math teacher. Jesse thought Spiegel wouldn't be as in tune with his students as Heather's other instructors, maybe because he was older and a math teacher. But he was the one with the available free period, so Jesse found himself in the teachers' lounge, which at that hour was pretty busy, with a few late arrivals grabbing coffee and hurrying out to their classrooms. Some, the ones who probably hadn't yet heard about Heather, gave Jesse curious looks as they left. *What's that all about?*

"What can I do for you, Chief?"

Jesse had a lot of people to talk to and didn't want to go through the whole "Call me Jesse" routine with everyone. Besides enjoying the informality of first names, Jesse often used the "Call me Jesse" thing to throw people off balance. He had no reason to believe he needed to throw Harvey Spiegel a curve.

"Heather Mackey," Jesse said, leaving it at that.

"Lovely girl." Spiegel wrinkled his nose, reminding Jesse of a rabbit. "A shame."

"You had her last term for"—Jesse referred to the papers Freda had given him—"calc and this term for trig."

He did that thing with his nose again, then he leaned forward and spoke in a whisper. "I did. Chief, I heard that drugs were involved. Is that the case?"

Jesse nodded.

"It wasn't . . . suicide, was it?" The word stuck in his throat.

Jesse answered with a question of his own. "You're the second person to ask me that. Why would you say that?" There was nothing accusatory in Jesse's tone.

"Do you have children, Chief?"

"A son," he said, still unused to the sound of his voice uttering those words.

"Well, then you know. I've got two of my own and I've worked with teenagers for thirty years now. Some of them look like adults, but I assure you they are not. They lack experience and are often ill-equipped to modulate the strength of their emotions. They're also feeling things like romantic love and jealousy as they have never felt before, and sometimes they just aren't able to make sense of what it is they are going through. Sometimes they make stupid choices, very stupid choices, from which there is no return."

Jesse must have looked dumbfounded, and Spiegel laughed a sad laugh at him.

"Surprised by a math teacher's expounding on the emotional lives of teenagers?"

"Uh-huh."

"I'm a guidance counselor as well. I imagine I'll have more kids coming to see me today than usual. Unfortunately, it's the ones that don't come who probably need my help more than the ones who do. The ones who come have a self-awareness of their feelings. The ones who don't come worry me. But I'm going on. Sorry, Chief."

"But about Heather, Mr. Spiegel, was there anything specific about her that caused you to mention suicide?"

Spiegel rubbed his chin as he considered the question. "Nothing I could put my finger on, no. Her grades were steadily declining." He shrugged. "But that's not always a sign of anything negative, per se. Maybe she was in love or having trouble at home. Some of these kids are very bright and have been able to navigate their way through school without working at it. That's less easily done when it comes to subjects like calculus or trigonometry. It wasn't as if she was in danger of failing."

"How about her attendance?"

"I'd have to check on that, Chief. Is it important?"

"At this stage, I don't know what's important or what isn't. Let me ask you, Mr. Spiegel, are you aware of a drug problem in the school?"

Jesse could see Spiegel was troubled by the question and working hard to formulate an answer.

"There have always been some problems with drugs," the math teacher said. "I'm afraid drugs have become another one of the minefields these kids must navigate, along with all the emotional baggage that comes with near-adulthood. It's been this way since I taught my first year. The drugs change, but their presence has not."

"That was a very good, politically correct non-answer," Jesse said.

Spiegel did the nose thing again and laughed. "I was afraid you were going to ask me to supply the names of specific students. I would be uncomfortable with that. It would ruin any credibility I have with the kids if word got out."

"But there are kids with drug problems."

Although Jesse and he were the only two people left in the lounge, Spiegel looked around him to make sure no one was watching or within earshot. He didn't answer the question with words but nodded yes.

Jesse didn't stop there. "Heroin?"

Spiegel nodded again, hesitated, then added, "Pills, too."

Jesse thought about pushing some more but decided he might need Spiegel as an ally if the investigation turned anything up. He didn't want to alienate him by making him any more ill at ease than he already was. Instead he tried a different tack.

"Do you know who Heather hung out with?"

"Sorry, Chief. Heather was my student, but she wasn't assigned to me as her guidance counselor. You'd have to speak to her home-room teacher and some of the others about that."

Jesse stood, shook Spiegel's hand. "Thank you. You've been helpful."

"Have I? I don't see how."

Jesse winked. "It's only important for me to know how."

Seven

Jesse wasn't often surprised, but he was when he entered the art room. There was a teacher's name listed, Clay Mckee. That wasn't who he found there seated on the desktop, facing the class. The students were busily rendering the colorful bowl of waxed fruit on a table by the classroom window.

"Maryglenn, what are you doing here?" Jesse said in a whisper, tapping her lightly on the shoulder.

She lit up at the sight of him. Maryglenn was a local painter who lived in a loft above an old carriage-house-cum warehouse next to Gayle Pembroke's art gallery. Maryglenn and Jesse had met a few months back during all the trouble with the white supremacist group that had tried to start a revolution in Paradise.

"Keep working," she said to the class. "Remember, this isn't about getting it right. It's about getting it." She turned back to Jesse. "Let's take it into the hall."

Maryglenn, dressed as she always was in a loose-fitting black T-shirt, black jeans, and running shoes, all rainbow-speckled in paint, led him through the door. When the door closed behind

them, Maryglenn grabbed Jesse's right hand. It was the most intimate thing that had ever passed between them.

"You're here about the dead girl, Heather," she said.

"I am, but that doesn't explain—"

"—what I'm doing here. No, it doesn't." She let go of Jesse's
hand. "I'm a certified art teacher and I've been subbing for the last
year. It's a way for me to get some partial health benefits and I like
working with the kids. There's never enough funding for the cre-
ative parts of education. These days it's worse than ever. All the
money gets poured into math and sciences." She caught herself.
"Sorry, Jesse, I'll get down off the soapbox now."

"No problem. So you're subbing today."

"Actually, I'm not." She smiled a crooked, disarming smile at
him. "The regular art teacher, Mr. Mckee, took an unexpected
medical leave of absence for the term and I was asked to take his
spot." She shrugged. "I figured, why not? The money is good and I
get full benefits and—"

"—you like working with the kids."

Her smile was in full force now. There had always been a low
spark of attraction between them, though neither was the other's
type. Jesse was usually drawn to beautiful blondes like his ex-wife,
Jenn, and his late fiancée, Diana. Women who were always conscious of their appearance. Maryglenn wasn't like that at all. Besides her paint-splattered black uniform, she had let gray creep
into her short-cut brown hair. She didn't always wear makeup and
didn't spend much time at the gym. But she always seemed so
comfortable with who and what she was that Jesse kind of liked it.
There was no pretense about her. And for Maryglenn, an artist
and onetime social activist, the idea of being attracted to a cop,
even one as ruggedly handsome as Jesse, would normally have
been an anathema. But there they were, smiling at each other.

"Did you know her, Heather Mackey?" Jesse asked, breaking the spell.

"A little, I guess. She had some talent for line drawing. Would you like to see her work?"

"Maybe later. What I need to know is did she display any outward signs of depression or . . . I don't know."

"I do. One thing that art class does is give kids a place to express themselves freely . . . well, as freely as they can in this setting." She nodded at the classroom door. "I know it's unlikely the next Basquiat or Weiwei is sitting in there. I just try to let them let go and express themselves without judging too harshly. They get enough of that in their other classes."

"And."

"Look, Jesse, I don't really know these kids like a teacher who had seen them develop over a period of a few years, but, yes, Heather seemed . . . distracted and a little withdrawn. At least, that's how she seemed to me. Yet she produced good work, so I'm not sure it means anything."

"Did she have any close friends in class?"

Maryglenn thought about it before answering. "Megan Alford, Darby Cole, and Rich Amitrano."

"Are they in that class now?"

She nodded at the door. "Those are sophomores, Jesse. Heather's class doesn't meet today, and my guess is they wouldn't be in class today anyway."

"You're right."

"I should get back in there."

"Okay," Jesse said. "Thank you."

"I don't know how much of a help I was."

"You were honest."

She looked perplexed. "What does that mean, 'I was honest'?"

"I was a Robbery Homicide detective in L.A. for ten years. People are hesitant to speak ill of the dead, especially when the dead person is a pretty young girl. People don't mean to hurt investigations. I know it's not malicious. Anything but. Still, I can't tell you how many times we were hindered in getting to what really happened. Sometimes, by the time the truth came out, it was too late. There was this one case I worked, a housewife, a very attractive former actress, rich husband, two kids. Her body was found in a shallow grave in the hills. She'd been raped, her body brutalized. But to hear it from her friends and family, she was a saint. No one is a saint, Maryglenn. After weeks of getting nowhere, her best friend came to us and told us that the victim had been working as a high-end escort two afternoons a week because the whole Suzy Homemaker thing was boring her to distraction. The case is still unsolved. If the friend had told us the truth to begin with, we might have caught the guy. When we asked the friend why she hadn't come forward sooner, she said she didn't want a woman she loved to be remembered as a whore."

Maryglenn nodded in understanding. With her hand on the door, she turned back to Jesse. "I'm not very good at this . . . but can I buy you a drink sometime? I mean, we've been dancing around each other for months and I don't enjoy this kind of dancing very much."

"Not a drink. I don't drink anymore." He felt both silly and proud saying it.

That didn't scare her off. "Dinner, then?"

"I'd like that."

"What's your phone number?"

He smiled. "Nine-one-one."

"A wiseass, huh?"

He handed her one of his cards with his cell number on it. "If you hear anything else about Heather, anything at all, call me about that, too."

After Maryglenn disappeared behind the classroom door, he stood in the hallway, remembering that long-ago case and how hesitant people were to speak ill of the dead.

Eight

When he got off the bus and saw the police chief's Explorer parked out in front of Paradise High, he decided to ditch school and walked around to the athletic field. He'd heard about Heather but hadn't expected the cops to already be sniffing around. He knew they would come eventually. *Where else are the cops going to look?*

Under the stands of the stadium, he punched in a number on that week's new burner phone. New phone every week. Sometimes two a week. That was how it worked. No one picked up on the other end and he didn't leave a message. That was how that worked, too. In five minutes or so, he'd get a call back.

In the meantime, he lit a cigarette, blew the smoke out the other side of his mouth, and peered through the empty spaces in the aluminum bleachers. One gangly, pimply-faced kid in a PARADISE HIGH PANTHERS JV track shirt ran a slow lap around the dark red track. As he puffed on his cigarette, watching the kid's awkward, loping strides, he remembered his own freshman year, sitting in the stands under which he now stood. He recalled those stupid pep rallies. He hated all that school spirit, rah-rah bullshit. But he didn't hate looking at the cheerleaders and the majorettes. No, sir, he did not. He remembered the first time he ever saw Heather, how he thought she was looking up into the stands right at him, but when she waved, he realized she was waving at the junior sitting directly behind him. He heard the junior lean over to his buddies and call him a dork. *As if any girl as hot as Heather Mackey would wave at him. Doofus.* Still hurt him to think about it. He crushed the cigarette out beneath his foot.

Heather had always been nice to him, though. She wasn't stuck up or anything, in spite of being so pretty and popular. He'd always wanted to ask her out but never had the nerve. He knew he wasn't bad-looking and that he wasn't anything like his freshman self, the doofus in the stands. The braces were gone, his voice was deep, no longer cracking when he got worked up. He'd grown into his body and a few girls in school had said he had the most beautiful deep blue eyes.

He remembered the first day of school this year, when she came over to him at his locker. She put her hand on his wrist and stared right into his eyes. And he thought, stupidly, *Is she looking at me or the guy behind me?* But she wasn't. She couldn't have been, because the only thing behind him was his open locker door. Then she brushed her hand across his cheek.

"We can't talk now," Heather had said, "but can we meet later, after school? Please."

His heart was beating so hard, the sound of blood rushing so loudly in his ears, he wasn't sure he'd heard her right. And then, when he convinced himself that he had heard her, he could barely speak.

"Sure." It was the best he could manage.

"Where?"

"Come to my house," she said. "My folks won't be home and we can, you know, talk."

Even as he was celebrating in his head, fighting the desire to click his heels and scream or to run to tell his friends that he would finally be with the girl he had dreamed about since his first day as a freshman, he knew there was something in her eyes besides wanting him. It was a very different kind of wanting. He knew what it was. Since he'd begun working for Arakel, he'd seen it many times: desperation. With some of the others, he hadn't even bothered to pretend and had slept with them. He had never forced himself on anyone or made it conditional. He had learned at an earlier age than most what desperation does to people. But with Heather, he wanted to pretend it was something more than that.

He remembered that when he came to her house that day, she was dressed in a black satin blouse and stilettos, nothing else. Remembered the feel of the satin. She didn't waste time getting him upstairs and into her room. And he was grateful that when she moaned she didn't make it feel like a transaction. Heather hadn't asked for anything until he was sore and coming out of her shower, mopping his hair with a bath towel. The truth was, he had hated washing the scent of her off him. She was everything he had ever fantasized about her and more. Still, he knew what was coming. He couldn't bear to hear her ask. Instead, he placed a small vial of pills on her nightstand. When she started to speak, he kissed her.

"Shhh," he said, when she tried to speak again. "But I do need the money."

That wasn't a problem.

As he left, she grabbed his hand. "I wanted to be with you," she said. "This wasn't about . . . you know. At least not all of it. We can do it again. I loved the way you tasted and how you felt inside me."

He had never gone back to her bedroom. If she hadn't said that last thing, he might have. But once she said it, there was no pretending. He'd felt dirty about it ever since.

When the phone rang in his pocket, he realized he was crying and that he would never see her again. He could never let her pretend to like him. He picked up.

"Kid, are you all right? What is wrong?"

"I'm good. I just got a cold."

"Why do you call?"

"One of my, um, clients . . . she died last night."

There was a long, loud silence on the line. Then, "Who?"

"A girl from my school."

"What were you giving to her?"

"Talcum powder."

"The cheap powder or the expensive?" Arakel asked.

"The cheap shit." He lied but didn't know what else to say. The truth was Heather had asked for the strongest stuff he had. She'd promised to be careful and to dose it out wisely. He was stupid to do as she asked, but when it came to Heather, he could never think straight. Now she was dead. He'd figure something out to cover his ass. Maybe he'd blame it on wrong packaging or say she stole the stronger stuff out of his stash. For now, he was just buying time.

"Okay, kid. You must remember, the good talcum is only for the very wet. Stay on low profile for a few days. Give people only what is necessary for staying dry. No more than that."

"I understand."

"Today, get a new phone."

The line went dead and he went back to crying.

Nine

By one that afternoon, Jesse had spoken to all the teachers on the list except for Heather's cheerleading coach, Brandy Lawton. He figured he would catch up with her eventually or just put in a call to her. Some of the teachers he did speak to said they had noticed the same things about Heather Mackey that Maryglenn had alluded to, that she had seemed withdrawn and distracted. But others hadn't noticed any change at all. *Oh, not at all, Chief. Heather was still the enthusiastic, intelligent young woman I have always known her to be.* They were all very troubled by her death, some so much that they broke down during the conversations. And they all mentioned Heather's circle of friends: Megan, Darby, and Richie.

As he rode back to the station, the ringing of his phone interrupted the Terry Jester song coming out of his speakers.

"Jesse?"

"Who else you think is answering the phone in my car, Molly?"

"Jesse, I'm curious. Do you have any of the bats from when you played ball?"

"I do. Why?"

"I'd like to borrow one to smack you over the head."

"Fair enough," he said. "What's up?"

"The ME called. He's released the body to the family. The tox screen isn't back, but the state crime lab called him. There was enough of a sample in the hypo to test. COD is cardiac arrest due to an overdose of—"

"Heroin and fentanyl," he said.

"Why do I bother?"

"Because you love me."

She laughed. "No, that isn't it."

"Because if something happens to me, you get to be chief again."

"Bingo."

"You might want to remember that the next time you're tempted to smack me over the head with a Louisville Slugger."

"Point taken. So, Jesse, how did you know about—"

"ODs like Heather's are rampant. The stats are scary bad, Crane."

"I've seen them."

"Now they're not just stats anymore. Heather was one of ours."

Molly tried to talk, but Jesse could tell she was choked up. There'd been a lot of that today, and there promised to be more of it in the days to come.

"Fentanyl is fifty to a hundred times more powerful than heroin," Jesse said, giving Molly time to compose herself. "It kills even longtime addicts. Someone like Heather, a new user . . . She had no chance. Any word on the funeral arrangements?"

"That was the other thing I was calling about," Molly said, her voice less shaky. "Selectman Mackey's sister called and said since the body has been released, the viewing would be tomorrow night. Are you going?"

"We are, if your husband can spare you."

"He can spare me. What will I be there for?" Molly asked, though she suspected she already knew the answer.

"People are comfortable around you, Molly. You're a cop, but you're also part of the fabric of Paradise."

"So are you, Jesse. You even said it before. Heather was one of ours."

"That's how I feel, but it's not how I'm always perceived."

Molly couldn't argue with that. Small-town people are slow to trust outsiders, and she guessed that no matter how long Jesse had been police chief, no matter how many times he had proved himself and his loyalty, some folks would always see him as an outsider. And with all the downstaters moving in, the locals weren't exactly in an accepting frame of mind.

"I hope this is an isolated incident, Jesse."

"C'mon, Molly, you're too good a cop for hoping. You know how this works."

"I guess I hope it's not another high school kid."

"If it means anything, I hope so, too. But where did hoping ever get us?"

"You think we've got a drug problem in town?"

"Every town has a drug problem. What I don't want is a drug network operating in Paradise."

"A drug operation in Paradise?" Molly was skeptical.

"Heather got the hit somewhere."

"But we're such a small town. What have we got to offer to a drug operation?"

"Small towns have small police forces, and we've got proximity to Boston."

"I guess."

"I'm going to grab some lunch."

"At Daisy's?"

"Uh-huh. You want something?"

"How are things with you and Cole?"

"We've kind of settled into . . . I'm not sure. A kind of truce, I think. When I was in the hospital after the old meetinghouse explosion, I thought we had something. But he's still angry at me, even though he knows the truth of what happened between me and his mom."

"Then the problem is his, Jesse, not yours. Tough thing for a parent to not feel responsible for everything and every feeling your children have."

"Yeah. When did you get past it?"

"Never. I don't think good parents ever do."

"So you don't have all the answers, Molly?"

"Nope. I just have more of them than you do."

Ten

Daisy's was busy. That was kind of like saying the sky was blue. Paradise was a great town, but it wasn't blessed with myriad restaurant choices. The Gray Gull was okay, but the food was never more than passable. The food at the Lobster Claw was better, though still not Michelin-star material. Both the Gull and the Claw owed the majority of their business to well-run bars, their waterside locations, and a lack of serious competition. There were a few pubs in town, mostly in the Swap, where you could get a good burger, but if you wanted a good breakfast and a great lunch special, you had to go to Daisy's.

Since Cole had arrived in town and gotten a job at Daisy's, the frequency of Jesse's visits had increased from once or twice a week to three or four times a week. He sometimes still couldn't believe he had a son, and he so badly wanted it to work out between them that he had made a lot of missteps. Nothing he did worked. He paid either too much attention or not enough. Like he'd explained to Molly, he thought they'd turned a corner when they finally spoke about how Jesse had been involved with Cole's mother, but that understanding had seemed to evaporate. Some progress had been made, just not enough. The thing of it was, Cole's existence shook Jesse's famous self-containment to its core, even more so than marrying Jenn or being with Diana ever had.

Daisy smirked at Jesse. She'd noticed his seemingly unquenchable hunger for her food.

"You keep showing up here like this, Jesse Stone, and people will say we're in love," she said, pouring him some coffee.

He smiled. "Would that be so bad?"

"I'm not your type. Besides, they'll take my lesbian membership card away."

"We can't have that. Let the kid wait on me."

She raised her eyebrow at that. "I would, but he's not here. Took today off. Didn't he tell you?"

"Tell me? Tell me what?"

Daisy cleared her throat, made some fidgety movements, and excused herself. "I'll be back in a minute to get your order."

That's odd, Jesse thought. Daisy was one of the toughest, most forthright, and least tactful people he'd ever known. It wasn't like her to be so uncomfortable around him or to dance around a subject, any subject. He shrugged. He was hungry and already had enough on his mind, if not on his lunch plate.

Studying the menu, Jesse became aware of someone standing near his booth, and he began to recite his order. "I'll have a Cobb salad, no bleu cheese." He held the menu up.

But when the menu wasn't snatched out of his hand, he raised his head and saw it wasn't Daisy standing there. It was Maryglenn McCombs. He handed her his menu.

"Twice in one day," she said. "May I sit?"

He smiled again, a different smile than the one he'd flashed at Daisy. "Might as well. You've already got a menu."

She sat across from him. "I suppose I can buy you that meal now."

"I love this place, but you'll have to do better than a Cobb salad at Daisy's."

She smiled. It was a shy, crooked smile. "I don't eat here very often. What's good?"

"Everything."

Maryglenn looked around her, worried she might be overheard. "Daisy, the owner, she's kind of intense."

"She sure can be. That's one way to put it."

"Last week when I came in, there was a good-looking young waiter here. Handsome, but sullen."

Jesse laughed. "My son, Cole."

"You have a son? But I thought—"

"I'm not married and I didn't know about Cole until a few months ago. Long story."

"Maybe you'll tell it to me over that dinner."

"And what's your story?"

Maryglenn's demeanor changed, the shy smile disappearing from her face as if a mask had been yanked off it. What was beneath the mask was unreadable to Jesse.

"I'm sorry," Jesse said. "Did I say something wrong?"

She deflected. "No, no. I'm just really hungry. Let's order." She looked at her cell phone. "I've got to get back to school."

Daisy came to get Jesse's order and twisted up her face at the sight of Maryglenn sitting across from him. Her expression was equally unreadable.

Maryglenn seemed not to notice, keeping her eyes on the menu. "I'll have the yogurt-and-granola fruit plate. And I'll have a Diet Coke with lemon." She handed the menu to Jesse.

"I'll have the Cobb salad, no bleu cheese, and coffee."

He gave the menu to Daisy and waited for her to give him grief about something or other, but all she did was walk away.

"I don't know what's up with her," Jesse said.

Maryglenn ignored that. "Any progress on Heather?"

"I can't really talk about current investigations. Sorry."

"I understand."

Jesse leaned forward. "If you had a kid in class you thought was in some kind of trouble, what would you do?"

She thought about it before answering. "Depends. I think I would probably speak to the student first. I'd ask what was going on, if there was something they wanted to talk about. We owe the kids at least that much. Then I might speak to the parents. But if it was something I thought was serious, I would definitely be obliged to tell Principal Wester and maybe Jane Phelan, the school psychologist."

"Thanks."

"Still not going to share?"

"Not yet."

She smiled. "'Yet.' You mean there's hope."

He smiled back but didn't say anything.

Eleven

The next day, Arakel waited until Mehdi came into the warehouse in the early afternoon to tell him about the girl's death. His first instinct had been to call on a secure phone, but there was nothing to be done yet and he had learned from experience that it was always better to tell Mehdi bad news in person. From the outside looking in, they were a strange pairing—an Armenian and an Iranian, a Christian and a Muslim. Still, their boss, a Bulgarian, had somehow known they would work well together. "Money," Nikola liked to say, "is making for people to coming together, not silly men who make bullshit lies in some stupid skyscraper in New York City. Money is making the UN a joke."

Arakel could not argue with his logic. He didn't know all the details of the supply chain, but he knew that people who would normally be blowing themselves up or shooting rockets or firing artillery at one another were all part of the syndicate, and that their little branch in the Boston area was relatively small and un-important. Unimportant to everyone but Nikola, Mehdi, and him-self. This was their market to grow. There was no other option. In this business, one did not file for Chapter Eleven if things went badly or Chapter Seven when things went completely belly-up. There was no protection from the people who carried your note in the drug trade, and certainly no help from the government. Arakel was all too well aware of how quickly a business could go under, and it had left a bitter-almond taste in his mouth. He and his brothers had owned a fine Oriental rug shop. The competition from cheap, machine-made rugs had squeezed them out. Sure, many people still had an eye for fine rugs, but not enough to keep them afloat.

For the moment, though, the rug shop was the last thing on his mind. No, he was worried about what Mehdi would want to do about the dead girl and the kid. Mehdi was a harder, tougher man than Arakel. He admired him for that and feared him for it, too. Arakel's wait was at an end when he heard the squeak and squeals from the old motor that raised and lowered the corrugated-steel bay door. Arakel turned and faced out the warehouse office window, but because of the lighting and the angle of the sun, Mehdi was in silhouette. It made him look more sinister than he was.

"Hello," Mehdi said, a smile on his face. "Things are good?" But he saw Arakel's face and knew the answer. His smile vanished and that hardness emerged from beneath it. "What is it?"

"We have a problem in Paradise," Arakel answered, trying and failing to keep his voice firm and steady.

"It would be too much to hope you are somehow being ironic."

"No, I am not being ironic."

"Do not make me guess at it, my friend."

But they weren't friends, not really. In fact, it was Mehdi's business that had hurried along the failure of Arakel's family's shop. They were more allies than friends, if that. Arakel knew that Mehdi had brought him into the business for his people skills.

Certainly not for his business acumen or his strategic thinking. He was all right with that. He liked people and was good with them. They trusted him and he had the knack for putting them at ease. All businesses, even the drug trade, needed people like him.

Arakel said, "The kid, I think he screwed up and gave a fentanyl load to a teenage girl."

"Dead?" He said it as if he was asking about a bug.

Arakel nodded. "Do you want to talk with the kid?"

Mehdi rubbed his cheeks as he thought. "Not yet. It would be a mistake to cause more trouble now. Make sure the kid has enough to maintain his clientele, but tell him not to bring in any new customers, not to either end of the business."

"I will make it so."

"Yes, you do that, my friend."

"I will call."

Mehdi turned, walked several steps away toward his office, turned back. "Remember, Arakel, it was you who brought this kid in. He is your responsibility."

"I am aware."

"Good. It is a good thing you are aware."

Mehdi looked long and hard at Arakel before heading into his office. It was not lost on Arakel that Mehdi was not smiling when he'd reminded him of his responsibilities.

Twelve

Jesse and Molly came in separate cars. They made sure not to get there too early, or as early as they might have if Heather's death were a homicide. Instead, they waited until the parking lot at the funeral home was nearly half full. Just inside the viewing room door, they were greeted by Selectman Tom Pluck, a big, burly guy from the Swap. He clapped Jesse on the back, shook Molly's hand, and, on behalf of the Mackeys, thanked them for being there. Another selectman, R. Jean Gray, nodded hello, the corner of his lips bending up in what passed for a smile. Unlike Tom Pluck, Gray lived on the Bluffs and was descended from one of the founders of Paradise. In his fifties, tall and lean, Gray was all old-school, with the patrician bearing that came with an Exeter, Dartmouth, and Wharton education. Not much ever seemed to disturb Selectman Gray, but he was clearly knocked off his pins by Heather's death. With a flick of his long right index finger, he indicated that he wanted a private word with Jesse. They strode into a dimly lit and empty viewing room.

"What can I do for you, Mr. Selectman?"

"This won't do, Chief Stone. It cannot stand. She was a lovely girl, and, if you were unaware, my goddaughter."

"I didn't know."

"As always, you are ever so effusive."

"I'm already looking into it."

"And?"

"And nothing yet. We know what killed her. Now we have to find out where she got it and why she was using it."

"Keep me apprised."

Jesse was tempted to say some things he would regret. Regardless of his time on the job here and in L.A., he could never stomach people who thought any one victim was more important than another simply because of their good looks, the color of their skin, or the size of their bank accounts. If Heather Mackey had been the daughter of a family from the Swap, Jesse wouldn't have cared any less. But Jesse, who had never enjoyed playing politics, had come a long way because of the things he had learned in AA. He couldn't control what R. Jean Gray thought, said, or believed, but he could control his own actions.

"I will let you know when we make progress, Mr. Selectman," Jesse said. When Gray walked away, Jesse said a few other choice things only he could hear.

MOLLY HAD GONE back into the viewing room, and Jesse saw she was visibly shaken. Two of Molly's girls were in college, but two were still at home and one of them was a junior like Heather. He wanted to throw his arm over her shoulders but was very careful to never show any form of intimacy with Molly in public. Her job was difficult enough without having to deal with whispers about the two of them. If there was one lesson about small-town life that

Jesse had learned early on, it was that rumors spread fast and there was no way to fight back.

The casket lid was raised, and all the ugly autopsy stitchery on her body was covered by her dress. Owing to his past, Jesse had always found those brutal stitches reminded him of the seams on a baseball. Not just then. He had been through this ritual hundreds of times in L.A. and here in Paradise, but this was the first time since Cole had come into his life. Jesse both hated and loved the ways in which Cole had changed him. It bothered him that he was having trouble distancing himself the way he had always been able to previously.

It occurred to him that he might already have been changed if he had seen Diana in her coffin, but her family blamed Jesse for her death and had banned him from attending. They weren't alone in their beliefs. Jesse blamed himself, too, and there was no way they could punish him any more than he punished himself. His guilt over her murder is what had driven him so deeply down into the bottle of Johnny Walker Black. When he finally hit the bottom he made the choice, with help from Tamara and Molly, to swim back up and climb out forever. Forever was a long way away. Jesse was concerned only with each individual day.

Molly wasn't the only person shaken by Heather's death. Obviously, her parents were devastated, and both were up front, both were crying. That wasn't exactly unexpected, but the death of a teenager sends shock waves through a community. It also reminded everyone of just how fragile and vulnerable they all were. There were lots of tears and stunned faces in the room and very little talking.

Jesse checked his watch. He had to get something to eat and get to a meeting. He tried not to skip too many days without a meeting if he could help it, and Heather's death had rattled him more than he wanted to admit. That used to be a prescription for a half-bottle of Black Label in the company of Ozzie Smith's poster. These days it meant a meeting and/or a call to Bill.

"Molly," he said in a whisper. "I've got to get to a meeting. Please give our condolences and tell the Mackeys I'll be by tomorrow to share what progress I've made with them."

"Not tomorrow, Jesse. Funeral is tomorrow. Besides, you haven't made any progress."

"The next day, then. I'm going to ask them questions, but I don't need them to be any more tense and upset than necessary."

"Got it. And you don't want them to prepare answers."

"Yeah, Molly, that, too."

OUTSIDE, JESSE SAW the parking lot was filling up, and many people passed by him on the way into the funeral home. Some stopped to shake his hand. Some nodded. Others waved. Most walked by him, zombielike, girding themselves for what they knew awaited them inside. When he got to his Explorer, he noticed a kid, a teenage boy by the parking-lot entrance, smoking the life out of a cigarette and pacing along the sidewalk under a streetlamp. There was something about the kid, dressed in black jeans, hundred-dollar red Nikes, and a black hoodie, that held Jesse's attention. He wasn't sure what it was, maybe the way the kid paced or his fidgety hand movements with the cigarette. He clicked the Explorer doors closed and walked toward the kid. He was on the short side, broad-shouldered, his dark blond hair spilling out of the left side of the hood. He was obviously distracted, lost in his own head, maybe, but whatever the reason, he didn't seem to notice Jesse's approach.

Jesse was no more than ten feet away when the kid looked up. Jesse could see in the kid's expression and in the reddened rims of his very deep blue eyes that he recognized him. The kid hesitated a beat, turned, and ran. Jesse wasn't sure what to make of that. It wasn't like a kid had never run away from a cop before, even an innocent kid. Still, there was something about the kid, and Jesse meant to find out what it was. He took off after the kid but lost him after he turned the corner.

Thirteen

After the meeting in the synagogue's basement in Salem, Jesse debated whether to head straight home or to do what he was about to do. Though he had put in his work at the meeting, the kid in front of the funeral home kept pushing his way into Jesse's consciousness. Some of Heather's friends were at the viewing, but he could speak to them tomorrow, after the funeral. The kid with the blue eyes had been crying, but if he was that close to Heather, why not go in like everyone else? During the coffee break at the meeting Jesse realized the kid outside the funeral home was acting guilty. The question was, guilty of what?

One of the things Jesse had learned early on in uniform was to watch the crowd that gathered at a crime scene. Some of them were there out of idle curiosity. Some were simply nosy. Some had no life and fed off the woes of others. But sometimes the guilty party was right there in the crowd, behind the sawhorses or the yellow tape, watching. They were curious, too. But their curiosity was neither idle nor innocent. Some, like arsonists, got off on seeing the results of their handiwork. They enjoyed watching the thing they'd lit up burn down. Others hung around to see what they could see and hear what they could hear about the investigation. It was amazing what you could learn at a crime scene if you knew how to observe one. Still others felt guilty for what they had done. They were the ones you saw in movies, the ones detectives said wanted to be caught. That was how the kid had seemed to Jesse, and that was why Jesse was standing next to the Pembroke Art Gallery and at the door of the adjoining warehouse.

He pressed the buzzer to Maryglenn's apartment/studio above the warehouse. He knew he could just as well have waited until morning and gone back to the high school, but there was something else on his mind besides the kid. Yesterday at lunch, both Daisy and Maryglenn had seemed odd. And when Jesse had asked about Maryglenn's past, she changed the subject. Through the big old door Jesse heard Maryglenn coming down the steps.

"Who is it?"

"Jesse Stone."

The locks clicked and the door pulled back. Jesse was surprised to see Maryglenn out of her usual artist's black pants and shirt. Instead she was wearing an elaborately patterned Asian robe made of a fabric that hung loosely off parts of her body and tightly to others.

"I'm not used to seeing you out of uniform," he said, smiling.

There was a brief moment of confusion on her face. Then, when she realized what Jesse meant, she smiled back at him.

"I do indeed own clothing that isn't black or splattered with paint. Do your boxers have your badge number embroidered into them?"

"How did you know?"

She shook her head at him. "What's up?"

"I need to talk. Can I come up?"

"This official business or some other kind of business?"

"A little of both, I guess."

"Come on. Lock the door behind you."

JESSE HAD BEEN in Maryglenn's place before, seen some of her work in progress, but those visits were during the madness surrounding the most violent incidents in Paradise since the assault on Stiles Island. This would be different on many levels. He knew it. She knew it, too. After scaling the stairs, Maryglenn pushed the door open and gestured for Jesse to go on in.

"Tea?" she asked, closing her apartment door behind him. "Coffee?"

"I just came from an AA meeting."

She seemed to understand. "Lots of coffee and cigarette breaks."

"Exactly. How do you know?"

There it was again, the smile disappearing just like at lunch. "Water?"

"Fine."

Maryglenn dug a plastic bottle out of her fridge and handed it to Jesse. Their hands touched as she gave it to him, and there was a spark there. They both felt it and they both knew it. But Jesse twisted off the cap and drank, while he stared out the windows on the backside of her studio and admired the view of the harbor area and of Stiles Island.

She cleared her throat. "Jesse, not that I'm unhappy you're here, but do you suppose you could fill me in on your reasons."

Jesse told her he had been at Heather's viewing. He described the kid pacing out front, smoking a cigarette. "He had dark blond hair and red-rimmed blue eyes."

"Oh," Maryglenn said, obviously disappointed, and plopped into a beat-up and scarred brown leather chair. "That's Chris G."

"G.?"

"Chris Grimm," she said. "Told me once the family had changed their name from Grimolkowicz."

Jesse laughed. "I could understand that. Tough name to handle. Tell me about him."

"Kind of a shy, intense kid. A lot going on inside his head."

"Did you ever see him together with Heather?"

"Not that I recall. Different types, Chris and Heather. She was a cheerleader and he was, you know, the brooding punk type. An outsider."

"You sound sympathetic to him."

"I was him, sort of," she said. "Artists aren't usually the popular kids with the rah-rah, sis-boom-bah ethic. You were a star athlete, so you probably knew lots of Heathers."

Jesse wanted to deny it, but lying wasn't his thing. "I did."

Then he did something he couldn't quite believe he was doing. He walked over to where Maryglenn was sitting, put down his bottled water, and lifted her out of the chair. He started to say something but just kissed her instead. The first kiss was a tentative one. He had to be certain he hadn't misread her. The way she kissed him back indicated that he hadn't, and things took their course from there.

Fourteen

Things happened so quickly after she kissed him back that neither of them thought to stop to make sure this was what they wanted. On some level, of course, it was. They knew that. *For the most part,* Jesse thought, opening his eyes in the darkness, *people do what they want.* He also understood there were many times a second's hesitation would save people a lot of heartache. He climbed out of Maryglenn's bed and stumbled his way into the bathroom. He tried not to make too much noise as he showered, but as he showered he got lost in thought.

The sex had been good, a little awkward for both of them, as it was bound to be with people unfamiliar with each other's body. And Jesse realized there was a small part of him that felt a twinge of guilt. Maryglenn was the first woman he'd been with since Diana. It was also true that Maryglenn was the first woman he'd been with since he was sober. Problem was, he couldn't be sure what their being together like this meant. Was this going to be a casual, itch-scratching kind of thing he'd shared with many women over the years, or was it something more? Less?

Maryglenn must have been reading his mind, because when she pulled the curtain back and joined him in the shower, she kissed him on the cheek, looked up at him, and said, "I really needed that, Jesse. I haven't been with a man in a very long time. But don't worry, I won't be showing up at your doorstep or cooking your pet rabbit on the stove. Let's just see how this goes."

"Works for me."

Then she handed him the soap and a washcloth and asked him to wash her. Ten minutes after that they were back in bed. Only this time, things were much less awkward and less fraught.

THE NEXT TIME he opened his eyes, the sun was just coming up over the edge of the Atlantic and its light making itself known to the sleepless and early risers. Maryglenn was already up, dressed, and at her easel, painting. She didn't look back, but said, "There's coffee waiting for when you get out of the shower."

Jesse climbed out of bed, walked over to her, put his arms around her shoulders. She kissed his forearm.

He said, "Thank you. Can we do this again?"

"I believe there's a dinner pending." She looked back at him and smiled. "We'll see about it after that. Go ahead and shower. I put some fresh towels on the rack."

Dressed in his clothing from the night before, drinking coffee, and admiring the sunrise, Jesse said some things he had meant to say to Maryglenn sometime before they got close to doing what they had spent the night doing, but the moment never seemed right. And before last night, they hadn't really spent much time together.

"Do you know about me?" he asked.

"I've heard some things."

"About Diana?"

She kept her focus on her work. "Your late fiancée? Yeah, I've heard."

"I haven't been with anyone since."

Maryglenn turned to look at him finally. "I don't know how to respond to that, Jesse. Am I supposed to be honored or something? Can't we just be happy about what it was?"

He laughed, realizing how she might take it that way. He wasn't very good with this part of relationships. Sharing his feelings—in spite of his time with Dix, in rehab, and at AA meetings—was still a challenge for him. Volunteering them at all was a new behavior. He guessed what Molly said about his self-containment was more accurate than he wanted to admit.

"That's not what I meant," he said. "I guess that was pretty clumsy of me."

She was back at her painting. "I take you at your word, Jesse. Look, I like you. I'm obviously intensely attracted to you, but I'm not on the hunt or anything."

"Got it."

She put her brush down, stood up, and came over to where he was standing. "Good, because I really enjoyed last night a lot."

He answered with a smile. "I've got to get going."

"Where to?"

"Home first to get back into what passes for my uniform, and then back to Paradise High. I need to look into this Chris G. kid."

"You think he knows something?"

Jesse nodded. "After that, Heather's funeral is this afternoon."

That knocked the smile off Maryglenn's face, which, in turn, reminded Jesse of the other thing he'd come to get answers about. But he didn't think this was the right moment to start asking about her past and the weirdness between her and Daisy, curious as he was. He leaned over, kissed her gently on the lips, and left, putting his coffee cup down on the kitchen counter as he went.

Fifteen

He stopped in at Daisy's on his way home, figuring he'd catch up with Cole. He figured wrong. And Daisy was as strange and evasive as she had been the other day. Jesse could be as patient as need be, but maybe because he was tired or because this involved his son, he didn't feel like being patient.

"Look, Daisy, what's going on with Cole?"

"Didn't you ask him when you saw him last night?" she asked, her smart-aleck expression and tone more in keeping with the Daisy Jesse knew and loved. "He is your son, last time I checked, and you do still live together."

"I wasn't home last night."

Daisy raised an eyebrow and gave him a sour look. "Were you with her?"

"'Her'?"

"Little late in the game for the both of us to start playing coy, Jesse Stone. You know exactly who 'her' means."

"What if I was?"

Daisy said, "Forget it. None of my business."

"Since when did that ever stop you?"

"Since right now."

Jesse shook his head. "Little late in the game for us to start playing coy, Daisy," he said, throwing her own words back at her.

"Ask her, Jesse."

He supposed Daisy had a point. If he was curious about Maryglenn, he should ask Maryglenn.

"Fair enough. What about Cole?"

"Same answer. Just know he's got my blessing to not be here. So don't go giving him a hard time about that. You may not have raised up that man, but he has a lot of your qualities . . . for better or worse."

"Thanks, I think."

That got Daisy to smile in spite of herself.

"All right, Jesse, how many coffees and what would you like to eat?"

MOLLY WAS AT THE DESK when Jesse came into the station. He put a large coffee and an egg sandwich down in front of her. Then he did something he rarely did. He pulled a chair over, put his own breakfast down at the desk, and ate with her.

"What's the occasion?" she asked.

"I wanted to talk."

"You don't need to ply me with food to get me to talk to you. You're my chief."

"And your friend."

"And my friend. So this isn't business?" she said, unwrapping her sandwich and sipping her coffee.

"What do you do when your kids keep secrets from you?"

"This isn't a hypothetical, I take it."

He shook his head. "Cole hasn't been at work for the last few days, with Daisy's blessing."

"Have you asked him about it?"

"Not yet."

"Then you've got two choices: ask him or let him tell you when he's ready."

"What if he's never ready?"

Molly laughed, almost choking on her food. "Don't be an ass, Jesse. People have secrets, and don't you dare bring up Crow."

Now it was Jesse's turn to laugh. "Never."

"Liar."

"Never again."

"Better, but I don't believe you. Listen, Jesse, as far as it goes with Cole, you can't force things. He wants to have you be his father."

"How can you know that?"

"Sometimes, for such a smart and perceptive man, you can be a real jackass. Cole's here, isn't he? He came looking for you. He hasn't left. For twenty-plus years you were the object of his scorn, resentment, fascination, and yearning. We only ever get one set of biological parents. He's figuring stuff out. Let him, and let him come to you. Ease off the gas a little bit."

Jesse didn't say anything to that, because it rang so true there was no point.

"Has your daughter ever mentioned a kid from school named Chris G., Chris Grimm? He's a junior."

Molly stopped chewing. "Why?"

Jesse explained about seeing the kid outside the funeral home.

"No, she's never mentioned him, but I can ask."

"Do that, but I'm going over to the high school to ask about him after breakfast."

"A lot of kids are going to be absent today because of Heather's funeral."

"I know, but there's something about this Chris G. kid. Looked guilty, but also like his heart got ripped out. He definitely wasn't a Heather type of boy."

"I don't know, Jesse. Girls sometimes really like bad boys." As the words came out of Molly's mouth, she realized she was putting her foot in it.

Jesse grinned. "Oh, kind of like you and Crow."

"I knew it."

"Don't you worry, Molly Crane. That secret dies with me."

Secret . . . There was that word again.

Sixteen

Molly was right. She usually was. The high school wasn't quite a ghost town, but it wasn't nearly as busy as it had been the other day. Once again he found himself in Principal Wester's office.

"It's a bad day for this, Chief Stone."

"There's never a good day for it."

She thought about it for a second and realized he was right. "No, there isn't, is there? Never a good day to bury a seventeen-year-old girl. So, what is it you think I can help you with?"

"Chris Grimm."

The principal's face remained neutral. That meant that the kid wasn't a constant problem or a real troublemaker. The administration always knows the kids at either end of the behavior spectrum—the superstars and the disruptive ones.

"What about him?"

"Can I see him?"

"I have no problem with you talking to the faculty, but I'd prefer you not do interrogations on school grounds," she said.

"I just want to talk to the kid. This isn't an interrogation."

"If you say so. Let me get him up to the office. You can use one of our meeting rooms, but I want to be present. We can't have the school liable."

Jesse didn't object.

Principal Wester picked up her phone, punched in two numbers. "Freda, please locate a student named Chris Grimm—" She covered the mouthpiece and asked Jesse what grade Grimm was in. "He's a junior . . . That's right. Please have him come up to the office."

"Thank you."

Wester's phone rang almost immediately. She picked up, made some unreadable sounds, and hung up.

"Sorry, Chief. Christopher Grimm's been absent for the last several days."

"Can you give me his contact information?"

Wester frowned but didn't put up a fight. "I'll have Freda get that for you. Will there be anything else?"

"No. Thank you for your help."

AS JESSE WAS heading out of the building, he bumped shoulders with Brandy Lawton, the head of the girls' physical education department and coach of the cheerleading squad. Brandy and Jesse were friendly if not exactly friends. They had known each other for many years. Brandy had had Jesse in to give some instruction to the girls' softball team and to talk about the life of a professional athlete. Brandy was cute, compact, and athletic, with short brown hair, hazel eyes, and a winning smile. Her eyes were red. There was an epidemic of red eyes in Paradise since Heather's death. She also seemed nervous and distracted. There was a lot of that in town, too. Brandy was usually dressed in a warm-up suit and running shoes. Not that day. Jesse barely recognized her in black slacks, a black jacket, a gray blouse, and gray flats. He smiled at her and then realized why the change in dress.

"The funeral," he said.

"Will you be there, Jesse?"

"I will."

"It's terrible."

"Can we talk for a minute?"

She looked at the hallway clock. "Five minutes?"

"Sure."

He followed Lawton into a dark classroom. She flicked on the lights and sat on the edge of the teacher's desk. Jesse stood.

"What can I do for you, Jesse?"

"Tell me about Heather."

"She was a great kid. Enthusiastic, dedicated, a good team-mate . . ."

Jesse gave Brandy a hard stare. He was tired of making no progress. "She's dead, Brandy. She ODed. You don't start with drugs the way she died. You move up to it. So if you want this not to happen to some other kid in the school, tell me what's really been going on with Heather."

Lawton's face turned down. "It wasn't like she became a different person, Jesse, but she hadn't been as into it as she used to be. She missed a few practices, made some slip-ups in the routines, and, frankly, was in danger of losing her spot."

"Did you talk to her about it?"

"Of course. She seemed to understand and promised to do better, but she was also distracted. Look, Jesse, I was a seventeen-year-old girl once, too. Things can get confusing when you start growing into your body and you notice boys, and you're thinking about college, and your parents get on your nerves."

"Were her parents getting on her nerves?"

"Something was, but she didn't want to talk about it. I was her coach, not her confessor."

"Relax, Brandy, I'm not accusing you of anything. This is helpful. Can you remember when Heather's attitude changed?"

Lawton didn't answer immediately. "I guess it was a gradual thing. I didn't notice anything different until late last spring. I thought that she'd straighten out after the summer."

"Were there any incidents with Heather last year? Something that might have signaled a change?"

She shrugged. "The only thing I can remember with Heather was an injury. She hurt her back during a routine at the Holiday Show in December. She slipped going into a jump and missed the landing, but she finished the routine. I got a note from her doctor the following week, saying that Heather would be out of action for at least a month. By March, she was back at it." Brandy looked at her watch. "Sorry, Jesse, I've got to move. I still have classes."

"Just one more thing. Did you ever see Heather with Chris G.?"

Unlike Principal Wester, Brandy Lawton made a decidedly unneutral face at the mention of that name.

"I'd see him with Heather after practice occasionally."

"You didn't like him?"

"I didn't know him, but he looked like one of those kids who'd come to school with an AR-15 one day."

"Did you talk to anyone about that?"

She laughed a laugh that had nothing to do with joy. "Half the boys in school look that way."

"But what was it about him in particular?"

"I guess I just didn't like him with Heather."

Old story, Jesse thought, *good girls and bad boys.* "Thanks, Brandy."

Jesse watched Lawton leave. He stayed behind to consider what Brandy had said. On the surface, she hadn't said a lot, but Jesse knew by instinct alone she had given him his first real opening.

Seventeen

Jesse Stone had been to funerals, burials, and memorials of every description, but he had never hardened to them. Even at the funerals of vicious gangbangers, he had an open heart for their families. Regardless, he had to remain stoic to do his job. More often than not, he would hang back, off to one side or another, far away from the altar or the podium. He was there to observe, to see if anyone in attendance showed his hand. At Heather's funeral, he wasn't looking for suspects. This still wasn't a murder case and it probably wasn't ever going to be one, though he was keeping an eye out for Chris Grimm.

The service was held at the same church Suit and Elena had been married in, and Ross Weber, the man who'd married them, conducted the service. *It was strange,* Jesse thought, *that grief and sorrow almost had a particular smell.* The sweet notes in the air came from the huge number of floral arrangements arrayed on either side of the cherrywood coffin. There were roses—red, pink, yellow, and white—hundreds of them. There was the herbal and choking alcohol infusion from perfumes and colognes. It took the young years to figure out the right amount of the stuff to wear.

The old had lost their senses of smell and wore too much to cover the odor of creeping decay. And there was the stink of stress sweat. None of the other odors could ever quite take the edge off that smell.

The church was full. Heather had been an only child, but both sets of grandparents were in attendance. There were lots of aunts, uncles, cousins, and family friends. Blank-faced, all. Jesse recognized many of the teachers he'd spoken with and some that he had not. Principal Wester and Freda were there, as were Maryglenn and Brandy Lawton. Three kids in the third pew from the front—two girls and a boy—were distraught, sobbing, rocking, clutching and clinging to one another. Jesse guessed those were Heather's closest friends: Megan, Darby, and Rich. He would catch them later, at the cemetery. That's when they would be most vulnerable to his questions.

There was no sign of Chris G. inside the church, and Jesse hadn't seen him outside, either. Just in case, he'd stationed Suit in plainclothes in his pickup truck out front. Jesse had already stopped by the Grimms' house. No one was home. At least, no one had answered the door. He'd also left a message on the phone machine. He hoped he wasn't chasing his own tail around with this kid. His cop instincts were usually spot-on, but he wasn't infallible. Jesse knew that believing you were was the biggest mistake of all.

THERE WERE ABOUT half as many people and twice as many tears at the graveside. When that casket gets lowered into the dirt, there's no more pretending that it just isn't real or that it's all some kind of crazy, sick joke. It's as real as it's ever going to get. One of Heather's grandmothers fainted, and Selectman Mackey fell to his knees as the first shovel of dirt rang against the cherrywood.

Jesse stayed far back, waiting for the crowd to break up. He kept a careful watch on Megan, Darby, and Rich as they walked away from their friend's grave. As they approached a beat-up Jeep Cherokee, Jesse came over to them.

"I'm Jesse Stone, and I was wondering if I could talk to you."

They looked at him with a mixture of hurt and confusion.

"You're the police chief, right?" Rich said, pointing at Jesse's PPD baseball cap.

He was a thin, handsome kid with fine, delicate features.

"Uh-huh. And you're Rich. Which one of you girls is Megan?"

A very slight girl with long brown hair and a face reminiscent of Bette Davis said, "I'm Megan."

Jesse turned to the other girl. "That would make you Darby."

Darby was a striking girl, about five-six, with long red hair, tortoiseshell glasses, and a nose ring.

"That's right," she said. "I'm Darby."

Jesse didn't like doing it, but he didn't waste time on preliminaries or small talk. They were off balance and raw with emotion. That's what he needed.

"How long had Heather been using?"

They didn't answer. He didn't expect them to.

"She's dead," he said, pointing behind them at Heather's grave. "I don't want to hurt her reputation and I don't want to get anyone in trouble, but I also don't want to be at another funeral."

"She wasn't using," Rich said.

"C'mon, kid. She didn't die of old age."

Rich shook his head furiously. "That's not what I meant. It wasn't that she did it for fun. She hated it, but—"

Megan, grabbed Rich's arm. "Shut up, Richie."

"No. I have to say this. She would want us to."

Darby said, "She would, Meg."

Jesse stood there, quiet, letting the friends work it out. Pressure from him would've ruined it.

"It was Oxy," Rich said. "She never told us too much about it, because she didn't want us to get in trouble."

Jesse asked, "Was this after she hurt herself at the Holiday Show?"

They all nodded.

Darby spoke up. "We didn't really notice until the end of school last year. She was acting a little weird and she was borrowing money all the time. She never used to need to borrow money."

Tears rolled down Rich's cheeks.

"What is it?" Jesse wanted to know.

"She stole things from me. My iPad, some jewelry . . . nothing important. I just told my folks I lost stuff."

That was when Meg and Darby admitted that Heather had stolen from them as well. There was sad laughter among the tears as they acknowledged what they had kept secret from one another. They had loved Heather so deeply that they let her steal from them.

"I tried to get her to go for help," Darby said. "The three of us tried doing one of those stupid intervention things, but she just got mad at us."

Jesse asked a few more questions, but it was clear Heather had worked hard to insulate herself and to keep her friends away from the other life she lived. But when they were ready to leave, Jesse mentioned Chris G.

"Loser," Megan said.

"A cute loser." Darby was less harsh.

Jesse could see that Rich wanted to say something, but not in front of the girls. Jesse gave him a nod—*later*—when the girls were distracted. Rich got behind the wheel of the Jeep and they were gone. As Jesse turned back to his Explorer, he caught a glimpse of Chris G. running among the tombstones. Jesse took off after him.

The kid was quick and the grass was slick from a shower that had passed an hour or so before Heather's burial. Jesse would make up some ground and then fall behind as the kid zigged, then zagged, among headstones, stone benches, and fences. As he chased the kid, Jesse shouted to him that he only wanted to talk. But Chris wasn't having it. Jesse couldn't blame the kid, especially if he had stuff to hide. After about a hundred yards, Jesse gave up, bending over at the waist, trying to catch his breath. When he stood straight, Chris G. was gone.

Eighteen

Jesse got Molly on the phone, told her about his suspicions, and gave her Chris Grimm's address.

"Send somebody to sit on the house."

"For how long, Jesse?"

"At least until morning."

"I'll send Gabe. What if Grimm shows?"

"There are no grounds for arrest. Officially, there's no crime, so tell Gabe not to do anything but call me directly. I just want to talk to the kid. He's already spooked."

"Why's he spooked?"

"Because I just chased him through the cemetery."

"If it was anyone else, I'd think you were trying to be funny."

"Nice," Jesse said.

Molly shifted focus. "How was it today?"

"About how you would expect."

"Bad?"

"Never good, putting a kid in the ground."

Molly choked up. "No, I guess not. I've got to go, Jesse."

HE THOUGHT ABOUT HEADING home but realized that would be the first place the cops would go looking for him. After Chief Stone had chased him through the graveyard, he no longer doubted that the cops were on to him. Now calling Arakel was a matter of survival. He had to get out of Paradise and find a place to lie low until this thing with Heather blew over. His mom didn't really give a shit about him anyway, and his stepdad would probably crack open a bottle of champagne at the idea of him splitting for good. He headed for Kennedy Park to make the call.

Arakel was impatient. "What is it? I have no time for this."

Chris hesitated. "The cops tried to grab me today."

"Where was this?"

"Outside of my school." The kid lied, knowing that if he told the truth, Arakel would lose his mind.

The lie seemed to placate him, and now it was Arakel who was momentarily silent. "Where are you?"

"I'm in a place where they won't find me for a while."

"Stay there. I will call you soon. Do not worry. We will fix this."

ARAKEL DREADED GOING to Mehdi with the problem. Mehdi had always thought his choice of the kid was a mistake—*too weak and no toughness*. The last thing he wanted to hear was an I-told-you-so. He had no choice, really. He was not an operations type of guy. He *was* good at taking instruction and following through, but thinking on his feet had never been his forte. He banged his knuckles on Mehdi's office door.

"Come."

Arakel stepped in.

Mehdi read his partner's face as if it were a Times Square bill-board. "There is trouble."

"In Paradise, yes."

"With the kid?"

"He says the police are after him."

Mehdi wagged his finger. "I told you so." He frowned, gave it some thought, and flipped a set of keys at Arakel. "Go pick him up in the van. Take Stojan and Georgi with you."

"Why do I need—"

"They will know where to go." Mehdi stood up and patted his partner's cheek. "Try not to disappoint me more than you already have."

"But he is only a boy."

"A boy, yes. A boy who can have you spend the rest of your life inside a federal prison. Think of it this way. A hand grenade will kill you no matter who pulls the pin, a child or a monster. The trick is to remove the possibility of explosion. Stojan and Georgi will find out what the boy has said and . . ." Mehdi turned back to his desk, opened the top drawer, and removed a sleek black pistol. He released the magazine into his palm, inspected it, replaced it in the handle, worked the slide, and checked the safety. He handed it to Arakel. "And when they have gathered all there is to know from the boy, you will make sure there is no possibility of the hand grenade exploding."

Arakel took the pistol. He handled it awkwardly, shoving it into his jacket pocket. But Mehdi wasn't finished.

"Alert everyone in the supply chain in that area. Obviously, we need a new recruit. Make it happen."

Arakel turned and left. He prayed silently for the situation to somehow resolve itself without the use of force. He might as well have prayed for peace on earth. Neither was going to happen.

Nineteen

The white, unmarked van crunched along the stone-and-dirt service road in the last flicker of sunlight. The kid had assured Arakel that the service road was hardly ever used and that even if they were stopped, they could claim they were lost.

"It's easy to screw up. People do it all the time. The roads in the park aren't very clearly marked."

Arakel had already made the calls to the people he had been ordered to alert, and as the van bounced, tires spitting out gravel, his hands shook and the nausea rose up in him. It was all he could do not to have them pull over so he could get out to vomit. Stojan, at the wheel, and Georgi, in the front passenger seat, looked back at Arakel, then at each other. They smirked, shaking their heads.

Stojan said, "What is wrong, Boss, you are being seasick?"

The two men in the front seats had a good laugh at that. They exchanged some words in their native tongue and laughed harder still. Arakel knew both men up front as brutal, unfeeling thugs. That was their niche in the organization, but Arakel also suspected one or both of them as plants, spies for the men above Mehdi and himself.

"Slow down," Arakel said as they neared the equipment shed. "Stop."

The van skidded to a halt on the loose gravel. Stojan turned to face his boss. "Open the door for the kid."

Arakel pulled the handle and slid the side door open. Chris Grimm stepped out into the open from the side of the metal shed and hopped into the van. He grinned at the sight of Arakel and slid the door shut behind him. The van started moving almost immediately. The grin slid right off the kid's face at the sight of the men up front. Arakel noticed.

"Don't worry about them," he said, patting Chris's shoulder, smiling. "They're here to protect you. No one will bother us with them around. Come on, once we get out of town, we'll get you something to eat. You haven't eaten all day, have you?"

The kid relaxed. There it was, Arakel's talent on display. In spite of Chris's troubles and fear of the men in the front of the van, Arakel had put him at ease.

"Stojan, stop at a McDonald's or a place like that once we get out of Paradise."

"But—"

"Do not defy me," Arakel said, not quite believing he talked to the brute that way. "We have time for the boy to eat."

The big man shrugged.

"So, Chris, where have you left your stash? Will the police find it in your home if they search?"

The kid smiled at him. "I'm not stupid. No. I have a storage unit that I pay for with some of the money I make."

Arakel raised his eyebrows. "Can we stop there and pick up the stash? We do not want to leave anything that might incriminate you here. This way, the police can prove nothing when you come back to town."

"Okay, sure."

"Good. Good. We get your stash and then you eat."

TWO HOURS LATER, Chris was very grim indeed. He was tied to a chair in a warehouse Stojan and Georgi used for such things. Chris's face was a bloody, pulpy mess covered in tears and snot. Unconscious, his eyes were already purple and swollen shut. The thugs had first broken all of his fingers, then worked their way up his legs. But Arakel put a stop to that when Stojan took out his knife and threatened to emasculate the boy.

"No!" he had shouted. "You will not do that."

"We will know the truth," Stojan said, as if he were about to cut the heel off a loaf of bread.

"We already know the truth. He never spoke with the cops and he's told us the names of the people who knew he dealt."

"You are being a foolish, foolish man, Boss," Georgi, the quieter of the two enforcers, said. "We have to be knowing if anyone knows people more than him. Is he telling anyone about you? This we must be sure of."

Arakel couldn't argue with Georgi's logic. If Chris had shared anything with his clients about Arakel, it could be a major problem. "All right, but not that," he said, pointing at Stojan's blade. "Not that."

Again, Stojan and Georgi shook their heads at him. Stojan closed his knife, and that was when they went to work on the boy's face. After a half-hour of that, it seemed to Arakel that the two thugs were hurting the kid more for their own amusement than to get anything more out of him.

"I swear. I swear," the boy had said a hundred times. "I didn't tell anybody anything."

No matter how they hurt him, he kept repeating it. Arakel believed it the first time he said it. Stojan and Georgi didn't believe it or didn't want to believe it regardless.

Stojan looked at his phone for the time, looked at Chris, then nodded to Georgi. He said something Arakel understood, even if he didn't speak their language. They were going to wake the kid up and start in on him again. Two thunderous explosions echoed in the cavernous warehouse. It was only after some of the smoke had cleared that Arakel realized the pistol Mehdi had given him was in his shaking hand and that he had ended Chris Grimm's suffering forever.

Stojan took the weapon from his hand and thumped him on the back. "You are having more balls than we thought, Boss." He waved to Georgi. "Get the bottle. Someone is needing a drink."

Twenty

After his meeting, Jesse stopped by Gabe Weathers's stakeout across the street from Chris Grimm's house. "Anything?"

"Nothing," Gabe said. "No sign of the kid."

"Parents?"

"Home." Gabe picked up a pad on the seat next to him. "Mother got home at six-fifteen. The father got in about twenty minutes later. That's his truck in the driveway."

"Good work. Head back to the station, pick up your cruiser, and go back on patrol. Let Perkins know what's going on."

"You taking over here?"

"I'm going to talk to the parents. I think the kid's in the wind."

"Why'd he split, do you think?"

"Same reason everybody runs. He has something to hide."

"Like what?"

"I'll know more after I talk to the parents." Jesse slapped the doorsill on one of Paradise's two unmarked cars. It was an old Honda Accord the Staties had seized in the process of breaking up a criminal enterprise and sold to the Paradise PD for a pittance. "Get a move on."

Jesse waited for Gabe to leave and turn the corner before approaching the Grimms' house. The darkness covered up the multitude of sins the exterior displayed in the daylight. It was like many of the houses in town: a simple two-story with a detached one-car garage, a small front lawn surrounded by a low picket fence, and a small backyard. When he had stopped by earlier, Jesse noticed the clapboards were five years past needing a new coat of paint, the roof was sagging like the seat of an old chair, the windows rattled in a light breeze, and the garage was already partially collapsed. The lawn was more weeds than grass and more dirt than either. The letters WE were worn out on the front mat, the C, too, so that it read L OME. He got the sense that the original sentiment on the mat was now an afterthought, if even that. There wasn't much welcoming about the place. He rang the bell twice but didn't hear it buzz on the inside of the house, so he knocked long and loud.

A blowsy woman with messy black-and-gray hair answered the door. Dressed in a cut-sleeve sweatshirt and yoga pants, she was forty-five going on sixty. She had fading yellow bruises on her arms. Her face was lined and gaunt. A lit cigarette dangled from the corner of her yellow-stained lips. Her deep blue eyes gave her identity away, as they were the same shade and shape as her son's. And those eyes got big at the sight of Jesse's PPD hat, uniform shirt, and jacket. Then, almost unnoticeably, they became sneering and suspicious.

"What'd Chris do now?" she asked, voice full of resignation.

But before Jesse could respond, an unseen man called out from inside the house. "Who's that? Is it your little fucking angel?"

She turned into the house. "It's the cops." When she faced Jesse again, her expression had changed. There was real fear in it. She said, "Well?"

"I'm Chief Jesse Stone." He gave her a smile in hopes of keeping things calm. "I just want to talk with Chris, Mrs. Grimm."

"Mrs. Walters. Grimm was my first husband's name, the lousy prick. Chris kept the name just to spite me and his stepfather."

"Is Chris in?"

She shook her head, but it wasn't a protective gesture. Jesse already got the sense she wasn't the maternal type who would lie for her kid or throw herself in front on an oncoming car to save his life. "Haven't seen him. What's this about?"

"You've heard about Heather Mackey's death?"

"She was a little hottie. Too bad, Chris had a thing for her. But what's this got to do with him?"

Jesse lied. "Probably nothing. I'm just talking to kids who knew her or were friends of hers."

The mother wasn't buying it. "Well, he ain't here."

There were the sounds of heavy footsteps coming from behind her, and when they did that fearful expression returned. Jesse looked over her shoulder to see a fireplug of a man coming their way. He was in a dirty blue work shirt that had been pulled out of darker blue work pants. He had on blackened work boots, the laces untied. The laces slapped the floor as he walked. He had thick arms, a thick neck, and a nasty face. The main feature of which was a bent nose covered in gin blossoms. As he got close, Jesse could smell sweat and alcohol coming off him in waves. Jesse wasn't exactly disgusted by the smell of alcohol since he stopped drinking, but he was now very sensitive to its odor coming off other people.

He said, "This the cop?"

She rolled her eyes at him. "No, it's one of those male strippers dressed as a cop, come to give me a birthday greeting from my girlfriends."

He snickered an ugly snicker. "Well, shit, it ain't your birthday and you don't have any friends, so he must be a real cop."

Jesse introduced himself again. That got another ugly snicker out of the stepfather of the year.

"The kid ain't here. Didn't she tell you that already?"

"She did."

"Then what are you still doing here? You," he said to his wife, grabbing her by the arms where those fading bruises were and shoving her behind him, "go finish doing what you was doing. I'll handle this."

She didn't protest, about-facing and heading down the hall without acknowledging Jesse.

The husband leaned against the open front door. "Listen, Chief, she lets the kid get away with murder. Yeah, she's way too lenient with him and maybe should've smacked him around a little more when he was younger, but I'm sure he never did anything serious. He's weak and too much of a pussy."

Jesse was getting angry with him, so pulled a card out and handed it to him. "Please give that to Chris when he gets home and let him know I just want to talk with him about Heather."

"Yeah, whatever," the stepfather said, waving a dismissive hand. He made to shut the door.

Jesse stopped him, holding his hand against the door. "Do it, because otherwise I'll be back, and I'd hate to interrupt your drinking every night. Do we understand each other?"

"Yeah, yeah, yeah. Cops are all the same."

He slammed the door shut. As Jesse walked back to his Explorer, he realized that his chasing Chris through the cemetery probably wasn't the only reason the kid wasn't anxious to come home.

Twenty-one

Arakel stood at the door, duffel bag in hand, waiting for her to answer. He had called her before killing the boy. In spite of the vodka Stojan and Georgi had practically forced down his throat, his hands were still shaking. He felt, as the English say, legless. Paradoxically, his shooting Chris felt simultaneously unreal and like the most real thing he had ever done. Since squeezing the trigger, he had told himself a thousand times he had done it for the kid's own good. That the two thugs enjoyed inflicting pain so much, they would have kept him alive if only to keep hurting him. But none of his rationalizations could chase away his guilt or extinguish that little piece of himself that felt perverse exhilaration. He had proven himself, finally. He had done something no one thought him capable of, and while he was mostly disgusted by what he'd done, he was also proud of it. He wanted to rush back to the warehouse and have Stojan and Georgi describe to Mehdi in detail how he had put a bullet into Chris Grimm's chest and one in his head.

See, partner, I am not weak like you think. Ask these two pigs. They will tell you. I am strong.

He was so caught up in his thoughts, he didn't notice the door had pulled back and that the woman he had come to see was standing just inside the doorway, bathed in darkness.

"Come up," she said. "Hurry."

Arakel followed her up the stairs, taking note of her pleasing shape and how the grassy fragrance of her perfume filled up his head.

Once he stepped inside her flat, she quickly closed the door behind him. The apartment was dimly lit, but he had been there once before and knew the layout.

"Please, Mr. Sarkassian—"

"Arakel. Call me Arakel."

"Arakel." She tried smiling at him but failed. "I can't do what you ask, not again."

He stroked her cheek. "Of course you can. You have already done it once."

"But—"

For the second time that night, he did something he had never done before. He swung his fist into her abdomen. The air went out of her in a rush and she fell to her knees. He grabbed her by the hair and put his lips close to her ear.

"You will do exactly as you are told."

"But the girl," she said, her voice cracking.

"Yes, it was a shame about the girl. That was the boy's fault. We chose badly with him. We must make a better choice with the new person."

The woman was sobbing. "I can't."

"You can, darling. And you will. You will do anything I tell you to do." He got down on his knees next to her, removing his phone from his pocket as he did so. He showed her the picture of Chris Grimm's battered, bloodied body. "This can just as easily be you."

She tried to stand and run, but he yanked her down and pushed her onto the floor. "But I have no desire to threaten you. There are better reasons for you to do as I wish."

He let go of her and reached into the stash bag. He came out with a prescription vial. He shook it. The woman stopped crying, as if a turnoff switch had been thrown and the circuit broken. Arakel removed one of the green pills with 80 stamped into it from the vial and held it in his palm for the woman to see. She grabbed at it, but he snatched it away, closing his fingers around the pill.

"This vial will be yours after we discuss the candidates and you make the call."

She didn't argue, but asked for the pill in his palm as a gesture of good faith.

"No. First we do as I say, then the pills."

AN HOUR LATER, she had fulfilled her obligations as he had described them. He had chosen the candidate to replace the Grimm boy.

"Now?" she asked, clicking off the phone and placing it down on the counter.

"No," Arakel said, still feeling the rush of his newfound strength. "Come here and get on your knees."

She opened her mouth to object, but he shook the vial of pills. When he did, she strode over to him and got down on her knees. She didn't need to be told what to do. The doctor in Boston had made her do the same. She pulled his zipper down and reached into his pants, but just as she was about to put him in her mouth, he pushed her away. He wasn't going to become a killer and a rapist on the same night. He tossed the vial into the air and she lunged for it as if it were a newborn baby tossed from a burning window. She clutched the vial to her chest.

"The other pill," she said. "The one you put in your pocket. Can I have that one, too?"

He reached into his pocket and handed it to her. She reached onto the counter, grabbed a homemade pill crusher, and got to work.

"Remember," he said, "those pills and those pills only are for you. We have made a very careful inventory of what is in the stash bag. We expect every other pill and package accounted for. Do you understand?"

But the woman had made fast work of the crushing and had already snorted some of the pulverized Oxy. He walked over to her, grabbed her hair, and put his face very close to hers.

"Do you understand?"

She nodded.

He took out his phone again. "Good, because I would hate to see you in that chair. You get the supply line up and running again in this town within two days and maybe there will be another reward."

He let go of her hair and left.

All that newfound strength of his had seemed to vanish. Now all he wanted was to shower and to sleep.

Twenty-two

When Jesse got back to his condo, he found his son in his default position—on the living room couch, watching something from one of the streaming services Cole paid for.

"Hey," Jesse said.

Cole hit pause. "Hey. Late night."

"A meeting and then work."

"About the dead girl?"

"Uh-huh."

"Getting anywhere with that?"

"Yes, but not sure where. Once I find where she got the drugs, I'll have a direction to pursue. For now, it's hit and miss. Welcome to police work."

Cole laughed. Jesse thought maybe a little too loudly.

"I say something funny?"

Cole shook his head. Jesse changed the subject.

"I'm not spying on you, but I've been by Daisy's. You've missed a few days."

"With Daisy's blessing."

Jesse held up his palms like he was on traffic duty. "I know. She told me. Also told me if I was curious that I should ask you about it."

"Are you asking?"

"I am."

"It's not like a secret," Cole said. "But I'd like to tell you in my own time. Okay?"

Jesse thought about pressing the issue, then remembered what Molly had advised. She'd told him to back off and let the kid come around by himself.

"All right. When you're ready to tell me, I'll be here. Did you eat?"

"Yeah, but I could eat some more."

"Omelet work for you?"

"Sounds good."

Jesse had never been good at small talk, and he was even worse at it with Cole. There always seemed to be an eight-hundred-pound gorilla in the room sitting between them that neither of them could quite bring themselves to talk about. Jesse had tried talking baseball, but Cole wasn't a big fan. No doubt that was part of Cole's resentment over the father who he had grown up believing had abandoned his mother and him. Cole's presence made Jesse very conscious of his own limitations. Jesse hated politicians and politics, so they didn't talk about that. He didn't drink anymore, so he avoided that as a subject for discussion. Whenever he tried raising the subject of Cole's life with his mother back in L.A., Cole shut down. And, frankly, Cole's job at Daisy's didn't exactly supply a lot of material. The one thing that Cole seemed genuinely interested in was when Jesse discussed police work. Of course, that was the one subject Jesse wanted to get away from when he was home. But as they sat there eating their omelets, Cole broke the silence.

"So, are you dating this Maryglenn woman?"

That took Jesse by complete surprise. He literally sat up from his food. "I guess Daisy must have mentioned it."

Cole nodded.

"Dating? I'm not sure *dating* is the word."

"Sleeping with?"

"Let's use the word *seeing*."

"Are you seeing her?"

"I am. Why do you ask?"

He hesitated but answered. "I don't think Daisy likes her very much."

"Yeah," Jesse said, "I got that feeling, too."

"Did you ask her about it?"

"Did you?"

"Are you kidding me? Daisy would bite my head off."

"Any guesses?"

"This may sound a little weird, but Daisy almost sounds a little jealous."

Jesse chewed on that for a minute before saying something. "Maybe protective more than jealous. We've always kind of watched out for each other."

"I don't know. You two are close. I get that, but it seemed more like jealousy to me."

Jesse wanted to dismiss what Cole was saying, but recalling the looks on Daisy's face and on Maryglenn's, he just couldn't.

"I'm beat and it's going to be a long, hard day tomorrow," Jesse said. "I have to interview the dead girl's parents."

"Good luck with that. I've got to get up early. Back to work for me in the morning."

Jesse went to wash the dishes, but Cole told Jesse to get to sleep.

"Old folks need more rest," he said, smiling at Jesse.

Jesse laughed and felt closer to his son than he had at any time since he visited him in the hospital after the old meetinghouse explosion. *Maybe,* he thought, *Molly had a point.*

Twenty-three

Jesse usually liked to catch people he was questioning off guard, but the Mackeys had just buried their daughter and he didn't suspect either of them of being involved in her death in any way. He had Molly call ahead to let them know he was coming.

"How did they sound, Molly?" he asked, calling her back as he turned the corner of their street.

"Not like I expected."

"How do you mean?"

"Jesse, this may sound weird, but they almost sounded happy. Well, not happy exactly. Just . . ."

"Don't struggle with it. I understand."

"What do you understand?"

"Since the night Heather died, their lives have been filled up with grief, but also with plans and phone conversations, and people dropping by. Now the real mourning starts. Today is the day when it will hit them that they will never see their girl again. Today marks the day she will be dead forever. They're thankful for anything that takes even a little of that sting away. And they don't

want to feel so helpless. They want to make her life worth something."

"For such a self-contained, stoic bastard, Jesse Stone, you do
know people."

"Hard-learned lessons, Molly. Hard-learned."

The Mackeys' red front door pulled back even before Jesse had
gotten halfway up the walk. He removed his hat before entering.
There, Steve Mackey was waiting for him, shook Jesse's hand, and
thanked him for coming to all the services.

"She was a great girl, Steve. I'm so sorry."

Fact was Jesse had barely known her, but this exchange between the selectman and Jesse was more ritual than anything else.
What else would Jesse say? What else did a father want to hear? He
took Jesse by the elbow and showed him into the kitchen, where
Patti Mackey was fussing with the coffee machine. Steve Mackey
gestured for Jesse to sit. He did. Mackey sat across from him. Patti
offered him coffee.

"Sure. I'd like that."

She put the cup in front of him and sat close to her husband,
clutching his hand. She looked a wreck. Her red eyes were the
least of it. For his part, Steve Mackey looked like he wanted to
crumble but was holding it together for Patti . . . or not. It was just
as likely, Jesse thought, Mackey was afraid of what would happen
if he let himself go. Jesse understood that. He had let himself
crack after Diana's murder and it had nearly ruined him. He made
a show of fixing up his coffee the way he liked it and making a
satisfied sigh after taking a sip. Then he got to business.

"Thank you both for talking to me today."

"We want to help," Patti said, voice brittle.

"I know you do. Let me say that the best way you can help is to
be totally honest with me. Nothing you say to me that might seem

to shine a bad light on Heather will ever leave this room. The only thing I want is to not have to repeat this same conversation with someone else's parents."

Both the Mackeys nodded.

Jesse waited a full thirty seconds. He was curious to see if either Steve or Patti would offer something without prompting before he asked his questions. He got the sense that Patti might have had something to say, but in the end, neither spoke up.

"Okay. Did either one of you have any idea Heather had a drug problem?"

The question was greeted by silence. Again, Jesse sensed Patti had something to say. He made a mental note to circle back to Patti and speak to her without Steve present.

"I didn't have a clue, Jesse. I swear to God," Steve said. "I mean, who understands teenage girls? Was she moody sometimes? Sure she was. Could she be a pain? Yeah. But I couldn't have asked for a better child."

Jesse turned to the wife. "That the way you saw it, Patti? You were a teenage girl once."

"Once," she said, "a million years ago, before everyone had a cell phone. Before social media. Before . . ." Her voice drifted off. "It's hard being a teenage girl, even a pretty one."

"I heard Heather hurt her back during a routine at the Holiday Show. Did she see a doctor for treatment?"

"First we took her to Doc Goldfine," Steve said. "He'd taken care of her since she was born."

"Then he recommended we take her to a spine and back specialist, Dr. Nour at the hospital."

"And?"

Steve Mackey raised his palms to the ceiling and shrugged. "Patti took her and dealt with it."

"She did an MRI and found a few compressed vertebrae. She prescribed rest, massage, PT, and gave her something for the pain. Motrin, I think. Eight weeks later she was back at it, dancing, cheerleading, all as if she hadn't been hurt in the first place."

Jesse said, "I know Doc Goldfine, but could you give me a number for Dr. Nour?"

It went on like that for fifteen or twenty minutes. Everything according to Steve and Patti was fine up until the moment Patti found Heather unresponsive in her bed. Jesse thanked them and gave them the usual line about calling if there was anything else they could remember or if something had slipped their minds. But just as he was about to leave, he stopped.

"Did Heather ever mention a boy named Chris Grimm?"

Steve Mackey's face was blank. It was clear to Jesse he had never heard the name before. "No, sorry. Should I know him?"

"Not necessarily," Jesse said. "Patti?"

"No."

Jesse knew she was lying. He also knew this wasn't the time for accusations or to bring up the things Megan, Darby, and Richie had said about Heather stealing from them. He shook Steve Mackey's hand, hugged Patti, and left, once again saying how sorry he was.

At the door of his Explorer he looked over the roof toward the Mackeys' house and wondered again if Heather's death would bind Steve and Patti together or blow them apart.

Twenty-four

She paced along the worn-out rug of the motel room, tried ignoring the cloying odors of pine-scented ammonia and sex that seemed to seep out of the mattress and the harvest-gold quilt. She managed to deal with the odors, but what she couldn't deal with were the mirrors—the cheap imitation Deco mirrors on the walls and the heart-shaped mirror above the bed. She couldn't deal with the mirrors because, for the time being, hers was the only image reflected in them. And she was disgusted by what she saw and what she was about to do.

Oh, she had seduced men and women before. She had no issue with seduction, per se. She liked it, was good at it, and up until she seduced Chris Grimm, she enjoyed her conquests. Before she got hooked, sex was sometimes the only thing that helped her get through the day. Now only one thing really mattered in her life. It was what she woke up yearning for, spent her days fantasizing about, and went to bed dreaming of. A little green pill. Sex was now a distant afterthought. She still kind of enjoyed it, but only once she was sure she knew where her next high was coming from.

The thing was, what she had done with Chris, and what she

was about to do, was like shooting fish in a barrel. But she was already in too deep to complain about the dirt in the pool she was swimming in. She needed those pills and, as she had proven yesterday with Mr. Sarkassian, she was willing to do just about anything to make sure she wouldn't get cut off. She remembered what her uncle Ted used to say about people. "You take food, electricity, and warmth away from folks for two days and the façade of civilization and morality is quickly stripped away."

Oxy, too, Uncle Ted, she thought. She supposed her sense of right and wrong had gone out the window that first time she was gripped by fear and desperation at the thought of not being able to dose herself. At that moment she knew she would do anything. Forget just fucking for it, or seducing a teenage boy. She knew that she would kill for it if she had to. And that realization shook her to her core. She also knew what would be waiting for her at the end of the road without her connection to Arakel. What waited for all opioid addicts when there were no more doctors willing to write prescriptions because of back pain, or knee pain, or . . . When the pills ran out, there was heroin. That was a step she never wanted to take.

She considered herself lucky that the last doctor she tried to con into giving her pills saw potential in her and introduced her to Sarkassian. He kept her in pills and, to her shame, she was willing to do whatever he asked to stay in his good graces.

There was a knock on the door. Now she used the mirror, trying not to look too carefully into her own eyes. She took a deep breath, loosened the knot of her blue satin robe, making sure her cleavage showed. She strode to the door, opened it, smiled a crooked come-and-get-it smile at the girl standing in the doorway.

"Come on in, Petra," she said. "I've been waiting."

Petra was the "everybody's friend" girl in school. The heavyset girl with the lovely skin and the pretty face who lacked confidence and was always willing to melt into the scenery. Maybe she would have matured beyond that in college and blossomed into a more secure and confident woman. But since she had slipped and broken her femur last fall, she had become a prisoner of those same little green pills. Petra stepped in, closing the door behind her. She started to say something about how she had never done anything like this and how she had been desperate to try and . . .

"Shhh!" The older woman placed her index finger across Petra's lips, placed a few strands of long black hair behind the girl's ear. Then she leaned over and pressed her mouth against the girl's.

Petra was shaking but soon gave in to the moment, opened her mouth, and let herself be kissed deeply. She kissed back. The woman let her robe fall to the floor.

An hour later, Petra lay with her head against the woman's left breast, tucked under her arm. And as insecure teenagers are prone to do, she asked if she was any good at it and wondered if she had been pleasing. The older woman tilted Petra's head back and kissed her.

"You were wonderful."

Petra smiled so earnestly that the older woman almost threw the girl out. In the end, though, she didn't. She couldn't, and continued holding the girl as if this was the first step in a long, true romance. Looking up into the ridiculous heart-shaped mirror, she was horrified at the level to which she had sunk. But as she felt the hunger beginning to gnaw at her, she pushed ahead with the reason any of this had come to pass.

The woman straddled the girl, stroking her hair, kissing her softly on the lips.

"Petra, I need you to do something for me," she said, cooing.

"Anything. God, anything for you."

There they were, the magic words—*Anything for you.* Chris had said the same.

"Would you like to be with me again, Petra?"

The girl tensed, fearing her dreams would collapse like all of her other dreams of the girls and boys she had wanted to be with. She fought back tears.

"Yes, more than anything. Please don't hurt me."

The woman lied. "Never, baby. Never." She stroked Petra's face, stopped, and reached under the bed. When she came back up, she held a vial of pills in her hand. "These are for you." She gave the vial to Petra. The girl's eyes lit up. "And you'll never have to worry about getting them or having me ever again. There's a new locker number. I've written it down for you. The combination will be the same. Do you understand?"

Petra repeated. "Yes. Anything. Anything."

The woman kissed the girl deeply once again, then told her what was required of her.

When she had seen Petra safely away, she called Arakel Sarkassian and told him everything was in place.

Twenty-five

Short, with a wispy head of steel-gray hair, Dr. Abraham Goldfine was a sprightly man a year or two past his seventy-fifth birthday. He was the most popular pediatrician in town. He had seen one generation of Paradise kids grow into parents themselves. Now those second-generation kids were almost grown and there was no reason to believe he wouldn't get to see the beginnings of a third generation. Goldfine was one of Jesse's favorite people in town. The doctor, who'd been widowed for many years, loved baseball. When he'd get tickets from a patient's family, he would always invite Jesse to come along. The free tickets were great, but what Jesse really enjoyed was Goldfine's deep understanding of the game.

"Used to be a pretty fair second baseman, Jesse," the doctor would say. "We would've made a hell of a double-play combo, you and me."

But Jesse hadn't come to the office to talk baseball. The doctor lived in a grand Victorian in Pilgrim Cove, with his practice around back of his house. His neighbors were often a little less than pleased with him, because his house, while a lovely specimen of the Queen Anne style, was never kept in the pristine condition of the surrounding homes.

The doctor once confided in Jesse, "I think they would try to sue me, but since I saw to all their children, they make allowances."

When Jesse came into the office that day, he was greeted by a young woman who looked vaguely familiar. He guessed she caught him trying to figure it out.

"Morning, Chief Stone," she said, pointing to her chest. "Anna Marantz. You know, my dad owns the card shop."

"Sure. Good morning, Anna. How's your family?"

Anna, a petite blond woman with coppery eyes, said, "They're good."

"I thought you were at school."

"Amherst, yeah," she said, shrugged. "I did a year there, but I didn't like it or it didn't like me. I'm taking some time off and I figured I'd make a little money for when I go back to another school."

"Doc in?"

"He's just finishing up with a patient. I'll tell him you're here."

Anna went into the back. When she returned, she told Jesse the doctor would be out in a few minutes. While they waited, Jesse thought he would use the time to see if Anna, a fairly recent graduate of the high school, knew Heather Mackey.

"No, I didn't know her at all, really," Anna said. "We were two years apart." But Anna didn't leave it there. "I mean, I guess we passed each other in the hall sometimes, and everybody knows her father because he's a selectman and all."

Jesse supposed she would have gone on, but the door to the office opened and out came a young Hispanic couple, the mother holding a very young baby in her arms. Doc Goldfine trailed behind them, a reassuring hand on the mother's shoulder.

"Rosa will be perfectly fine. It's nothing more than a cold. If she's not better in a few days, give us a call and bring her back in."

"Thank you, Doctor," the husband said, and shook Goldfine's hand. "I will mail you the check on Friday."

The doctor smiled. "That will be good. Whenever you can. You just take care of these two."

He walked the family to the door and saw them out. He turned to Anna and told her to fit the Ramirezes in if the mother called for another appointment. Then he shook Jesse's hand and said hello.

"First-time parents . . ." Goldfine laughed and shook his head. "With the first one, the bottle falls on the floor, they make a new one. By the time the second one comes around, the bottle falls, they wipe it off on their nightshirt and stick it in the baby's mouth. So, you wanna talk baseball? No, I guess not. Come on in. I don't have another appointment for about fifteen minutes."

Jesse trailed the old man into his office. As he followed, Jesse marveled at the hop in Goldfine's step and the sparkle in his eyes.

"You know, Doc," Jesse said, sitting in one of the old chairs across the desk, "I think we might draft you for the PPD softball team. I don't know about your range at second, but you could be our designated runner."

"Please, Jesse, I'm old enough to carbon-date. So, what's up? How's that boy of yours?"

"Good."

"Molly and the girls?"

"Good."

"Oy, Jesse, with baseball, I can't shut you up. With everything else, one-word answers. So, what's doing?"

"Heather Mackey."

The sparkle went right out of Goldfine's eyes. He bowed and

shook his head. "I delivered her. I held her in my hands before her own mother. Did you know that?"

"No."

"This was when Steve and Patti still lived in Old Man Mackey's house around the corner from here. The baby decided to come in the middle of a nor'easter. You couldn't see your hand in front of your face and it was impossible to drive or for ambulances to get through. Steve called me in a panic. My Bea was still alive then. We walked around the corner. Got there just in time, too. But what can I tell you? How can I help?"

"Patti says when Heather got hurt last year, they came to see you first."

Goldfine held up his right index finger. "Wait." He called Anna into the office and asked her to get Heather Mackey's file.

"Good kid, Anna," the doctor said when she left. "John Marantz came to me last spring when he heard I was looking for some help. Said Anna was a little lost and could I think about her for the job. What could I say? I've known her also since she was like this." He held his upturned hands close together.

Anna came back, handed him the file, and left. Goldfine looked it over.

"Yeah, bad fall. Wrenched her back. She was in a lot of pain. There wasn't anything I could do but refer her to the back and spine specialist at the hospital, Dr. Nour."

"You didn't prescribe anything for her?"

Goldfine shook his head. "Prescribe? No. I suggested she use Motrin or Tylenol for the pain until she saw the specialist. Backs are quirky things, and you know my first duty is to do no harm. I was going to leave Heather's treatment to Dr. Nour. Good at her job."

Jesse stood up. Thanked the doctor and asked if he was sure he didn't want to play for the PPD softball team. Goldfine laughed, but not for long.

"You find out what really happened with Heather, let me know. Opioid addiction is going to kill off a generation if we don't watch out. I care for these kids too much to see that happen."

Jesse promised he would do everything he could and left, saying goodbye to Anna as he went.

"Take care," he said. "And give my regards to your folks."

Jesse sat outside in his Explorer, remembering the two babies he had delivered while in uniform in L.A. He wondered about what happened to those kids. He didn't wonder too long.

Twenty-six

Dr. Nour wasn't anything like Doc Goldfine, neither in temperament nor demeanor. Five-foot-six, with shoulder-length jet black hair, eyes nearly as dark, rich brown skin, and a downturned mouth, she was more the type of doctor Jesse had known at hospitals in L.A.—terse, impatient, and preoccupied. No matter what they said to him, it always seemed to Jesse that it translated into "What? What? I'm busy. Go away." He didn't judge them for it. He knew there wasn't much glory in the profession. As with police work, the public's perception of the medical arts was television-based.

"Dr. Nour," Jesse said, "I'd like a minute."

The doctor barely acknowledged his presence, tapping away at a mobile computer. "Yes, yes, Officer, what is it?"

Jesse couldn't help but laugh.

That got her attention. She looked up. "I wasn't aware I said something amusing."

"I'm actually the Paradise police chief, but that's not what I was laughing at."

"Pardon me, Chief. I meant no offense."

"None taken. And please, call me Jesse."

"All right, Jesse. But may I ask what you found so amusing?"

"Your impatience."

She shrugged, and Jesse wasn't inclined to explain any further.

"You saw a patient here last year, Heather Mackey. She was sixteen at the time. She'd taken a fall and was diagnosed with compressed vertebrae." He repeated the course of treatment Patti Mackey had described to him. "Do you recall treating her? I would like to discuss her case with you."

Nour's expression lost any hint of friendliness. "As police chief, you know I am legally and ethically prohibited from discussing my patients with—"

Jesse cut her off. "She's dead."

"My goodness. How?"

"Heroin overdose."

"I see, yes, follow me."

Dr. Nour led Jesse to a conference room. At first, they both sat, but when Jesse described how Heather was found by her mother, Dr. Nour rose out of her seat and paced.

Jesse asked again, "Do you remember her?"

Nour looked devastated. "I'm sorry, but I don't. I treat many, many patients here and in Boston, where my practice is based. You say I diagnosed her with compressed vertebrae and that I prescribed rest, physical therapy, massage therapy, and that Dr. Goldfine gave her Motrin for the pain?"

Jesse nodded.

"That sounds consistent with a course of treatment I might suggest, but without looking at her charts . . . wait. Will you excuse me for a few moments?"

Ten minutes later she returned, holding a batch of papers in her hand. "I had the staff make a copy of the report from Heather's visit here and I had my office scan and email the notes from her follow-up visits in Boston." She sat and reviewed the files. "Yes, Heather had compressed vertebrae." Dr. Nour stood, came around to Jesse, and slid MRI images in front of him. "See, right here. And, indeed, I did prescribe that exact treatment."

But something else had gotten Jesse's attention. "You said 'follow-up visits.' How many?"

She checked the files. "Four . . . yes, four visits in total, including her initial visit with me here at the hospital."

"Is that unusual?"

"Each case is different, especially with spinal injuries. For instance, I'm sure that if I were to do an MRI on you, Jesse, I might find that you, too, have compressed vertebrae or possibly stenosis of your cervical spine. The general population all have injuries of some form or other. Give me a group of ten men or women with MRIs indicating the identical issue and there's a likelihood that six of the ten would be asymptomatic and completely unaware of the damage. The remaining patients would likely display a range of symptoms with varying levels of distress."

"Uh-huh. Fascinating, but what about Heather? Where did she land on the curve?"

"I'm afraid she wasn't tolerating the pain very well with the Motrin. I prescribed Vicodin."

"Is that usual, prescribing an opiate for teenagers?" Jesse asked, his tone calm and nonaccusatory.

"I prefer not to prescribe it for anyone, but my notes say she was in obvious distress and she was accompanied by her mother. See the notation here. Whenever I prescribe any controlled substance, I discuss with the patient the drug's potential lethality and addictive characteristics. I prescribed a fifteen-day course of the drug for Heather. With Vicodin, I am loath to renew the prescription unless the patient reinjures herself or sustains a new injury. My file shows that was not the case with Miss Mackey."

Jesse said, "That accounts for three visits. What happened on the fourth visit?"

"It was routine. She reported a considerable reduction in pain. Her physical-therapy report showed a marked improvement. She did not return for further treatment or consultation. I hope this has been of some help."

"Thanks, Doc. At this point, I can't say."

"If you think I can be of any further use, please do not hesitate to contact me. Here." She held a card out to him but pulled it back. When she did, she wrote a number on the back. "That is my cell phone number. I find this very distressing, so I don't want you to have to go through my office to get in touch."

Jesse stared at her after taking the card from her, then said, "I understand your distress, but is there any reason in particular Heather's case disturbs you?"

"Heather's is not the first such story I have heard. Several of my colleagues have had to deal with similar cases."

Jesse didn't say what he was thinking but knew the moment she said what she had about other similar cases that either he or Molly would definitely be getting in touch. A pattern was always easier to track than an isolated case, and if he could establish a pattern, he might find out why Heather Mackey was dead.

Twenty-seven

Jesse called Molly as soon as he got back into his Explorer.

"I need you to do a little investigative work. You might have to charm Lundquist a little bit to help you."

"What do you need?"

"Dr. Farah Nour. She's a spine and back specialist at Paradise General and her practice is in Boston. I need to know whatever you can find out about her."

"You suspect her of something?"

"No, but she is the first link to Heather's addiction. She prescribed Vicodin for her last year. I doubt she's involved beyond that, but we should do our due diligence. See if we can connect any other cases like Heather's to her."

"Sure thing, Jesse. Where are you headed now?"

"I think I'll circle back to the Mackeys."

That was met with a curious silence. Jesse sensed Molly had something to ask but was holding back. And since Jesse was still working his way through things on gut feelings, he wasn't ready to share.

He said, "I'll check in later," and clicked off.

JESSE APPROACHED THE Mackeys' house slowly. He wanted to be certain Steve Mackey wasn't around, and when he saw that the selectman's BMW wasn't parked in the driveway, as it almost always was, Jesse pulled over to the curb.

Patti Mackey was a wreck. The other day, when he'd come by to ask about Heather's recent behavior, Patti had acted the part of the brave parent. The woman who would push on in spite of her girl's death. The woman who would somehow find a way to make Heather's death mean something. None of that was in evidence today.

"Jesse!" she said, gasping as she realized the state she was in. "God, I'm a mess. I'm sorry."

She was dressed in a ratty pink bathrobe and slippers. She wore no makeup and, from the smell of her breath, had been using vodka as a mouthwash.

"What parent wouldn't be?" he asked. "No need for apologies."

A light went on behind her reddened eyes. "Have you found something?"

"Can I come in?"

"Oh, please forgive me. Sure, Jesse, come into the kitchen."

The kitchen. It was almost always the kitchen where people felt most comfortable talking to him. He was suspicious when people asked to speak to him in libraries, offices, or dens. There was just something about kitchens that put people more at ease and made people more willing to speak the truth.

Patti tried to excuse herself once she made coffee for Jesse, but

Jesse grabbed her wrist, gently, and guided her into a seat at the breakfast nook.

"It will only get harder," he said, holding her hand, "if you don't just talk to me."

Patti Mackey broke down, sobbing, laying her head on the table. Usually Jesse made sure to never act in any way that could be misconstrued, but Patti was a friend and in pain. He stroked her hair until she was ready to talk.

"The other day, when I was here," he said, voice soft as he could make it, "I knew there were things you wanted to say to me without Steve present. That's why I'm here, Patti. I spoke with Dr. Nour. She told me about your other visits with Heather. She told me about the Vicodin."

Patti Mackey's hand tensed. All of her muscles tightened at the mention of the drug, but she didn't stop crying. And then, finally, she lifted her head up from the table, wiped the tears away, and said, "It was me, Jesse. I killed her."

His first instinct was to be a friend, to tell her she was wrong and that she wasn't responsible. But as a cop he knew to just let her talk and let the guilt that was eating away at her out into the open.

"I let the doctor prescribe Vicodin even after she explained the possible side effects, but Heather was in so much pain, Jesse. She couldn't sleep, couldn't eat. Sometimes I even had to help her up in the bathroom. I didn't know what else to do. It's hard to watch your child be in that much pain."

"Steve doesn't know about the follow-up visits and the Vicodin?"

She shook her head. "You know Steve, Mr. Straight Arrow. He doesn't even like it when I have a few vodkas when we're at the Gull with friends and everyone's drinking. He would have disapproved. But I didn't know what else to do."

"I might've done the same thing. I hurt my back a few times when I played ball and the spasms were so bad sometimes I couldn't stand up straight."

"I swear, Jesse, I didn't know she was hooked for a long time."

"I'm not here to judge or punish you, Patti. Just tell me what you have to say."

"Heather seemed much better after the fifteen days on the drugs. The PT and massage therapy were kicking in. Like Steve said, eight weeks after the injury, Heather was back at it. She said she didn't want a refill on the Vicodin. She was herself again. And then one day in the spring I was cleaning her room and—"

"You found pills."

Patti nodded and turned away. She was embarrassed. "I'm so ashamed, Jesse. How could I not have known? How did I miss the signs?"

"Come on, Patti. Teenagers are often strangers to their parents. Even parents close to their kids can't really know them or what's going on in their heads. What did Heather say about the pills?"

She laughed a sad laugh. "What you'd expect. That they weren't hers and that she was holding them for someone else. When I asked who she was holding them for, she said she wouldn't rat out her friends. I wanted to believe her. I guess I almost did until I went to pour the pills into the toilet and Heather flipped out. She was like a wild animal, Jesse. She grabbed them out of my hand, scratched my wrist when she did, and swallowed a pill right in front of me. I didn't know what to do or where to turn. I was afraid to tell Steve and afraid to ask around for help because of Steve's position. Heather begged me not to tell and said she could kick it with my help, that she could cut back gradually."

Jesse said, "It seemed like it was working, didn't it?"

She laughed that sad laugh again. "I financed her habit for a few weeks, doling out the pills as we had agreed. By May, I thought we had done it. I even took her into Boston, shopping to celebrate. What an idiot I was, a prize fool. In July, I noticed some of my things started to go missing: a pair of diamond earrings, my iPad, a watch. I pretended with myself for a week but knew in my gut what was going on. It was Heather. I confronted her and told her she had until the end of summer to kick it or she was going to re-hab. And voilà," Patti said. "She did it . . . I thought she did. What an idiot I was. Arrest me, Jesse. I killed my daughter sure as you are sitting here. I killed her with blindness as faith."

"Patti, there's nothing I'm going to say that will make you feel better, but drinking isn't going to help. That I am sure of. I think you need to talk to someone about this, someone more qualified than me."

Twenty-eight

Patti wasn't listening to him. Stood up, went into the living room, and came back with an open bottle of Grey Goose. She didn't bother with a glass, taking a big swallow from the bottle. These days, this kind of punishment drinking was hard for Jesse to witness. He had been where she was.

He sat patiently and watched as Patti took another swallow. As painful as it was for him to watch, he knew better than most how futile it would be for him to try to stop her. He remembered how he'd taken any attempt to stop him from drinking as a kind of personal challenge. He saw it so clearly now and had been utterly blind to it when he was still actively drinking. He imagined Patti would see it the same way.

"Chris Grimm," he said, when he thought Patti could refocus.

That got her attention. "What about him?"

"You know him?"

"Of him," she said.

Jesse stayed silent. He wanted to hear where Patti took this and he didn't want to lead her in one direction or the other. As silence usually did, it got to Patti, and drunk as she was, she needed little prompting to fill in the quiet.

"I came home from shopping one day at the beginning of the school year and went to change the sheets in Heather's room. It was pretty obvious she'd been sleeping with someone. I also found a condom wrapper on the floor under the bed. I'm not a prude, Jesse. I never thought a girl as pretty as Heather wouldn't be sexually active. I mean, I was at her age, but when I asked her about it, she was oddly honest. She told me she had slept with a kid named Chris Grimm and that she had kind of always liked him even though he was sort of a loner. I figured that his name would come up again and they might become girlfriend and boyfriend, but . . ." Patti made a face and shrugged. "Heather never mentioned him again."

"Is that it? When I was here the other day and mentioned his name, you denied knowing about him."

Patti bowed her head. "I love my husband, Jesse, but he can be hard to deal with. I don't know, I think he didn't see Heather for who she was. His upbringing was old-fashioned, and I think he still suffered from the whole Madonna/whore thing. He wouldn't have been able to accept the idea of Heather having casual sex. And the drugs . . . he would have totally lost it."

"Uh-huh."

"Why did you bring this Chris kid up?" Patti said, her body language hardening, her eyes focused and intense. "Did he have something to do with—"

"I don't know. All I can tell you is that he was outside the funeral home and at the cemetery. It's pretty clear he felt something for Heather, too. More than that, I can't say."

Jesse stood up to go. He figured he had gotten all the information he was going to get from Patti, but he reminded her to call him if she remembered anything or thought of anything else that might help him.

Patti tried to stand to show Jesse to the door, but he put a hand on her shoulder to hold her down in her seat. He knelt beside her.

"Patti, I'm an alcoholic. I'm sure that's not a surprise to you."

She smiled at him.

"Yeah," he said, "I thought you knew. I'm not going to preach to you. I hated it when people did it to me."

She was impatient. "But?"

"But whatever answers you're looking for, they're not in there." Jesse pointed at the bottle of vodka on the table.

"That it?" she asked, grabbing the bottle in defiance, just as he would have done a year ago.

"That's it." He stood. "You ever just want to talk, you call me."

With that, he left.

OUTSIDE THE HOUSE, he headed straight to the car. He used to be good at separating himself from the victims' families, from their grief and anger, their guilt and recriminations. It had been one of the great benefits of his self-containment, but it was tough to separate himself from the torture Patti Mackey was inflicting on herself. He had been there, right there in the wake of Diana's murder. It was all so painfully familiar. Patti Mackey seemed about ready to take the dive off the high board into the deep end of the bottle and, unlike him, she wouldn't even have Ozzie Smith for company.

He drove away from the house and headed back to Chris Grimm's address. Maybe he would catch the kid's less-than-charming mother at home alone, without his even-less-charming stepfather. And if he really got lucky, he'd catch the kid there unsuspecting, though Jesse never counted on luck. He took it when it came his way. All cops did. Luck had solved more cases than law enforcement types would ever admit, but relying on it was just plain dumb. Jesse was a lot of things. Dumb wasn't one of them.

Twenty-nine

Chris Grimm wasn't there, but his mother was. As he hoped, Kathy Walters was alone. No hard-assed husband to deal with. Maybe that was why she seemed more welcoming, or maybe it was something else. Just like the other night, she had a dangling cigarette at the corner of her mouth. But this time she asked Jesse in and headed straight to the kitchen.

"Coffee?"

He wasn't really up for it, but he didn't want to ruin the vibe. "Sure."

She put a mugful in front of him, got milk out of the fridge, and slid the sugar bowl over to him. There was already a mug and ashtray in front of where Kathy Walters settled down. Jesse sipped his coffee and, just as he'd done earlier with Patti Mackey, waited for her to fill in the void. Didn't take long.

"He ain't been home for two nights," she said, taking a long pull on the cigarette. "I'm worried."

"Is that unusual? His stepfather didn't seem to be a big fan of Chris's."

She smiled. "They ain't exactly fans of each other. Chris usually comes home. There's been times when he comes in real late, but he does come home. Sleeps in his bed and then leaves before Joe gets up."

"He hasn't called?"

She shook her head, blowing smoke in a steady stream out the side of her mouth as she did.

"Nothing. Not a word."

"Why didn't you call me?" Jesse asked. "I left a card with your husband."

"Joe . . . he . . ."

That was answer enough for Jesse. "Can I have a look at Chris's room?"

She didn't like that, hesitating to answer.

"Listen," Jesse said, "if you want me to start looking for your son, you're going to have to cooperate."

She didn't say anything. She stood up and nodded for him to follow her. Kathy Walters walked slowly up the carpeted stairs. The carpet worn thin, the steps creaking as they went. At the landing, she pointed at the third door to her left.

"He keeps it locked," she said.

"Key?"

She shook her head, doing that smoke-stream thing again. "He wouldn't trust me not to give the key to Larry, our neighbor, and he wouldn't trust Joe as far as he could throw him."

"You mind if I break the lock?"

There was that hesitation again. Jesse supposed that she was more afraid of her husband's reaction than of what he might find in the kid's room. He understood her fears. Just because she didn't bear any obvious scars or because those fading yellow bruises from the other night were now almost gone, it didn't mean she wasn't in an abusive relationship. He'd answered enough domestic abuse calls in his time to get the picture. He knew how easy it was to judge people like Kathy Walters. *Why stay with a man who hurts you and hates your son? Why not leave?* Always easier to quarterback on Monday morning than on Sunday afternoon. The problem was, there wasn't much Jesse could do for her in this instance.

"Any way this plays out, he's going to be mad at you."

"I know," she said, voice quivering.

"I can get you into a shelter, if that's what you want."

She shook her head furiously. "No. No. I want to be here when Chris gets back. I really do love him, but it's hard for me to show it. And Chris doesn't make it easy. I'm not a good mother, but I'm the only one the kid's got."

Jesse waited.

"Go on, do it."

Jesse gloved up, stepped a few feet back, built up some momentum, and kicked the door just below the lock. The door swung open violently. He turned to Kathy and asked if she'd like to accompany him to make sure he handled things properly.

"No, that's okay. I'm going downstairs. I need a drink."

Jesse said he'd come down when he was done and waited for her to leave before heading into the kid's room. The moment he entered, he knew something wasn't right. The kid had a huge wall-mounted flat-screen TV, every video game system in the known universe, three classic guitars in his closet, including a classic Les Paul with a sunburst finish, a Fender jazz bass, and a Rickenbacker twelve-string. He had a drawer full of gold chains, diamond rings, watches, and iPads. A lot of the jewelry was women's jewelry. The watches ranged from cheap Timexes to Rolexes. The Rolexes had different people's names inscribed on their backs. It didn't take an experienced detective to figure out that some, if not most, of the items in Chris Grimm's room were stolen goods. Only issue was, Jesse saw every report of theft and robbery in town and he recognized only two of the items in the kid's room—the jazz bass and one of the watches—as reported stolen.

Jesse's instincts about how the kid had acquired all these goods were confirmed when he found a box of off-the-shelf, disposable cell phones under Chris's bed. All the phones were still in their clear plastic packages. Chris Grimm hadn't stolen any of the items in his room, but Jesse was willing to bet most of them were bartered for drugs and that Chris eventually turned these items into cash. It occurred to Jesse that there were now several possibilities as to why Chris Grimm hadn't returned home for the last two nights.

He called Molly and told her to send Peter Perkins over to the address and to prepare paperwork for a search warrant on the entire premises. Jesse stepped out of the room and went downstairs to have a different kind of talk with Kathy Walters. The kind of talk no mother, not even a bad one, wants to have.

Thirty

While Peter Perkins did a more thorough search of the upstairs rooms, Jesse remained in the kitchen with Kathy Walters. She was really shaken, as much by the fact that the cops were going to have to search the entire house and garage as by the probable truth of her son's drug dealing. He could see in her face the regret over having opened up the door to Jesse and the fallout that would likely ensue.

"Kathy," Jesse said, "I'm not here to make your life or your marriage any harder, but if there are things we are going to find in the house that shouldn't be here, tell me now and I'll see what I can do. If we find something when we're searching for more of the stolen goods, it will be out of my hands and up to the DA."

Her deep blue eyes, the blueprints for which she had passed on to her son, were darting from side to side as she thought about what Jesse had said. That meant only one thing to Jesse: She and/or her husband had something to hide.

"Joe's really not as bad as he seems," she said, making a case for her husband. "He just gets worked up sometimes when he drinks. He don't mean nothing by it. He loves me in his way, and let's be honest about it, I'm no catch anymore. A forty-three-year-old woman with a seventeen-year-old son who hates the world."

Jesse had heard this same sort of thing many times when he was in uniform in L.A. and occasionally in Paradise, battered wives making excuses for their abusers. It was one of the reasons why answering a domestic call was so dangerous for cops. The women who had called for them often feared their husbands' reprisals. There were hundreds of incidents each year when domestic disturbance calls turned violent, even deadly, for the responding officers. It wouldn't do any good for Jesse to try to talk her out of it, so he didn't bother.

It was then that Joe Walters came through the front door, crazy-eyed and smelling of scotch.

"Get the fuck outta my house!" he said, charging right at Kathy. "What the fuck did you let them in here for?"

Jesse stepped between husband and wife. Jesse held the warrant out to Joe Walters. "We have a warrant to search the premises."

Walters grabbed the warrant and ripped it in half. "Fuck you and fuck your warrant. Get outta my house."

Jesse didn't budge.

"Why didn't you call to tell me about this, you stupid bitch?" Spit flew out of Walters's mouth as he yelled at his wife. "Instead I gotta get a call at work from Larry next door, telling me there's cops over at my place."

"I wouldn't let her call you," Jesse said. It was a lie, but he figured it was worth a shot.

"Bullshit! You can't stop her from making a call. This is her house. She ain't under arrest, and all you're doing is executing a search warrant."

"You know a lot about the law," Jesse said. "You a real lawyer or a jailhouse lawyer?"

That didn't go over well with Joe Walters.

"Fuck you! Who do you think you are?"

Jesse had had enough. "Sit down, Mr. Walters."

"And what if I don't?"

"Unless you took a cab here or walked, I'll arrest you for DWI."

Walters sat down, but Jesse knew it was only a matter of time. He could see Walters was seething, and seething drunks can control themselves for just so long.

"Jesse, you better get up here," Peter Perkins called from upstairs.

"In a minute, Peter." Jesse turned to Kathy Walters. She was on the verge of panic, because she also knew about seething drunks and what awaited her the minute the cops left. He wagged his index finger at her. "You come with me. You, Mr. Walters, stay right there."

"It's all your fault," Walters said, his voice getting louder and louder as he worked himself up. "You and that mutant brat. He's poison, that fucking kid. He caused all of this. You shoulda smothered him in his crib."

When he was done with his rant, he charged. Jesse stepped around Kathy Walters and threw a forearm into Joe Walters's face. His nose broke in a spray of blood and mucus. But Walters was a tough guy and didn't go down. He came at Jesse again. This time, Jesse planted his foot in Walters's crotch. Nobody was tough enough to shake that off. Walters crumpled to the floor, bloodied and breathless.

Jesse knelt down beside him and spoke loud enough so that only Walters could hear him. "Listen to me, you piece of crap. I'm going to make you my personal business from now on. I come by here and see one mark on your wife or your stepson, what I did to you just now will be nothing. Stay down and stay down here. I hear you on the move, I'm charging you with DWI and assaulting an officer. Nod your head if you understand."

Joe Walters nodded.

Upstairs, Peter Perkins pointed toward the door on the far right and held up an evidence bag containing a nine-millimeter pistol. "Loaded. Found it in the master bedroom in the nightstand."

Jesse asked, "Your husband have a permit for that?"

She shook her head.

"I didn't think so." Jesse could see in Perkins's expression that he had something to say out of Kathy Walters's earshot. He turned to her and asked her to wait in her bedroom. She walked into the bedroom, zombielike. Her world was coming apart at the seams, with no sign that the seams would hold.

Perkins walked toward Chris Grimm's room. Jesse followed him in.

"Beside the swag," Perkins said, "there's a passbook account with thirty-five grand in it. I found a few keys, business cards, and slips of paper with phone numbers on them."

"Any drugs?"

"None."

"He probably kept them somewhere else," Jesse said. "Okay, I'll send Gabe over to help finish the search. In the meantime, I'm arresting the husband on weapons charges. Come downstairs and witness the Miranda. I don't want this guy slipping through our fingers."

Thirty-one

After the arrest, Jesse had Gabe Weathers took Joe Walters to the hospital to get his nose reset and have him checked out. The last thing Jesse wanted was to give a belligerent abuser like Walters a way to game the system and hand him a get-out-of-jail-free card. So it was all by the book.

"Stay with him, Gabe. He doesn't leave your sight until we book him and put him in a cell."

Jesse drove back to the station and asked Molly to come into his office. She sat opposite him. Jesse explained what had gone on at the Walterses' house and what they'd found in the kid's room.

"So you think Chris Grimm was Heather's connection?" Molly asked.

"Uh-huh."

"But you didn't find any drugs in the kid's room."

"None, but that just means the kid wasn't stupid."

"He was stupid enough to keep stolen property in his room."

Jesse smiled a sad smile.

"What's that smile about, Jesse?"

"I'm smiling because I heard your voice in my head, Molly."

"And what did my voice say?"

"It said that Chris Grimm wasn't stupid, he was just being a kid."

"A kid selling drugs."

"I didn't say I thought he was a saint or that he was even a good kid. My guess, he pawned a lot of the stuff he got in trade for the drugs and held on to the stuff he thought was cool, like the stolen bass and the Rolex. We have to remember, this is a kid with a kid's sense of the world. A pro wouldn't have kept any of it, would have unloaded it immediately for ten, twenty cents on the dollar if necessary. One thing I can say, there did seem to be something between Heather Mackey and him."

"Yeah," Molly said. "The kind between a user and a dealer."

"It was more than that. Why else would the kid show up outside the funeral home and at the cemetery?"

"Fear. Guilt."

"Maybe. Doesn't matter now."

"I guess we'll find out when we get him."

Jesse shook his head. "I don't think so."

Molly was confused. "He's a seventeen-year-old kid scared out of his mind. Where's he going to run? We'll get him or the Staties will."

"My guess, the kid's already dead. He was working for someone else."

"Who?"

"You tell me, Molly. But he wasn't a criminal mastermind. He must have been recruited for the job. He was the school-level connection. There's always layers of insulation between the real supplier and the users."

Molly didn't love hearing that. It reminded her how easily her own daughters might have come in contact with Chris Grimm or someone like him.

Jesse said, "First thing we have to do is go through the stuff we collected at the kid's house. When Peter gets back and logs in the evidence, I want you to carefully go through it and call all the phone numbers on every slip of paper and every business card. Most will be dead ends, but maybe not all. I need you to individually catalog every piece of jewelry we found so we can put it up on the PPD website. And I need you to pull the reports on the theft of the Fender guitar and a Rolex."

Molly's expression turned down. "Do you really think the kid's dead?"

"If not already, he soon will be. Selling such potent stuff to Heather was a bad mistake. We didn't even know there was a ring in our area until Heather's death. The people the kid was working for can't afford to have him roll over on them to save his own neck. Not if they want to keep their operation going. That's the other thing."

"What is?"

"Assign someone on the night shift to collect all the digital surveillance footage from the town's cameras and see what the private security cameras captured."

"Will do. But, Jesse, if the kid really is dead, what do you hope to find?"

"The next person up the food chain from Chris Grimm. I think that's the best we can hope for now. I don't know, maybe I'm wrong and the kid got away. Maybe we'll get lucky and he'll turn himself in, but we have to work on the assumption that we're not going to get much help from Chris Grimm. Drug cases are built one step at a time."

Molly left. A minute later, Jesse grabbed his new baseball mitt off his desk, stood, and turned to face the window. He stared out at Stiles Island and the sun shimmering on the ocean as he pounded a baseball into the too-stiff pocket of the glove. The last of his old gloves had finally collapsed, the kangaroo leather beyond rescue or repair. Rawlings no longer made the model he'd used throughout his minor-league career. He'd been forced to buy a similar model online from a Japanese company, and it just didn't fit his hand the way his old gloves did. For the moment, it wasn't about the glove, but about concentrating on how to move forward with the case.

Thirty-two

Jesse put the glove back on his desk when he heard Joe Walters being hauled into the station. Molly printed him and photographed him, and Gabe brought him to a cell.

"Did you Breathalyze him?" Jesse asked Gabe, when he returned from the jail section of the station.

"Refused, but the doctors at the hospital drew some blood from him just in case. Molly will send it over to the lab."

"If the gun charges don't stick, his refusing to be Breathalyzed should stand up. Get him off the streets and away from his wife for a while. Good work. How'd he check out otherwise?"

Gabe laughed. "He puked a few times in the hospital. Not sure what made him more nauseated, the shot to his nose or the one to his—"

Jesse interrupted. "He ask for a lawyer?"

"Said he didn't have one."

"Thanks, Gabe. Get back out there." Jesse turned to Molly. "Call the public defender's office and get Mr. Walters some representation. Then call Lundquist and ask him to drop by."

———

BRIAN LUNDQUIST HAD taken the step up into Captain Healy's old job as the area's chief homicide investigator for the state police. Although Jesse and Lundquist had known each other for years, Jesse could never quite reconcile Lundquist's Minnesota farm-boy looks with his skill as an investigator. Always seemed to Jesse that Lundquist would have been a more natural fit as a guy out on a lake somewhere, ice fishing, drinking beer, and eating lutefisk. Then again, Jesse Stone, born in Tucson, wasn't much of a Yankee, either. It was odd that the two of them should end up knee-deep in murder in eastern Massachusetts.

Lundquist's hand didn't quite swallow Jesse's, but it was pretty big. The Statie plopped himself down into the chair opposite Jesse, but his attention was elsewhere.

"That a new glove?"

"It is."

Lundquist shook his head. "What's the world coming to? Jesse Stone bought a new glove."

"I also have a son I didn't know about until a few months ago. If that didn't make the world spin off its axis, my buying a glove isn't going to do it."

"Great news about your son, huh?"

Jesse was puzzled. "What?"

"The kid, Cole, didn't he tell you yet?"

"Tell me what?"

"Oh, no." Lundquist held his palms up to Jesse like a traffic cop. "I'm not saying another word. But if you didn't call me about Cole, what am I doing here?"

Jesse thought about pressing him on the thing with Cole but decided to let it go for now.

"We had a teenage girl OD," Jesse said. "Fentanyl and heroin."

"Was she a user?"

"She was opioid-addicted, but this was the first time she did it intravenously. Didn't stand a chance. Mom found her in her bed, cold and unresponsive."

Lundquist shook his bowed head. "A shame, but more and more frequent. Still, Jesse, what's it got to do with me? You want me to act as liaison between you and our narcotics team?"

"Nothing like that. I think we've tracked down her supplier. A Paradise kid named Christopher Grimm."

"Arrest him?"

"No, and I don't think we ever will."

"How's that?" Lundquist asked.

"My guess, the kid's already dead. So I need you to be alert for any John Does that turn up. Molly has all the particulars for you."

"How do you know the kid was her connection?"

Jesse explained about the stolen goods, the passbook account, and about how the kid showed up at the funeral home and cemetery.

Lundquist agreed. "Yeah, the people he was involved with have probably cut their losses and moved on. Victimless crimes, my ass. Sometimes I wish I could make people understand how crime shakes things up. If people who were thinking about murder ever had to do a family notification, I wonder if it would make them think twice about it. And their own damn families . . . Jeez, if they could only see how murder can destroy the killer's family the same way it destroys the victim's family . . . If, sometimes I think I'll choke on that word. You ever think about that stuff, Jesse?"

"Not as much as I used to."

"That it?" Lundquist asked, standing up.

"It is. Remember to stop and talk to Molly."

"Of course. A new glove . . . Will wonders never cease?"

"Get out of here."

At the door, Lundquist turned. "Listen, Jesse, don't spoil it for the kid. Let him tell you."

Jesse nodded.

Thirty-three

When Jesse arrived in Paradise, there weren't many African American families in town, except for a few who lived in and around the Swap. That was no longer the case, and the new diversity of Paradise was part of what Jesse enjoyed about Boston's encroachment. Although Paradise was relatively small, there were now developing communities of Indians, Chinese, and Hispanics, along with the Portuguese fishermen and their families who had lived in Paradise for a hundred years. Nor were African Americans consigned now solely to the Swap.

Moss Carpenter was a famous jazz guitarist who had lived on Stiles Island since before Jesse's arrival in town. Carpenter had always been the one prominent African American who the town fathers pointed to when outsiders complained about Paradise's lack of diversity. Their tone-deafness used to make Jesse cringe, because to him it always sounded like "Some of my best friends are black."

It was Moss who had filed the report of the missing Fender jazz bass. He had supplied enough detail in the report so that Jesse was one hundred percent sure the bass they had retrieved from Chris

Grimm's closet was Moss's stolen guitar. Jesse had brought the guitar with him just the same. The idea wasn't really to have Moss confirm the guitar was his, but to use it to get closer to the truth about Chris Grimm and the people who employed him.

Jesse pulled his Explorer up the stone driveway and parked next to Moss's Range Rover. Jesse had always liked the Carpenters' place, a large but simple farmhouse design with cut cedar shingles that the salt air had turned a lovely shade of silver. Many of the houses on Stiles were designed by famous architects and exuded about as much warmth as a dull steel blade. But Moss's house, garage, and studio seemed natural to their surroundings, almost as if they had grown up out of the ground on which they stood.

By the time Jesse got to the door, it was already open and Etta Carpenter was standing on the front step.

"Jesse Stone," she said, smiling at him. She was a lovely, dark-skinned woman with an oval face that was beginning, finally, to show her age. Etta, an English lit professor at the local community college, had that eternally young quality about her. Even now, with her age more obvious, she had a youthful exuberance. "Get in here and let me fix you some coffee and some breakfast."

Unlike the previous day, Jesse was in the mood for coffee and confessed to Etta that breakfast sounded great. She put a mug in front of Jesse and got to work at the stove.

"I'd like to think you came to flirt with me, Jesse, but I guess you're here to talk to Moss."

"Never could fool you, Etta."

She placed a fork and a plate of scrambled eggs, peppers, onions, and cheese next to Jesse's mug and sat across from him with her own mug of coffee.

"Now, what have you come to talk about with my husband?"

"The guitar he reported stolen last spring . . . We recovered it."

But instead of Etta reacting joyfully at the news, she stood up and went back to the stove, then to the kitchen sink, to be busy and not to face Jesse.

"You did?" she asked, washing the pan she'd cooked the eggs in. "Where?"

"In the closet of a missing teenager."

That stopped Etta cold. She turned to Jesse. "Moss will be pleased."

But there was nothing about her expression or the tone of her voice that reinforced the words coming out of her mouth. Mostly she just looked and sounded unnerved.

"Excuse me, Jesse, I've got to go upstairs for a moment. Finish up your eggs. There's more coffee in the pot if you'd like. Good seeing your handsome face again." She tried but failed to put a positive spin on her demeanor.

Jesse finished his eggs and coffee, retrieved the bass from the back of his SUV, and headed over to Moss Carpenter's studio.

Jesse knocked, but no one answered. He could hear the music coming from inside. He took a moment to let the beautifully complex guitar work wash over him as Moss would play a long riff, stop, start again. It was as if he was searching for something he just couldn't yet find. When there was a long pause, Jesse let himself in. There, on a high stool in the middle of the room, sat Moss Carpenter. His bald scalp and ears were covered with headphones. He held a blond-bodied Gibson Super 400 on his knee. Jesse waited for him to again stop playing before he approached.

"Jesse, man. How are you?" Moss said, carefully placing the guitar down and removing his headphones. But before Jesse could answer, Moss noticed the Fender bass in the evidence bag. His expression was a little bit more positive than Etta's had been, but it was clearly mixed. "You got it back?"

"Uh-huh." Jesse was careful to let Moss talk.

"If the people who had it only knew its value. That bass there used to be owned and played by the great James Jamerson, most talented rock bass player I ever knew. All those Motown hits from the sixties, that's him playing. But the man had demons."

"Older I get, Moss, the more I realize we all have them."

"True that. So are you here to return it to me?"

Jesse shook his head. "Still evidence. It will be returned to you, probably within a few months."

"If you're not here to return it and you could've just called me to let me know, then there must be another reason why you're standing in my studio."

"There is."

"I like solving musical mysteries, Jesse, like finding just the right key or chord. That's what I was doing when you came in, but generally, I just want things straight out."

"Fair enough. I came here for the truth about how this got stolen." He held up the bass. "And before you twist yourself up, let me say I'm not looking to hurt anyone or get anyone into trouble with the law."

Jesse then explained about Heather Mackey and what they had found in Chris Grimm's room. Moss, a slender man with a handsome face that might've looked like Sam Cooke's if he had lived long enough to make it into middle age, listened intently.

"Shame about the girl," Moss said when Jesse was finished.

"There's nothing either one of us can do for her, but I can't let it happen again in my town, in our town. I noticed that three weeks after you reported the bass stolen, Etta came down to the station and claimed the bass had just been misplaced. Yet here it is, Moss. I know your boy Django's down at Berklee, studying trumpet. He's nineteen and I don't need your permission to talk to him, but I'd like to go armed with the truth, so I don't have to waste time."

"You give me your word you're not looking to get anyone into trouble."

Jesse stuck out his right hand. "Unless he dealt the drugs, I'm not interested in him. I just need to find out as much as I can about what's going on with the stuff in town."

Moss took Jesse's hand and shook it. Then he detailed for Jesse how Django hurt his shoulder playing pickup basketball the previous autumn. Like Heather, he'd seen Doc Goldfine, who referred him to another doctor at the hospital. From there it followed almost exactly the same pattern as it had with Heather. The initial treatments didn't work and the pain got intolerable. Oxycontin had been prescribed and things seemed to have improved. Eventually, Etta discovered that Django was hooked and tried to wean him off the drugs. She thought she had done it and that Django was fine, but things started going missing from the house. Moss had been too absorbed in his work to notice until his James Jamerson bass had vanished.

"We got him help, Jesse. He did rehab over the summer. Thank God, it never got to where he was shooting heroin. I've seen what that does to people, close up."

"He ever tell you who was supplying him with his pills?"

Moss hung his head. "No, and we never asked. We just wanted our boy back and healthy. You got a boy now, so you understand."

"Moss, I would have understood anyway. I'm just glad you got Django some help. I know how hard it is to beat something alone. Tell him I'll be down in a day or two to talk to him and tell him not to worry. One thing I ask is that he doesn't hold anything back. You can tell Etta everything is cool. She looked scared."

"Will do, Jesse."

They shook hands again. Outside the studio, Jesse stopped and listened to Moss playing. Moss seemed to have found the answer to what he had been searching for when Jesse first knocked on the studio door.

Thirty-four

That night, after attending an AA meeting in Salem, Jesse went home, wondering about the odd conversation he'd had with Brian Lundquist about Cole. Jesse wasn't even aware that Cole and Lundquist were acquainted. Still, Jesse supposed it was good that Cole was making friends and contacts in town. It had been a little claustrophobic, just the two of them living in Jesse's condo. It wasn't that Cole never went out, but for a while there it had been a struggle.

Cole was in his usual position, on the sofa, watching some show on TV. But Cole seemed antsier than usual. He wasn't normally a fidgety person, but as soon as Jesse came into the apartment, Cole began shifting his position on the sofa.

"I got the mail," Cole said, reaching over and handing the pile to Jesse.

Jesse shuffled through the mail. It was the usual stuff: bills, ads, flyers. There was something else, an open envelope addressed not to Jesse but to Cole Slayton. Jesse's heart thumped harder when he saw the return addressee was the Massachusetts State Police.

"There's something here for you," Jesse said, voice steady, holding the open envelope out to Cole.

"No, why don't you read it."

He had a notion of what it would be, but when he actually read the letter stating that Cole Slayton had passed all requirements and had been accepted into the next class of trainees at the State Police Academy in New Braintree, Jesse was simultaneously filled with pride and worry. Pride was the stronger of the two emotions.

The next thing he knew, Jesse was hugging Cole, pushing him back, shaking his hand, and hugging him again.

"Easy, Dad, easy," Cole said.

"'Dad'? You sure you want to call me that?"

"For the time being. I reserve the right to change my mind."

"It's times like these I wish I still drank."

"No, you don't."

"You'd be surprised," Jesse said. "The desire comes and goes, but I don't think it ever truly just goes. Anyway, we should go celebrate. Come on, we'll go to the Gull or the Lobster Claw."

Cole waved for Jesse to calm down. "We can celebrate soon. I may even let you throw me a party before I go in next month."

"Why all the secrecy?"

"I didn't want you to try to talk me out of it. I've seen up close how dangerous this profession can be, and though I know deep down you love what you do, it's taken a toll."

"Can't deny that."

"And I didn't want you to think I was doing this to prove myself to you," Cole said.

"You're sure this is what you want?"

"It is."

"Then do it the best you can."

Cole asked, "So you're okay with this?"

"Truth?"

"Yeah."

"I would have rather you wanted to play shortstop for the Dodgers, but, yes, I'm good with your decision."

"I hate baseball, especially the Dodgers."

"So you've said. C'mon, get dressed. I'm taking you for a drink, whether you want one or not. I'm in the mood for a tall club soda on the rocks with a twist."

Cole hesitated but realized he wasn't going to win this one. He went into his bedroom to throw on some clothes.

TWENTY MINUTES LATER they were seated at the bar at the Lobster Claw, a beer in front of Cole and that tall glass of club soda in front of Jesse. Jesse toasted his son. Afterward, Cole shared some things with Jesse that he'd never spoken about with him.

"I've lived in Massachusetts for over a year now," Cole said. "It took me a long time to work up the nerve to confront you. I think that if I hadn't lost my job in Boston and wasn't nearly broke, I may never have come to Paradise. I was mad at you, mad at Mom for dying, mad at the world."

"Uh-huh."

"You say 'uh-huh' a lot."

"Uh-huh." But Jesse couldn't keep a straight face. "I don't want to get in your way, but if you ever need any advice about being a cop . . ."

"Advice like what?"

Jesse debated with himself about how to answer that question. In the end, Jesse shook his head. "No, Cole, you'll figure this stuff out for yourself. When you have trouble doing that, come to me."

"Okay."

"So who introduced you to Lundquist?" Jesse asked.

"Captain Healy. Both Captain Healy and Brian were great. They both think a lot of you."

"This isn't about me tonight. This is about you. Congratulations."

After that, they sat in silence, finishing their drinks. But unlike the silences between them over the last couple months, silences that were often awkward and strained, this one was comfortable.

"C'mon, Statie," Jesse said finally, clapping his son on the shoulder, "let's go home."

Thirty-five

Jesse didn't usually make it a point to attend arraignments, but he made sure to be at the one for Joe Walters. He had particularly strong views about men who abused women. It had gotten him into occasional trouble in L.A., trouble he was glad to bear. During his very first case in Paradise, he'd had to confront a musclehead who beat on his wife. He'd dealt with that guy much the same way he'd dealt with Joe Walters, with a swift kick and a warning. Sometimes the warnings stuck. Sometimes not, but abusers had to know there would be a price to be paid.

Jesse knew something was wrong the minute he stepped inside the courtroom and saw Kathy Walters seated in the front row behind the defense table. That wasn't a good sign. He knew that those first twenty-four hours after the cops interceded were crucial. That it gave the wife a chance to walk away, to get to a shelter or to a relative's house. Unfortunately, things often went the other way. The abused party, full of fear and regret, tried to make it up to the abuser. But he was sure it had gone ass-end-up when they led Joe Walters into the courtroom and he stared back at Jesse, a chilling sneer on his face. He mouthed the words *Fuck you.*

Seeing Joe Walters looking into the gallery, Dan Malmon, the new town DA, turned and saw Jesse. He shook his head. That was never an encouraging sign. And if Jesse needed any further proof of how things were going off the rails, the reading of the charges against Walters took care of that. Driving While Intoxicated was the only charge against him.

After the charge was read and before the judge could ask for Walters's plea, Malmon stepped forward.

"Your Honor, if it please the court?"

"Proceed, Mr. District Attorney."

"Thank you. Mr. Walters has agreed to plead guilty to the one count of Driving While Intoxicated. In exchange for this plea, the people have agreed to the following. Mr. Walters will pay a fine of two thousand dollars, will do fifty hours of community service, and agrees to undergo ten sessions with a town-appointed alcohol counselor."

The judge didn't seem any more pleased with the bargain than Jesse was.

"Mr. District Attorney," said the judge, "I note that the defendant has a prior criminal record and that this deal does not include a suspension of his driver's license."

"That is correct, Your Honor. Mr. Walters's past criminal behavior occurred over a decade ago and his business requires him to drive. My office has made Mr. Walters well aware of the consequences if he should in any way deviate from the letter or spirit of the agreement."

"Very well." The judge turned to Joe Walters. "Mr. Walters, do you understand the terms of this sentence and will you abide by them?"

"He will, Your Honor," said Walters's public defender, Ruth Jordan.

That didn't please the judge. "I'm asking Mr. Walters directly."

Walters said, "Yes, sir. I do and I will."

"You are free to go." The judge banged his gavel and that was that.

Jesse walked up to the DA, failing to hide his anger.

"What the hell was that about? What happened to the gun charge and assaulting an officer?"

"Let's take this to my office, Chief," Malmon said, nodding to the door.

Inside Malmon's office, he offered Jesse coffee.

"I don't want coffee. I want an explanation. We caught an ex-con with an unlicensed nine-millimeter in his bedroom. He assaulted me and it's pretty clear he's an abusive spouse. Now you explain to me how he's not spending five seconds in jail even though his blood alcohol level was one-point-six."

"Because the wife claimed the gun was hers, Jesse, and—"

"She claimed I was the one who precipitated the assault with her husband."

The DA was perplexed. "How could you know that? Are you a mind reader?"

"Old story. Kathy Walters got scared and his lawyer got to her. The trade-off is that Walters won't sue Paradise or me if you dropped the assault charges and let the wife walk away from the gun charge."

DA Malmon shook his head. "That's exactly how it went. His lawyer knew I wasn't going to let the wife do time for his having the gun illegally. At least I got them to surrender the weapon without a fight." Malmon handed Jesse a piece of paper. "That's a legally binding document that turns possession of the weapon over to the PPD. The gun is yours."

"This isn't going to end well," Jesse said.

"Sorry, Chief Stone, but without her testimony and with her claiming ownership of the weapon, this was the best I could do."

"I understand, but it still stinks."

"No argument from me."

They shook hands, neither of them smiling.

Jesse left the DA's office and began walking back to his SUV. Before he got twenty feet, his cell buzzed in his pocket. It was from the PPD.

"What's up, Molly?"

"I've been calling the numbers we got from the paper and business cards Peter collected in Chris Grimm's room."

"Anything?"

"Most go unanswered and to a generic voicemail message, but I got one hit."

"You did?"

"A Mr. Arakel Sarkassian. His cell number was on a business card for an Oriental rug business in Boston. The business number was disconnected, but he picked up when I called his cell. What would Chris Grimm have to do with an Oriental rug business?"

Jesse wasn't as surprised as Molly. "The kid had all sorts of stolen goods in his room. Maybe one of his customers stole a rug to barter for drugs. I'm no expert, but I know those rugs can be worth a lot of money."

"I don't know, Jesse. That makes sense, but Mr. Sarkassian was awfully nervous about the call."

"Cops make people nervous. Worries me when they don't. I'll call him back when I get in to the station."

"Something else."

"What?"

"There was a pawn receipt and chit from a shop in Boston as well."

"Boston? I think I need to take a trip to Boston. See you in a few minutes."

"How'd the Walters arraignment go?"

"It didn't." Jesse hung up before Molly could ask him to explain.

Thirty-six

Before heading to Boston, Jesse stopped at the high school. As he was now pretty certain Chris Grimm had been dealing drugs, he wanted to alert Principal Wester and to drop in on Maryglenn. No one except a victim is happy to see the cops, so Jesse wasn't offended by Freda's expression when he stepped into the office.

"Morning, Jesse," Freda said. "Hope this isn't terrible news."

"It's nothing tragic, but I do need a few minutes of Virginia's time."

Freda called in to the office to announce Jesse's presence.

"Go on in, Jesse. She's waiting for you."

Principal Wester stood back to the door, facing out the window, much the way Jesse looked out at Stiles Island. Except Principal Wester was peering down at the activity on the athletic field.

"I try not to think about it," she said, back still to her visitor.

"About what, Virginia?"

"All the responsibility that comes with my job. Come, stand by me."

Jesse did.

"Look down there, Jesse. Every one of those kids out there has his or her own story. His or her own pain. They have their own small victories and crushing defeats. They have to deal with it minus the benefit of perspective. Everything to them seems so large. It's all so overblown. And for seven or eight hours a day for almost two hundred days a year, I'm responsible for all of them."

"Heather's death has got you in a philosophical frame of mind."

She nodded. "It has. Why is it we only consider these things when tragedy strikes? I ask you, Jesse, because you, too, bear the same kinds of responsibilities. I'm sure after that horrible business with the white supremacists, you must have thought about what might have happened. It must have given you pause."

"For about five minutes." He smiled. "I just try to do what's right, Virginia, and leave the bigger questions to someone else. I've never been very good at figuring out the larger meaning of things, because I'm not sure there is one. I've dealt with too much pain and death to worry about it all now."

"How do you know what's right?" she asked, turning to look at his profile.

"I think once we're their age," he said, pointing out the window, "we already know what's right, and when we're not sure about what's right, we have a good idea of what's wrong."

Principal Wester was quiet for a few seconds and then asked Jesse why he'd needed to see her.

He explained about Chris Grimm being missing and about what they had found in his room. He avoided discussing what he thought the odds were of the kid still drawing breath.

"What do you think it adds up to, Jesse?"

"I believe Chris was dealing drugs and was probably the person who supplied Heather with the fentanyl-laced heroin that was the cause of her death."

Wester looked back out the window, that faraway stare return-ing to her eyes. "But if he's run, why tell me?"

"Because if he's run, someone will replace him. Someone prob-ably already has. You know how to handle these kids and your faculty. I think you should put the word out to your teachers, guid-ance counselors, and the school psychologist. Let them know if any students want to talk to me about Chris, I'm available. I'm not looking to get anyone into trouble."

"Understood. Thank you, Jesse."

FIVE MINUTES LATER, Jesse was looking through the window of the art room door, waiting for a pause in Maryglenn's lesson. When she stopped and the students began working on their projects, Jesse knocked and stuck his head into the room. A smile flashed across her face before she could stifle it. She was afraid that any student paying attention would know just how she felt about Jesse Stone.

"I was wondering if I might have a few minutes of your time?" he asked, and retreated into the hall.

She followed him out.

"This is a pleasant surprise." She wasn't trying to stifle her smile now. "What I'd really like to do is kiss you, but I think we'll have to table that idea for now. What are you doing for dinner?"

"I'm driving down to Boston right after I leave here. Tomorrow night?"

"Sure. Why are you here, anyway?"

He smiled. "Seeing you isn't good enough reason?"

"For me, yes. But really, Jesse."

"I had to talk to Virginia Wester about Chris Grimm."

"Anything you can share?"

"I think you'll have an idea by the end of the day."

"Okay."

He brushed his fingers across her cheek. "I'll come get you tomorrow night. You pick the place. Remember, you're paying."

"I was hoping you'd forget that."

"Unlikely."

"Okay, let me get back in there. They're probably already talking about us."

"Let them."

"They're teenagers, Jesse. I don't have a choice."

"Seven o'clock all right for tomorrow?"

"Perfect. Good luck in Boston with whatever."

"Thanks."

Before he could move, she kissed him quickly on the lips and smiled. "Let them talk."

Thirty-seven

He had five places to visit while in Boston. Only four of the visits were scheduled. His first stop was the unscheduled one. Precious Pawn and Loan was on Washington Street in the South End. Precious Pawn bore almost no resemblance to the old three-balls-above-the-door dumps he'd been familiar with in L.A. The ones on skid row, in East L.A., and in Compton. The ones that sucked the blood out of the poor and the desperate. But Jesse knew the days of those dives were over. He bet if he went back to L.A. now, the pawnshops in those places would look as cleaned-up and neat as Precious Pawn did. These days, pawnshops looked almost like respectable jewelry stores. Hell, there were even TV shows about pawnshops. Jesse knew the truth. Many pawnbrokers worked both sides of the street, as fences and as snitches for the cops. And if he wasn't already sure about the relationships among brokers, bad guys, and cops, Jesse's AA sponsor, Bill, knew the deal. He had once been a fence in Boston and had done time for it.

It made perfect sense. Pawnbrokers knew the real value of things and commodities. They were expert negotiators and traveled in many different circles. Still, to stay in business, licit and illicit, and to stay alive, pawnbrokers often had to skirt the line. Everyone involved understood the rules. It was not too dissimilar from how it worked in the drug trade. Even the soulless people at the top of the drug cartels understood that they had to occasionally sacrifice people in their own organizations to the law. It was the price of doing business.

Jesse had made sure not to dress in anything remotely coplike. He was in a blue sports jacket, a plain gray sweater, faded jeans, and running shoes. Upon entering Precious Pawn and Loan, he strode through the aisles, eyeing the rings, watches, bracelets. He stopped to look at the rare books, which included signed first editions of Zane Grey and Louis L'Amour novels. Jesse had a real weakness for Westerns, books and movies. Part of that was a result of growing up in Tucson. The larger part of it was simply a matter of who he was and what he stood for.

A woman's voice interrupted his reverie. "Are you a big reader or a collector?"

Jesse stood up, looking away from the glass. The woman on the other side of the display case was in her late thirties or early forties, blond, with light blue eyes. She was attractive if not exactly pretty, wore lots of makeup and enough jewelry to open her own kiosk at a mall. She had a bright white smile and clicked her long, silver-painted nails against the case, waiting for Jesse's answer.

"More of a reader," he said.

"My name's Jolene. I would be happy to show you one of the books if you'd like."

He smiled back. "No, thank you, Jolene." He reached into his pocket and came out with the pawn receipt and ticket Peter Perkins had found in Chris Grimm's room. He slid it across the glass to Jolene. "I'd like to check to make sure this item hasn't been sold. If it's still here, I'd like to see it. I might want to buy it back."

Jolene went white and her hand trembled slightly. There was something about the receipt or the ticket that set her off. Jesse knew what he was doing. If the transaction between Chris Grimm and the store had been legitimate, she would simply have excused herself and gone into the back to retrieve the item. Her reaction was anything but casual.

"I'm sorry, sir," she said, smiling, getting her legs back under her, her hand steadying. "I have to check with my manager to see if this item is on hand. We sometimes send items to our storage units, and I believe this item may be off premises."

Jesse acted his part. "You can tell that just by looking at the number on the ticket? That's remarkable."

She smiled at him again, thinking he was a rube. "Not the number, sir. The color. Items with blue tickets are often the ones we send to our off-site storage units."

"I see."

He was quiet, waiting for her to make the next move. He was sure she was hoping he would either leave or say he'd return the following day to give her time to retrieve the item. She might as well have hoped for him to sprout wings. Eventually, she caved.

"Let me go speak to my manager."

"Sure, Jolene."

Jesse watched her maneuver between the cases on high black heels and disappear behind a mirrored door at the rear of the shop. As he watched her, he was aware he was being watched as well. There were security cameras all over the place. Jesse just went back to admiring the books. Fifteen minutes passed. Clearly they were hoping he would leave. He didn't.

A man claiming to be the manager appeared in front of Jesse at minute sixteen. Fifty, white, clean-shaven, slightly overweight, and dressed in an expensive suit and custom-made shirt with French cuffs, he introduced himself as Jerry.

"I'm sorry, sir. I believe Jolene told you this item might be in one of our storage units."

Jesse smiled at him. "That's right."

"I'm afraid she was mistaken, Mr. . . ."

"Stone."

"Mr. Stone. Yes, well, the item was sold as per our agreement as stated on the ticket." Jerry pointed to some small print in high legalese written on the receipt. "If the person who offers the item up as collateral doesn't return within that specified period to reclaim the item and pay what's due, we have the right to offer the item for sale. I'm sure you understand. I'm sorry I couldn't be of more help."

Jesse wasn't quite ready to leave it at that. "You see, Jerry, my son ran away from home and there are items missing from our house. My wife and I hadn't wanted to pursue it, but it's been many months since he left and some of the things he took have great sentimental value to us. Is there any way you could tell me what item or items Chris pawned on this ticket?"

"I'm sorry, Mr. Stone. I don't have the time to search our records right now, but if you make an appointment to come back in, I'm sure we can do something. But take my advice, Mr. Stone, let it go. No matter what your son pawned, it's gone now and there will be no way for us to retrieve it. I'm sure you understand."

Jesse left it there for the moment. He had found out enough for the time being and didn't want to push so hard that they would become suspicious.

"Thank you, Jerry, and please thank Jolene."

"Good luck, Mr. Stone. I hope your son comes back and that things work out."

The insincerity in Jerry's voice got to Jesse, but he walked out without answering or looking back.

Thirty-eight

A rakel Sarkassian found little pleasure in alcohol. He didn't enjoy how it made him feel. Even the other day, after murdering the boy to save him further pain, he hadn't felt the release of tension. He certainly didn't reap the joy Stojan and Georgi had. Then again, they had taken joy in brutalizing the boy even after it was clear he had nothing to tell them. What good was pain for pain's sake? He would never understand thugs like Stojan and Georgi. There was one thing about alcohol he noticed the day he killed the boy—it numbed him. And he had kept himself numb ever since. Good thing, too, he thought, knotting his tie and staring at himself in the mirror.

He wasn't sure how he would have handled the phone call from the Paradise policewoman if he had been sober. The vodka had kept him removed just enough from his panic to sound equally calm and yet surprised to hear from the police. And when the second call came, the one from the chief of police, the alcohol had utterly saved him from himself. But the chief, this Jesse Stone, wasn't going to take no for an answer. Arakel couldn't get rid of him and had agreed to meet him for lunch. Lunch was a setting

Arakel was comfortable with. In his old business, he often met with the best results over a meal. In a business setting, clients have their guard up but often let their guard down when there is good food and conversation to be had. Good food and conversation, these were things Arakel was expert in. When he was certain he looked good, he ran his tongue over his teeth and swallowed the small bottle of vodka in a single gulp. As the numbness spread, he went into the bathroom, took a shot of mouthwash, rinsed, and spit.

JESSE GOT THERE twenty minutes early, owing to the fact that the Little Armenia Café was located in the South End, less than a mile from Precious Pawn and Loan. He wanted to watch Arakel Sarkassian's approach, see how he would react. There had been nothing about their phone conversation to make Jesse suspicious. Sarkassian had seemed reasonable, if slightly nervous, and had cooperated. In spite of the fact that Jesse had given Molly a perfectly rational explanation of why Chris Grimm might have the business card of a man in the Oriental rug trade in Boston, he wasn't sure he believed it himself. He would know soon enough.

Sarkassian walked into the restaurant and was immediately greeted by the hostess and the owner. They shook hands as well as kissed on both cheeks. There were smiles all around, and real warmth among all three. Jesse guessed this was why he had been treated with such deference when he arrived and said he was here to have lunch with Arakel Sarkassian. He had turned down the offer of a complimentary glass of wine but had enjoyed the bread and various dips they had provided him with. The owner, a friendly man, seventy-five if a day, with a serious gray mustache, had spoken with Jesse for a moment.

"A shame about Arakel's family business, no?" said the owner, almost as if thinking aloud. "They sold only top-notch merchandise, but these days . . . a shame, a shame. Well, I hope you enjoy the meal. I will send over something for you to eat while you wait." It hadn't been a question.

When Sarkassian came to the table, Jesse stood and they shook hands. It was difficult for Jesse not to notice the superior quality of Sarkassian's navy blue, gray-pinstriped suit. Like Jerry's at the pawnshop, Sarkassian's white shirt was custom-made with French cuffs, his initials embroidered in black into the cuffs. His cuff links were gold, encrusted with blue sapphires. His tie was gold silk. He wore a Patek Philippe watch, a simple gold wedding band, and a diamond pinkie ring. Jesse couldn't see his shoes in the low light, but he was sure they were handmade Italian. Even Vinnie Morris would have envied how Sarkassian was turned out. There was something else Jesse couldn't fail to notice, the smell of vodka and of the mouthwash meant to hide it on the man's breath.

Sarkassian made a gesture for Jesse to sit as if he owned the place. Now Jesse understood why Sarkassian had selected this restaurant. It was familiar ground, a comfortable place, an arena in which he thought he could control his lunch guest. That was fine with Jesse. He always believed it was a great advantage to be underestimated. Jesse reinforced Sarkassian's comfort by letting him order for the both of them and carrying the conversation. Jesse didn't bring up Chris Grimm or the business card until the coffee was served. But during the meal, he had asked about the restaurant owner's commentary on Sarkassian's failed business.

Sarkassian made a sad face, shook his head. "Tigran is old-school. He cannot imagine a world in which the traditional values are not kept. See the beautiful rugs on the wall." Sarkassian pointed. "We, my brothers and I, we sold him these. They tie Tigran to the home-land. We must make allowances for the old."

When Jesse had asked about what business the family was in now, Sarkassian's answer was just like the rest of his presentation—reasonable. "Now we import and export more than rugs. Traditional food, musical instruments. Like that."

Jesse left it there and Sarkassian seemed at ease with the subject. The same could not be said about the subject of Chris Grimm and the business card.

"Jesse, I have not any clue how the boy got hold of my business card," Sarkassian said, rubbing his fingers nervously along the edge of the tablecloth.

"Uh-huh. And did you two ever do business together?" Jesse made sure to be less than specific about what type of business.

"Not really. What I mean to say is that the boy said he had come across some small Oriental rugs for which he needed an appraisal. I explained that my business was no longer in existence, but that for a fee I could look at his rugs and give him an accurate estimate of their value."

"And you met?"

"Yes, here in this restaurant, as a matter of fact. He came, I looked at his two rugs and supplied him with a fair-market-value estimate. When I saw he was so young, I asked only that he pay for the meal as my fee."

"Armenian rugs?"

"Persian. Good quality, but nothing very valuable, a few thousand dollars each."

"Were you suspicious of a high school boy in possession of valuable pieces?"

"Looking back, I suppose I should have been." Sarkassian

shrugged. "But he was such a nice boy and polite . . . I did not think to suspect. I suppose I was foolish."

Jesse stood, but when he reached for his wallet, Sarkassian clamped his hand over Jesse's. "It would be an insult. It is my honor to pay."

Jesse let him and then dropped a bomb of sorts on Sarkassian. "Thank you for the meal and your time. I've been a cop of one type or another for a very long time now, and there's one thing I'm surprised at, Mr. Sarkassian."

"And that is?"

"That you never asked about why the police are interested in Chris Grimm in the first place. And one more thing, Listerine works much better with vodka than the minty stuff."

Jesse left before Sarkassian could react. As Jesse headed to his Explorer, he failed to notice the two men in the white van parked across the street from the Little Armenia Café.

Thirty-nine

Bill met Jesse at the Starbucks near the old Episcopal church, where they used to go for coffee after the AA meetings. Far from the eyes of Paradise's citizens, those were the first meetings Jesse had ever attended, and Bill befriended Jesse early on. Bill's encouragement really helped Jesse get through those early sessions and helped him buy into the plan. *Not everyone has to buy into it like it is the gospel truth,* Bill had told him, but Bill had also warned Jesse that too much doubt and straying too far from the twelve steps was also a route back to drinking. So when Jesse picked a sponsor, he chose Bill.

"You okay, Jesse?" Bill asked after they'd said their hellos and settled into their favorite table by the window.

"You could see the church from Diana's apartment windows," Jesse said, referring to his murdered fiancée. He smiled sadly. "That's why I picked the church for my first meetings, to feel close to her."

"Still miss her?"

"Every day."

"Seeing anyone?"

Jesse told Bill about Maryglenn.

"Serious?"

Jesse shrugged. "I'm not sure what that means, Bill."

Bill knew it was time to change the subject. "How about your boy?"

That chased away Diana's ghost and questions about Maryglenn for the time being and changed Jesse's mood. Jesse could feel himself smiling and his chest jutting out.

"He's going to be a Statie. Applied without me knowing about it. He's going into the academy next month."

Bill reached over and shook Jesse's hand hard. They held on to each other's hand a beat longer than usual.

"Bet you felt like having a double Johnny Black when you heard that news."

"You know it."

"But you didn't."

"I did not," Jesse said.

"So, Jesse, not for nothing, but I'm not sure you couldn't have told me all this good news over the phone."

"I was going to be in town today anyway, and I could use your expertise."

"In?"

Jesse showed Bill the receipt and ticket from Precious Pawn and Loan. Bill raised his eyebrows and gave Jesse a sideways glance. "I've been straight for twenty years. I'm not sure what I could tell you. If you're asking me if I know the people who run this shop and do I know if they're legit or not . . . I can't tell you. When I stopped drinking, I cut myself off from the people I used to drink and do business with."

"No, Bill, that's not it." Then Jesse explained about Jolene's reaction to seeing the paperwork and Jerry's explanation about the goods being sold and his being unsure of what the pawned item was.

Bill laughed. "Things have changed, but not that much. The game is still the game."

"Explain it to me."

"Look, a thief comes to me to get rid of some merch, but I want to cover my ass in case the cops are on to the guy. I pay the guy for the watches or the rings or whatever. I write him out a receipt for fifty bucks without describing the merchandise. Just like this one here you're showing me. I give him a claim ticket even though I know he's never coming back to get his stuff.

"If I can, I let a few weeks go by and then sell the merchandise. Somebody like you shows up in my store, I'm covered. There's nothing on the receipt says what the pawned goods were, and because I recognize the coded color on the claim ticket, I know the deal. I blow you off the same way this Jerry guy did. If you persist and make yourself a pain in the ass, I find some piece-of-junk watch or set of bongo drums and say this is what was pawned on that ticket. How can you prove otherwise? The hot merch is long gone. I'm surprised you only found this one receipt and claim ticket. This sort of arrangement isn't usually a onetime type of deal. It's not worth it to the broker. Too much risk, not enough return."

"There are probably plenty more receipts. We just haven't found them yet."

Bill asked what this was about. Jesse explained about Chris Grimm.

Bill asked, "You think the kid's dead?"

"I do."

"You headed back up to Paradise after we finish?"

"One more stop."

"Where?"

"Nowhere that would interest you."

"You sure about that?" Bill said.

"We'll never know."

Bill held his hands up in surrender. "I get it. Never mind. You should come back for a meeting down here when you can. We'll do dinner afterward."

"Sounds good. I know a place that has great Armenian food."

Bill gave Jesse another sideways glance but kept quiet and finished his coffee.

Forty

Arakel Sarkassian showed up at the warehouse at three that afternoon after making certain to stop at a bar to fortify and numb himself further. He knew now what he had to do, and he understood that doing it would imperil his life. He had thought the luncheon was going so well right up until the end. That was when this Jesse Stone had stripped him of his confidence and laid him bare. He had underestimated the man, badly. Always a mistake, but one he had made before. In business, he had underestimated the competition, underestimated their willingness to stoop low and sell cheap goods, their ruthlessness.

He had avoided telling Mehdi, his partner, about the calls from the police. He hated to listen to Mehdi lecture him and to constantly bring up his weaknesses and blind spots. It galled him and made him feel small. When he considered telling Mehdi about the police calls, all he could hear was Mehdi's voice in his head. *How stupid a man you are. How could you have been so stupid to give the boy a business card with your mobile number on it? Why not simply invite the police to your door? Do you ever think things through before you do them? Why did I choose you and not one of your brothers or one of a hundred other people I knew from the business?* It was one thing to hear the man actually rebuke him, but for Arakel to do it for him in Mehdi's imaginary voice . . . It was too much.

He had thought, maybe foolishly so, that killing the boy would put an end to Mehdi's lectures and sniping. It had impressed Mehdi, at least for a few days. He had even let Arakel keep the gun he'd used to kill the kid. At first he hadn't wanted it, but then he reconsidered. It would not do, he thought, to cede the respect he had earned at such a bloody cost by acting weak. Now was not the time for weakness, and he knew it.

After throwing some water on his face and hanging his jacket up in his office, Arakel walked on shaking legs into Mehdi's office. Mehdi was not an unattractive man. He had a deep olive complexion and short black hair that was showing some gray. He kept his beard neatly trimmed and short, but let his mustache grow out longer than the beard surrounding it. He had a square jawline and a wrestler's neck. But his brown eyes seemed always to be looking through the person or thing he was focusing on. It was his eyes that got to Arakel. It felt as if his eyes were staring through him into the truth, as if the truth were something physical, with a specific location inside his body. He knew such thoughts were madness, but Arakel could not deny them.

"Arakel," said Mehdi, smiling at his partner. "You are late today."

"I had business to attend to. That is why I am—"

Mehdi cut him off. "Things in Paradise, Salem, and Swan Harbor are good? They have been stabilized?"

"I have heard nothing to tell me otherwise, but that is not—"

Mehdi interrupted him again. "That is a nice shirt. You do not often wear such nice clothing into the warehouse. And you seem to be perspiring. Look at your underarms."

Arakel could no longer bear it and slammed his hand down on Mehdi's desk. "For heaven's sake, Mehdi, let me speak. This is not easy for me."

Mehdi smiled, a reaction Arakel thought strange, but he dared not stop for fear of never having the nerve to finish.

"Yesterday, I received calls from the police department in Paradise," he said, beads of sweat forming on his brow. "First from a woman, an Officer Crane. She asked about a business card the police found in the boy's drawer. The second call was from the police chief, a Jesse Stone. I tried to calmly talk my way around things, but he insisted on meeting with me to discuss how my old business card ended up in a teenager's dresser drawer."

"And how did you enjoy your lunch at the Little Armenia Café, my friend?"

Arakel froze, the sweat pouring off his brow onto his face. "You followed me?"

"Stojan and Georgi," Mehdi said. "After the other day with the boy, I felt it was good to keep an eye on you . . . in case you were overwhelmed with a bout of guilt or some other nonsense. I couldn't afford to have you go to the police and turn yourself in."

Arakel was wounded by that. "I would never dishonor my own family that way, nor would I harm you."

Mehdi bowed his head in thanks. "I appreciate that and I admire that you tried to handle this on your own, but no more." Mehdi wagged his finger at his partner. "You must never keep such things from me. Yet it is good you came to me. My respect for you grows, my friend, and gives me confidence that I made a good choice in bringing you into this business. Now, tell me what the conversation was between you and this police chief."

Arakel gave him a comprehensive account of the conversation between himself and Jesse Stone but could not bring himself to reveal the last things Stone had said to him. He wasn't going to risk the newfound confidence Mehdi had in him.

"Do not worry, Arakel," Mehdi said, standing and grabbing his partner's biceps. "The Bulgarians are keeping an eye on this cop, Stone. If his nose gets too long, we will see to him. For now, relax." Arakel turned, getting as far as the office door before Mehdi stopped him. "Remember, my friend, never withhold things like this from me again."

Arakel did not say anything to that and went back to his office. There, he collapsed into his chair and reached into his jacket pocket for another small bottle of vodka.

Forty-one

The sun was getting lower in the sky by the time Jesse turned off the Concord Turnpike into the bowling alley's parking lot. Vinnie Morris's name appeared nowhere on the deed to the building that housed the bowling alley, nor on the incorporation papers for the firm that owned and ran it. In fact, Vinnie Morris's name did not appear on a single document that in any way connected him to the bowling alley, but there wasn't a soul who knew anything about the Boston underworld who doubted the place was Vinnie's. Jesse had come to see Vinnie many times, and every time he did he was forced to dance the same dance with the person at the front desk. It didn't matter who was behind the desk, man or woman, young or old, tall or short, thin or fat. They all played dumb.

"Tell Vinnie Jesse Stone is here to see him."

This time it was a woman behind the desk, twentysomething, with a thick Irish accent. "Come again," she said. "Vinnie, you say? No, sorry. I don't tink there's anyone by dat name here, sir."

Jesse took out his chief's shield. "Just call in back and tell him I'll be at the bar."

He didn't bother to wait for her to parry with him, much as he enjoyed her brogue. He turned, walked straight to the bar, and sat down. He asked for a tall club soda with lime. The barman recognized Jesse from previous visits but was unaware that Jesse had given up the drink. He put a Johnny Walker Black on ice down in front of him. Jesse didn't hesitate to push it away.

"No offense, but I don't drink anymore," Jesse said. "I'll take that club soda."

"For real?" the barman asked.

"For real."

The barman took the blended scotch away and tossed it in the sink. He put the club soda up in front of Jesse. "Sorry."

"No need."

"So, you really did give it up?" Vinnie Morris had been watching and listening.

Jesse turned and shook Vinnie's hand. "Cute Irish girl up front. Better than the usual fat losers you have manning the desk."

Vinnie laughed. "She's Jewish, from Sharon, an actress. She likes screwing around with the customers' heads. Her dad's one of my accountants."

"She's good. Had me fooled."

"Hey, Jesse, you mind if I have a real drink?"

"Your place, Vinnie. Your rules. I'm fine, but thanks for asking."

The barman didn't wait and put a double pour of expensive bourbon in front of his boss. Jesse raised his glass. They both drank. Sat there quietly together for a minute, looking into the mirror behind the bar.

"What can I do for you, Jesse?"

"Not so long ago, you warned me that Boston's crime would creep into Paradise. You were right. It's arrived."

"I like being right, but you didn't drive down here to pat me on the back for being an oracle."

"Opioids and fentanyl-laced heroin," Jesse said.

"That stuff's all over the place. You know you got an opioid problem in this country when there's a drug just for opioid constipation that a pharmaceutical company pays millions of bucks to advertise on TV."

"We had a seventeen-year-old girl OD in town last week, and I think the trail leads down here."

"Not to me it don't."

"I mean Boston. Sorry, Vinnie. I know that's not how you make your money. But you hear things."

"I do. Word around is there's a cartel out there that sells franchises like a fast-food chain."

"Turks? Afghans? Russians? Mexicans? Bulgarians? Israelis? Colombians?"

"Everybody. That's the scary thing. It's not set up the traditional way. Word is the money comes out of China, and when it comes back to them it's squeaky clean. Their hands are so far away from the product that most of the investors don't know what their front money is for. You think the DEA is playing Wack-A-Mole with the Mexicans . . . this is worse."

"Did anyone come to you to make the offer for you to buy in?"

When Vinnie didn't answer immediately, Jesse had his answer.

"Yeah," Vinnie said, seeing Jesse had already guessed at the answer. "They came to me, but it was through lawyers and nothing was ever stated that could blow back on them. It was a discussion about product and shit. All neutral words, but what was really being said and offered was understood by everyone in the room."

"Was it a good deal?"

"I didn't get to where I was by turning over control of my whole life to some nameless, faceless syndicate. And you know the way I feel about drugs like that. Could you make money? Yeah, a lot more than someone who is a silent partner in a bowling alley."

Jesse asked about the lawyers, but Vinnie balked.

"Not crossing that line, Stone."

Jesse didn't push, but changed subjects. "Precious Pawn and Loan, you know them?"

Vinnie laughed. "I heard of them."

"Next time I go see them, can I use your name?"

"Sure, I think they probably heard of me, too."

"No doubt. What do I owe you?"

"Any intel you get on that drug franchise," Vinnie said. "I don't want them to get any ideas that they should expand into other areas."

"Deal." Jesse shook Vinnie's hand.

"How's things with your boy?"

Now it was Jesse's turn to laugh. "He's in the next class at the State Police Academy."

"Jeez! Like father like son. I hope he's not as good a cop. I'd hate to have to deal with the both of you." Vinnie stood, finishing his drink in a single swallow. "Watch yourself with these drug guys, Jesse. They don't fuck around."

When Jesse headed back to Paradise, a white cargo van followed.

Forty-two

Jesse drove from the bowling alley to the Back Bay. It hadn't been a disappointing day, but there hadn't been any revelations, either. He felt he wasn't much closer to finding the person who employed Chris Grimm than he had been when he'd driven away from the high school that morning. Sure, he knew more about how the scam with the pawn shop worked. He had his suspicions concerning Arakel Sarkassian and his story about Chris Grimm bringing Oriental rugs to him for an estimate.

It had been good to see Bill again and, he had to confess, it had also been good to see Vinnie Morris. Jesse and Vinnie would be bound together forever by how things had played out in the immediate wake of Diana's murder. And it wasn't only that. Jesse had to acknowledge it was more than respect and gratitude he felt for Vinnie Morris. There was an undeniable kinship between them. For now, though, Vinnie and the other events of the day were in his rearview mirror. He had a sense that this last get-together had more potential to get him closer to the drug scene in Paradise than those that had come before it.

The last thing Jesse wanted or needed was more caffeine, but he met Django Carpenter at a coffeehouse a few blocks from the Berklee College of Music campus. Django was a classic blending of his mother and father. Dark-skinned, with a radiating warmth like his mom and as stunningly handsome as his father, Django had yet to fill out the promise of his long limbs and broad shoulders. He bumped fists with Jesse as he approached. Jesse had known the kid since birth, so there was no feeling-out nonsense.

"Yo, Jesse," he said, seemingly at ease in these surroundings.

"How are you doing, Django?"

"It is what it is."

"School?"

"All good. Love my folks, but nice to be out of their orbit . . . if you know what I mean."

"Can't be easy wanting to be a musician and having a famous father for a musician. And then to hang Django on you . . ."

Django laughed. "This your way of easing into a talk about me and drugs? Well, Jesse, I didn't do drugs because I needed an escape or nothing, or because I was all neurotic about competing with my dad. I didn't get all bent because my folks named me after one of the greatest guitar players who ever lived. I didn't do drugs because my dad's a better musician than I'm ever going to be. Really, I'm good with that. I did drugs because I had to. First it was the pain relief. Then it was the high. Then it was the hunger. It's that simple."

Jesse laughed at himself. "Thanks for being honest with me. You straight now?"

"Totally. I never want to go back to feeling that desperate again. You can't know how that feels."

"I'm an alcoholic, Django. I know."

The kid smiled. "No offense, Jesse, but that's not exactly breaking news. Imagine being an alcoholic and having no open bars, no stores where you can buy a bottle, no way to quench that thirst. That is a sickening, lonely feeling."

"You get your pills from Chris Grimm?"

Django's eyes got wide. Suddenly, Django's openness and ease took a hit. Jesse could see the kid calculating how to answer.

"Relax, Django. I already know he dealt. I understand that you don't want to rat him out, but you might be doing him a favor."

The kid wasn't buying it, not yet. "That sounds like something a cop would say, that I'd be doing him a favor."

"Chris Grimm is missing. He might already be dead, and if he isn't, he soon will be. Did you hear about Heather Mackey?"

The kid nodded. "Always liked her. She was hot, yeah, but really nice, too."

"Well, the people who were using Chris to feed drugs to the kids in school can't afford to have him out there to talk if we find him first. You're a smart person. You understand."

"I don't know how I can help."

"You can help by telling me the truth," Jesse said. "I'm going to ask you some questions and I need full disclosure. I'm not looking to hurt any of your friends or get anyone other than the people in the supply chain in trouble. I will not reveal to anyone that you gave me their names. Understood?"

Django nodded.

"Do you know who Chris was working for or where he got his supply?"

"Sorry, Jesse, I don't. I swear."

"When you bought from him, how did the buy go? Did you approach him, give him money, and he gave you pills, or—"

"Nah, not like that. You slipped him a note with a number on it or if you saw him in the hall, you'd say like 'fifteen,' then you'd go to locker 113, undo the combo, and leave the money. Next day you went to the locker and there would be your pills."

"Was it Chris G.'s locker?"

"No. He had his own locker in the number-three section. Left it open a lot so we could see he didn't keep nothing in it we could use. If you know what I'm saying."

"I know. So it was never a direct exchange?"

"Never, no way."

Jesse asked, "What if someone stole?"

"First thing, it was made clear that there would never be big orders filled. Only enough for a few days at most. Second, if anything was taken, the locker number would change and we'd all get cut off for a while. Chris also said he worked with some bad dudes who would beat the shit out of anyone who even thought about stealing. Man, no one wanted to risk any of that. At least I guess. We never got cut off, and the locker number didn't change."

"How about phone orders?" Jesse asked. "He couldn't always be sure to run into his customers in class or in the hall."

"Every week he'd leave a slip of paper with a new phone number on it in the locker."

Jesse understood why he'd found all those prepaid phones in the Grimm kid's room. Different phone every week. Phone records for Chris's regular cell phone would be worthless. The same would be true of the people he worked for.

"Did you ever do a deal with him that deviated from this locker pattern? You had to have a way to get supplied over the holiday and term breaks."

"Only once," Django said, hanging his head in shame. "I met him by that self-storage place in the Swap. That's where I brought him the James Jamerson bass."

"How many pills did it buy you?"

Silent tears rolled down the kid's cheeks. He couldn't look at Jesse. Then, "I told him how much it was worth because of it being vintage and who had owned it and all."

Jesse pushed. "How many?"

"Ten."

It wasn't just tears now, and they weren't silent. Django excused himself and went to the men's room. In the meantime, Jesse called in to the station. Suit was taking his rotation on the night desk. It was interesting how marriage had changed Suit. He used to hate the desk, but these days he didn't mind his week of night shifts, answering calls, dispatching cars, entering data, and doing paperwork.

According to Suit, there was nothing going on in town and there was no word on Chris Grimm. Jesse said he'd stop by when he got back into town.

"Sorry, Jesse." Django was back in his seat, face dry, eyes clear. "That was the worst thing I did, but I was desperate. I think I would've done much worse than that if I had to."

"Well, the bass will be back in your dad's hands and you're doing well. Don't beat yourself up."

"I think I'll beat myself up over that for the rest of my life. Helps remind me about how bad and low I was."

"Makes sense."

"Anything else, Jesse? I have a rehearsal with my band in fifteen back at school."

"What was the combination to locker 113?"

"Six right, fourteen left, seventeen right, twenty-nine left."

"Last question, and it's the hard one." Jesse took his notepad from his jacket pocket. "Names of anyone else you know was buying from Chris Grimm."

"You give me your word they won't get in trouble?"

"As long as they're not selling, I give you my word."

This time they shook on it.

"Steve Parkinson, Petra North, Lidell Thomas, Sara York, Carl Bedell, Bob Mark . . . That's it, Jesse. I swear. Lidell and Bob graduated with me. Must be others, too, but I don't know them."

Jesse stood, replaced the notepad in his pocket, and bumped fists with the kid.

"Okay, Django. Thank you for your honesty. Get to rehearsal."

He watched the kid disappear into the night. As he did, he thought about the price people paid for their missteps. Not the price in money, but the cost in dignity and self-respect. Money could always be recouped. He wondered about the rest of it. Remembered how he almost drank himself to death and embarrassed himself after Diana's murder.

Forty-three

Suit was at the desk, reading a paperback. Jesse had stopped on the way up from Boston and bought Suit a jelly donut. The times of Suit devouring three or four donuts were over. Elena had seen to that. Suit even ate salads these days and went to the gym. His belly no longer strained at the buttons of his uniform shirts. He put down the book when Jesse came through the door.

Jesse held up the bag. "Only one."

"Jelly?"

Jesse nodded.

Suit smiled, but it was sheepish. "Elena will kill me. Hell, Jesse, I'm down to less than my football-playing weight in high school."

"How do you feel?"

"Great."

"So you don't want this?"

Suit's right hand swung out and snatched the bag from Jesse's hand. "Did I say that?"

Jesse enjoyed watching as Suit relished each small bite of the donut.

They hadn't discussed Suit's bravery at the old meetinghouse since right after it happened. Suit had been awarded a medal for his bravery, a plaque had been placed on the wall of the station-house, but like most real heroes, he was almost embarrassed by the attention. What mattered to Luther "Suitcase" Simpson had nothing to do with medals and plaques. He had always longed for Jesse's respect. Not respect as a person. Jesse had always afforded him that. It was that he had always craved Jesse's respect as a cop. There was no question of that now.

What still surprised Suit was not that he'd walked back into a building knowing he was very probably going to die inside. Nor was it that he'd done it only several months after getting married and finding true happiness for the first time. It was that when he walked into the old meetinghouse, it had nothing to do with win-ning Jesse's approval or respect. It was all about doing his duty and doing what was right in spite of being choked with fear. He had done it because that's what a good cop did.

"Did you hear about Cole?" Jesse asked, as Suit swallowed the last bite.

"No. What?"

"He's going into the State Police Academy next month."

Suit felt a twinge of something when Jesse said that and saw the smile light up his face. Suit hadn't much liked Cole when he arrived in Paradise. Truthfully, Cole hadn't made it easy for any-one to like him. And though Suit had earned everything he wanted from Jesse, he guessed what he felt was a touch of jeal-ousy. Suit had always acted the part of Jesse's surrogate son/ younger brother, and a piece of him didn't want to relinquish that just yet.

"Good for him," Suit said, in spite of himself. "How do you feel about it?"

"Proud and scared. I'm going to throw him a party before he goes in."

Suit changed the subject. "How did it go in Boston?"

"Mixed."

"What's that mean?"

"What it means," Jesse said, "is that we're going to change tactics tomorrow."

"How so?"

"We're going to put some people on notice at the high school."

"We are?"

"We are. You have tomorrow off, right?"

Suit nodded.

"Want some overtime?"

"Sure, Jesse."

"How long are the periods at the school?"

Suit thought about it. "If things haven't changed, the periods last fifty minutes. With ten minutes between classes."

"And school starts at seven?"

"Seven, yeah."

"You meet me for breakfast at Daisy's at nine."

"Then what?"

"Then we're going to the high school to shake the trees and see who falls out."

"Whatever you say, Jesse."

Jesse retreated into his office. Suit tried to go back to his book but felt too guilty about his reaction to Jesse's pride over Cole. Suit had to laugh at himself for the irony of his petty jealousy. But he no longer had to walk around in silence, burdened by his thoughts and feelings. He had a wife at home to talk to and share with. Now he smiled at the prospect of talking to Elena, and the guilt disappeared even faster than the jelly donut had.

Forty-four

At eight, before heading to Daisy's for breakfast to discuss what he wanted to do at the high school, Jesse was at the stationhouse, talking to Molly.

"Peter have any luck yet with the Grimm kid's computer?"

Molly shook her head. "None."

"We probably won't find anything on it, even if we get into it."

"I've gone over his cell phone records," Molly said. "Nothing there either. I checked the numbers in and out."

Jesse took out his notepad and tore off a sheet. "Get the home and cell numbers for these kids and match them against Chris Grimm's records. He was using prepaid phones, but when addicts are desperate, they don't tend to follow the rules. My guess is some of their numbers will show up."

Molly paled when she read the names on the list.

"My girls are on the field hockey team with Sara York and they've known Carl Bedell since they were little. We are in a supper club with the Bedells."

Jesse hadn't thought it through and realized he should have had someone else handle this aspect of the investigation.

"Molly, I can have Suit do this tonight."

"No, Jesse, absolutely not. I can do my job. But are you sure about them?"

"I got their names from a reliable source."

Molly was clearly upset, simultaneously angry and sad.

"But you can't say anything to these kids or their parents, and definitely not to your girls. Not yet. We can't compromise the investigation."

Molly bit her bottom lip. "I understand."

Jesse knew better than to ask again or to make Molly promise not to share the information or warn the kids' parents. Molly didn't frequently go ballistic, but when she did it was ugly, and Jesse was usually on the receiving end of her wrath. He moved on.

"I want you to go through the evidence from Chris Grimm's room. Look for receipts from Quinn's Self-Storage in the Swap. Also, see if you can find a key to a storage unit from Quinn's. I don't know if their units have their own locks or if the renters have to supply them. In any case, write up a search-warrant application for Quinn's and leave the unit number out. I want it ready for when we get that info."

Jesse rarely touched Molly, and when he did it was never in a manner that could be misperceived by anyone watching as even remotely romantic or sexual. It was the same when they were alone. They loved each other, deeply, in a way that would be hard for either one of them to explain or for anyone else to understand. From early on they understood that they were professionals and that the job was always the most important thing. Before heading to his office, Jesse put his hand on Molly's shoulder and left it there for several seconds. They did not look at each other. No words passed between them, but Molly knew Jesse was acknowledging how difficult it was for her to be a mother, a wife, and a cop.

When the phone rang, Jesse lifted his hand from her shoulder and went into his office.

Forty-five

Jesse sat with Suit and Gabe at a booth at Daisy's. Cole waited on their table. Suit, who had discussed his jealousy with Elena earlier that morning, stuck out his big hand to Jesse's son.

"Congratulations on getting into the academy. I know we haven't gotten on so well, but I'm happy for you."

Cole smiled and shook Suit's hand. "I didn't exactly make it easy for you or anybody else to like me. I'm sorry about that."

Jesse smiled but said nothing.

Gabe was confused. "What am I missing here?"

Suit said, "Jesse's son is going to be a Statie."

Gabe scowled. "A Statie! Watch out, kid, us local cops hate the Staties."

There was a second of hesitation and confusion on Cole's part. When the three cops at the table saw it on his face, they burst out laughing.

"Get used to it, Cole," Suit said. "These guys give you any trouble, come to me."

"Thanks, Suit. Now, what do you want for breakfast."

Once Cole had walked away from the table, Jesse thanked Suit for his gesture.

"That was a nice thing to do, Suit."

Suit deflected Jesse's praise and asked about what the plans were for the high school.

Jesse said, "I've been playing it low-key. I didn't want to cause a big stir after Heather Mackey died. The kids needed time to mourn and reflect. I also didn't want to send people running for cover. But since now I'm certain Chris Grimm was the connection and he's already split or dead, we're going to serve notice today and make people nervous."

Gabe, a former Boston cop, understood perfectly. "We're going to put on a show."

"Uh-huh."

Suit asked, "What kind of show?"

Not revealing his source, Jesse explained about locker 113 and how it was used as a transfer point for orders and deliveries.

"Between classes, while the kids are outside their rooms and going to their lockers, we're going to make a show of cutting the locker open."

"But you have the combination," Suit said.

Gabe answered, "That's part of the show, Suit."

"We want to make a lot of noise for as many people as we can, students, teachers, secretaries, administrators, and maintenance people," Jesse said.

This time it was Gabe who didn't understand. "Teachers? Janitors?"

Jesse nodded. "I was thinking about it last night. Who would have access to Chris Grimm? Who would approach the kid? How would Chris get a spare locker? I'm thinking that maybe the person next up the ladder from the kid works in the school."

Both Suit and Gabe were nodding now, too.

Suit said, "Do you think we're going to find anything in the locker?"

Jesse shook his head, taking a sip of coffee. "Unlikely, but it tells us something either way."

Gabe smiled. "If there's still drugs and unfilled orders in the locker when we open it, it means they haven't replaced the kid as the supplier and his customers are going to be in pretty bad shape."

"And if it's empty," Suit said, "then it means they have moved on and that there's either a new locker or a different system already being used. Also means that your theory about it being someone at the school who was the kid's connection makes sense."

Before they could discuss it any further, Cole arrived with their breakfasts.

Gabe said, "You sure you want to give up all this glory to be a Statie?"

Cole laughed. "Tough choice."

WHEN HIS COPS went outside and after Jesse paid the bill, he cornered Daisy. It bugged Jesse that Daisy, who had always been simpatico with him, had seemed to avoid him that morning. And he couldn't get past Cole's comment about how Daisy had seemed jealous of his relationship with Maryglenn. Jesse was a man who liked things to make sense. That's what being a homicide detective had been about, bringing order to or making sense of circumstances and events that, at first glance, seemed disconnected. Of course, there were and would always be cases that defied sense and reason, but most of the time it was simply a matter of doing the work.

"Are you going to give me a hard time about covering for your son?" she said. "Because if you are, mister, you can just forget it. I'm—"

"Not that. I'm glad you two trusted each other so much and that you gave him the space to go for what he wanted."

"You got quite a boy there. His mother did a good job raising him. Don't screw your part up."

"She did and I won't. But what's the deal with you and Maryglenn? And don't tell me to go ask her. I'm asking you."

"You know Swingline Sue's?"

"No."

"Then educate yourself." She pushed past Jesse, about-faced, "And congratulations. You have a party for him, I better be there."

She didn't give Jesse a chance to say another word before she disappeared into the back of the restaurant.

Forty-six

Jesse and Principal Wester understood each other's position.

"The kid is officially missing, so I don't need a warrant to get into his locker. Locker 113 is something else, but I could get a search warrant for it if you force my hand."

"I know precedent says that the students should have no expectation of privacy on school grounds, but this will hurt my relationship with the students, and the school board won't be pleased."

"They'll be even less pleased if there's a delay and another kid ODs."

As displeased as she was with the notion of giving the police access to the lockers, she was even less happy about Jesse's insistence on doing it as the kids moved between classes. Jesse's explanation of why that was the best time to do it made sense. Still, none of it was to her liking.

Inevitably, a crowd of students and teachers formed around Jesse, Suit, and Gabe. Peter Perkins, evidence bag in his gloved hands, had joined them as well. Principal Wester stood next to

Jesse. Things got surprisingly quiet, and when they did, Jesse turned and faced the crowd.

"We're cutting open the lock on number 113," he said. "I know for a fact that this locker was used as a transfer point for pill orders and deliveries. Heroin, too. Let me make this clear to you, I am not looking to get anyone in school in trouble. If you've got a problem, all we want to do is get you help. If you don't want to come to the police, I understand. Go to a teacher, your guidance counselor, the school psychologist, Principal Wester, or a friend. We don't want any more of you hurt. But let me put anyone involved in selling the drugs on notice: You have one chance to come forward. I realize you might be addicted yourself and feel trapped. You're not. We'll get you help. Here's the thing. I found out about this locker and I will find you. That's what I am paid to do. If I find you before you come forward, that won't be good for you." Jesse turned to Gabe. "Cut it."

Gabe Weathers placed the sharp jaws of the lock cutter on either side of the combination lock's U-shaped metal and squeezed the long handles together. The jaws cut cleanly through the curved metal. Peter Perkins stepped forward and put the lock in an evidence bag. He opened the locker. As Jesse expected, it was empty. Peter Perkins put the bagged lock away and got busy taking photos. It was all part of the show.

Jesse nodded to Virginia Wester.

"Okay, everyone, back to class," she said, looking at her watch. "The excitement is over and I don't want to hear any excuses about being late for class. Let's go. Let's go." She gestured with her arms, shooing them away.

Jesse had wished she would have repeated some of what he had said, but he understood why she hadn't.

He leaned over to Suit. "You stay here with Peter. Keep an eye

out for any kid who sticks around or seems like they want to approach you. When Peter's done, go home and get to sleep before
tonight's shift."

"Sure, Jesse. You think this did any good?"

"Too soon to tell, Suit." Then he walked over to Peter. "When
you're done with this locker, open Chris Grimm's locker. I want
everything in it bagged and cataloged."

"I will."

"Gabe," Jesse said. "You can go out on patrol."

AS THE SCHOOL'S FRONT DOOR closed behind Jesse, Maryglenn
raced to catch up to him. When he turned to face her, the expression on her face wasn't what he expected. Instead of smiling at
him as she usually did, she was scowling and there was very real
anger in her eyes.

"I didn't expect that of you," she said, brushing hair out of
her eyes.

"I was doing my job."

"Is it your job to scare the hell out of these kids? I heard that
was some display you and the troops put on."

"'Troops'?"

"Well, it was a show of force, wasn't it?"

He nodded.

"Word has already spread around the school."

"Good," he said. "That was the idea."

"What was?"

"I wanted word to spread and I wanted to scare some people."

"At what cost?"

"Trying to make sure Heather Mackey is the last casualty."

"There wasn't any other way to do it?"

"Look, Maryglenn, I can't discuss an ongoing investigation. But I will tell you this: Chris Grimm is missing. No one from the school has come forward to give us any leads." He turned and pointed toward the school. "There are kids in there hooked on Vicodin and Oxycontin, some probably pretty desperate to get hold of anything to make the hurt go away. If they can't get pills, heroin is probably their next best option. I think that might be the point of the whole operation, moving kids from pills to heroin. That's what killed Heather Mackey."

Maryglenn's expression softened, but not completely. "I know you have a job to do. I think maybe I'd like a raincheck for tonight. Maybe until this blows over."

"Sure."

He was tempted to ask her about Swingline Sue's. He didn't ask, not wanting to complicate things between them any more than they already were. Maryglenn said goodbye. There was no stolen kiss like the day before, but Jesse had been around long enough to know how fast weather changes and how romance could evaporate even more quickly.

Forty-seven

She stood close to Petra in a darkened classroom. She stroked the girl's hair, her cheek.

"Shhh . . . Shhh, lover. Calm down. Calm down. The police left an hour ago. They're gone, honey. Everything will be all right, I promise."

But the girl was so scared her whole body was shaking. She'd been in the hallway and watched the cops break into the old drug locker. Eight days ago, they might have found her pill order in that locker. She had listened to Jesse Stone's speech about getting help. That wasn't the part of what he had said that resonated with her. She was no longer just a kid hooked on pills. Now she was on the other end of things. She had taken Chris Grimm's place.

"I can't do this anymore," she said, tears rolling down her face. "You heard what the chief said. If they catch me doing this, I'll be in big trouble."

The older woman wiped the tears off Petra's cheeks.

"Listen, lover, we can't be seen in here together. Meet me tonight at the motel at eight and we'll work it all out. You'll see. I will make it all better. I'll text you with the room number."

She'd pushed the right button, at least for the time being. Petra stopped crying, smiled.

"Give me your hand. This is for you." She opened Petra's fingers, placed a little green pill in the girl's palm, and closed her fingers around it. "I will have more for you tonight. Now make sure no one is outside the door when you step into the hallway. I will wait a few minutes and leave after you." She leaned forward and kissed Petra softly on the lips. "Go. Until tonight."

When she was certain the girl had gone, she reached into her pocket, retrieved the prepaid cell phone, and dialed Arakel.

JESSE STOPPED AT THE STATIONHOUSE to collect another piece of evidence they had retrieved from Chris Grimm's room: a Rolex Submariner. It was a blue-faced watch with white markings on the dial. The bezel was colored blue with gold markings. The metallic wristband was predominantly silver in color, with a central, single line of gold-colored metal running along the full circumference of the watch from twelve o'clock to six o'clock. There was an inscription on the back of the watch. *To Ambrose North from his loving wife.*

Molly stopped Jesse on his way from the evidence room to the stationhouse door.

"How did things go at the school?" she asked. "My girls called me. Told me you guys really put a scare into everyone."

"If the kids are scared, that's good. But it may have cost me." He told her about Maryglenn's reaction to the show they'd put on.

Molly said, "You were doing your job."

"I was, but no one likes the police in their school."

Molly shrugged and moved on. "Where you headed?"

He held up the evidence bag containing the Rolex. "The Norths."

"Oh, Jesse, I almost forgot. I've got something on video."

"Chris Grimm?"

She nodded. Jesse stepped around and stood behind her as she tapped at her computer keyboard.

"This is from the camera at the service-road entrance to Kennedy Park the day of Heather Mackey's funeral. See the white van." She clicked the mouse and rollerball to enlarge the image of the van. "It's a Massachusetts tag, but I can only make out a partial number." She clicked the mouse again. "Here, less than a minute later. Look."

The footage showed the white van stopping, its side door sliding open, Chris Grimm emerging from a clump of overgrown bushes and entering the van. There was a silhouette of a man in the back who helped the kid into the van. Once he was in, the door slid shut and the van rode away.

"The rear tag is purposely obscured," Molly said, pointing to an enlarged still of the rear license plate. "It's got one of those dark tinted plate holders. Makes it almost impossible to read, even in daylight."

"Good work, Molly. Run the partial tag. Maybe we'll get lucky."

"More likely to win the lottery."

"Buy us a ticket and run the plate anyway. And see if you can't pick the van up on any other cameras. Anything on the storage unit?"

"No receipts, but I have a call in to the owners."

"Let me know when you hear back."

"You know, Jesse Stone, I'm not so sure I didn't like it better when you were in rehab and I was acting chief. There was nobody but the mayor to order me around."

Jesse took out his credentials case containing his chief's shield and put it on the desk next to Molly. "Just say the word, Officer Crane, and all this can be yours."

Molly ignored the offer, because they both knew the truth. Molly had hated her time as acting chief and Jesse had fought too many battles to keep his job to simply walk away.

Forty-eight

The North house was around the corner from Doc Goldfine's. It was a modest-sized Victorian, but unlike the doctor's house, it was kept in pristine condition. There wasn't a missing, rotted, or wrongly painted spindle on any of the complicated woodwork. There wasn't a chipped shingle—fish scale, diamond, square, or scalloped—on any of the siding. And the blue, turquoise, red, and pink paint job was refreshed every other year. The wrought-iron fencing that surrounded the home showed not an ounce of rust, and the English-style gardens on three sides of the home were meticulously maintained. But Jesse had learned long ago that the perfection on the exterior of the house wasn't a commentary on the people who resided within.

The North family, along with other prominent local families like the Cains, Grays, and Salters, went back to the founding of Paradise. As the Cains had, the Norths chose to stay in their Pilgrim Cove home and not build gaudy, oversized manor houses up on the Bluffs. While many of the descendants of those founding families had given up the pretense of their heritages, Ambrose North, like R. Jean Gray, played his patrician role to the hilt. Jesse wasn't fond of pretense, and he wasn't particularly fond of Ambrose North. North was a partner in an old Boston law firm and was a vocal leader of the "not in my backyard" movement in Paradise. He opposed anything that threatened to change either the face or the vibe of the town.

Jesse stepped up onto the wraparound porch and knocked on the front door. He was pleased to see that Annette North, not her husband, had pulled open the door.

"Chief Stone," she said, her voice and demeanor calm. "Would you like to come inside? Please." She made a sweeping gesture with her arm.

While her husband enjoyed throwing his weight around, Annette North was always proper and polite. She was thin, more handsome than pretty, and dressed the part of an upper-crust conservative New England housewife.

"Thank you, yes." He stepped in and followed her as she retreated into the parlor.

"Please, sit." She gestured at the period settee. "I fear Ambrose is in Boston and won't be back for several days."

"That's fine."

"How rude of me, Chief Stone. Would you care for some refreshments?"

"No, thank you, Annette."

She sat opposite him on a green leather wing chair. "How can I help you today?"

Jesse decided to play things a little differently with the Norths than he had with Etta and Moss Carpenter. He had felt comfortable with the Carpenters, knowing that they would eventually trust him enough to tell the truth. Although he liked Annette far more than he liked her husband, he wasn't at all as confident in the answers he would receive in the North household.

"Several months ago, Ambrose filed a report concerning a stolen watch."

Annette rolled her large brown eyes and looked up at the ornate plaster and woodwork on the ceiling. "That again! I told Ambrose he had simply misplaced the damn thing, yet he insisted on filing a report with your department. Would I be correct in assuming you've come as a courtesy to do your due diligence, to check to see if the watch has been recovered?" She leaned forward. "Thank you again, Chief, and please forgive Ambrose for wasting your department's time."

"So," Jesse said, baiting the trap, "you've found the watch?"

Annette North opened her mouth to answer, then thought better of it. She was sharp and sensed that she may have misjudged Jesse's reason for being there.

What she said was "No, unfortunately, the Rolex has yet to turn up. Why do you ask?"

Jesse removed the evidence bag from his pocket. It was barely detectable—a slight flinch, a twitch at the corner of her mouth, a fleeting widening of her eyes—but there was no denying the shock in Annette North's reaction. She had clearly never again expected to see the Rolex she had purchased as a gift for her husband.

Jesse thought she might be tempted to push back because it was pretty obvious he had tried to trap her. Wisely, she didn't go there.

"My goodness." She shook her head. "I owe Ambrose an apology. I must have told him twenty times since he filed the report that he was foolish to do so. Now I may have to buy him another watch to make up for my wrongheadedness."

"I don't know, Annette. I think he'll probably be happy enough to get this back."

"May I ask where you found it?"

Now it was Jesse leaning forward. He spoke in a soft voice, as if he didn't want anyone but Annette to hear. "In a drug dealer's bedroom."

That hit her a little harder than just showing her the watch, but instead of fighting it, she went with it, clapping her hand over her mouth.

"Goodness, no. How do you suppose it ended up there? Was this in Paradise?"

"I can't discuss that, Annette. Sorry."

She had regained her composure. "When may we retrieve the watch, Jesse?"

"A month, probably. I will let you know."

Annette North stood, letting Jesse know she was ending the discussion before it went any further. She made that arm-sweeping gesture again. "You'll excuse me, Chief, but I've got a meeting of the Paradise Women's Club and I have to get ready."

Jesse walked with her to the front door. "I saw your daughter today at school."

"Petra? Why were you at the high school?" Her voice cracked, though she cleared her throat to try to cover it up.

"Drugs. Since Heather Mackey's death, we've found there's a problem at the high school. I'd hate to see any of the kids caught up in the net." Jesse quickly said his goodbyes, not wanting to give Annette North any room to maneuver or to ask more questions.

He had little doubt that Django Carpenter's list was accurate. Even Petra North had been forced to steal to support her addiction, and she'd done it with the complicity of her mother. But Jesse didn't judge Annette any more harshly than he'd judge Etta or any other parent. As a drunk, he knew what the addict's side of things felt like, and now, as a father, he understood the parents' side, too.

Forty-nine

After his AA meeting that night in Salem, Jesse drove over to Maryglenn's apartment above the warehouse. Although he was pretty much consumed with the drug dealing in town and finding Chris Grimm, Maryglenn's reaction to his show at the high school had gnawed at him all day. It didn't matter that Jesse didn't see Maryglenn as his next great love. He wasn't sure what they would ever be. What counted was that Jesse Stone was a changed man.

The old Jesse would have kept it to himself, would have let it fester. Or he would have gone home and polished off half a bottle of Johnnie Walker Black. If he discussed it at all, it wouldn't have been with Maryglenn, but with his poster of Ozzie Smith. It had been a pattern that had persisted in spite of his years of therapy with Dix, in spite of breaking free of the destructive pas de deux he had done with Jenn, his ex. His relationship with Diana had helped open him up a little, but it was going through rehab and attending the AA meetings that allowed him to see how the old behaviors had been a trap.

He parked the Explorer and walked down Newton Alley. There was no parking on the alley, a narrow street that housed many of Paradise's art galleries. As Jesse walked down the dimly lit, quiet street, he smelled the salt sea air blowing in off the Atlantic and listened to the wind rattling clapboards and whistling through the gaps between the buildings. He also listened to his thoughts, remembering how the white supremacists' insane plan for a race war had begun with a murder here in Newton Alley, just a few feet from Maryglenn's door, and how it had led to him meeting Maryglenn. Before stepping to the door, he stopped on the spot where the murder had occurred. He hesitated for only a moment and then pressed the buzzer.

SHE PACED THE MOTEL carpeting again. Though she had done more with her hair and makeup tonight. Instead of wearing the robe, she dressed up for the girl. She wore leather and lace, her black stilettos. Wore the raw perfume that she had been told highlighted her own scent. Yet in spite of all she had done to seduce and manipulate Petra, she somehow knew that it was all going to fall apart. She had already spoken to Arakel Sarkassian and warned him that the girl was a risk.

"And before you start threatening me," she'd said to Sarkassian, "know that this girl isn't like Chris. You can't just be rid of her. Her father is rich and powerful. If she wants out, we have to let her go. I will keep her under control as far as the cops go."

"What about the cops there?" Sarkassian asked.

"Jesse . . ." She stopped, catching herself. "Jesse Stone, the chief, is very determined. He was once a homicide detective in L.A. He's a serious man."

Sarkassian had been silent for a moment and then said, "Yes, okay, let the girl go if you must, and do whatever it takes to keep her quiet."

She wasn't stupid. Even if Arakel hadn't said it, she understood that if Petra refused to carry on and he decided to cut his losses in Paradise, she would also be cut out of the picture. And if she was no longer important to Sarkassian, her supply would dry up. She heard a car pull into the spot in front of the room. She peeked through the curtains and saw Petra getting out of her BMW.

JESSE PRESSED THE BUZZER for a third time, but there was no response. He stepped back and looked up at the one window that faced Newton Alley from Maryglenn's apartment. It was only a small bathroom window, and it was dark. He was disappointed, not angry. He figured he'd try to call her and see where she was. If he got her on the phone and she was close by, he thought he might be able to join her and they could have that talk. His call went straight to voicemail. He left a message.

SHE SAW THE look on Petra's face and knew she was right. The girl was going to back out. Inside, she was sick, her guts tying themselves into knots, tightening by the second, panicking about how she would stay healthy if Arakel cut her out. When she tried to kiss the girl, Petra turned away. When she reached out for the girl to stroke her hair, the girl pushed her hand away. Tears poured out of Petra's eyes.

"I . . . I can't do this. I'm so scared all the time. I can't sleep."

"This?"

"The pills and the heroin. I can't. Please don't make me do this anymore. Don't hate me."

She stepped in close to the girl and kissed her forehead. "I could never hate you, lover. Never."

She put her mouth on the girl's and kissed her with an urgency and intensity that surprised even her. It wasn't out of love. It wasn't out of desire, but out of fear for herself. She needed to lose herself for a little while. She dragged the girl over to the bed and let herself go.

"Listen to me, lover," she said when they were done and reality was setting back in. "You have to give me the stash."

Petra was crying again. Through her tears she managed to say the stash was in the trunk of her car. Then, using all of her will to hold back the tears, asked, "Does this mean you won't be with me?"

She knew what she should have said. Knew she should have kissed the girl and said that they could see each other only if Petra promised to never talk to the police about her. But she was getting edgy, the last pill wearing off, and with that came anger and frustration. She reached for her phone and retrieved the photo Arakel had sent to her of Chris Grimm's brutalized body as a warning.

"If I was you," she said, her voice cold and nasty, "I would worry less about being with me than what will happen to me if you ever tell the cops about us." She showed Petra the photo.

At first the girl was startled and couldn't make sense of what she was seeing, but when she understood, she ran into the bathroom and vomited.

Fifty

Cole was already out of it on the couch. Jesse couldn't sleep. This happened to him occasionally since he had parted ways with alcohol. He paced around, read a little, and caught the end of *The Outlaw Josey Wales* on cable. It was one of those movies he could watch from any point in the movie to the end. He turned on his computer. When it booted up, he typed *Swingline Sue's* into Google, but never hit enter as his cell phone buzzed on the table. He saw it was from the Paradise Police Department and picked up.

"What's up, Suit?"

"There's a kid here to see you . . . Rich Amitrano. Says he was a friend of Heather Mackey's and that he really needs to speak with you."

"Ten minutes."

JESSE WALKED INTO THE STATIONHOUSE, waved hello to Suit, who nodded at the bench by the fingerprinting table. Rich was staring at his phone, which made him like every other teenager Jesse had encountered over the last several years. The kid looked as tired as Jesse felt. He guessed they could share at least a few minutes of insomnia together.

"Hey, Rich," Jesse said, offering his hand.

The kid shook it, placing his phone in his front pocket.

"Come on into my office. You want anything? Water, coffee, tea?"

"No, that's okay, Chief Stone."

"Jesse. C'mon."

When they went into the office, Jesse pointed at the two wooden chairs facing his desk. Jesse sat opposite the kid.

"I should apologize," Jesse said. "When I spoke to you, Megan, and Darby at the cemetery, I could tell you wanted to talk."

"That's okay. I understand. You must be really busy."

"Not too busy to talk."

Then Jesse waited the kid out. He had wanted to talk, so Jesse was going to let him do it without prompting.

"Is it true that Chris is missing? Do you think something bad's happened to him?"

"What makes you say that?"

"Is he missing?"

Jesse said, "Uh-huh, but I don't know what's happened to him. Do you?"

Suddenly, Rich, who'd come to speak to Jesse, had nothing to say.

"Look, Rich, you're the one who wanted me—"

"I'm sorry, Chief—Jesse. I really miss Heather. I love Darby and Megan, too, but it was different with Heather and me. We never judged each other. We could be totally honest with each other about stuff."

The kid had changed directions, but Jesse figured he would circle back around to what he'd come in to say. "Stuff like what?"

The kid squirmed in his seat a little, took a few deep breaths, and stared Jesse right in the eye. "I'm gay. I know that it's supposed to be easier these days to come out, but I can only know my experiences. I knew I could tell Heather and she would be totally cool about it. Telling her gave me the courage to tell other people."

"Does your family know?"

"My dad's accepted it. He doesn't like it, but he's okay. My mom . . . She prays a lot and ignores it. My brothers and sisters couldn't care less."

"I couldn't care less, either, Rich, but is this what you came to me to talk about?"

"Heather and I shared a kind of secret crush on Chris. That was okay. We could tell each other stuff like that. The thing is . . ." He stopped himself, stood up. "I shouldn't be here telling you this stuff. I'm sorry."

"Rich," Jesse said, "you came in here to tell me something. If you don't tell me now, I can't help."

"Heather slept with Chris to get drugs. She was ashamed of herself for doing it and she was ashamed about caring about what other kids thought. That's why she never told Chris how she felt about him."

"Did you tell Chris how you felt?"

Rich smiled, shrugged. "I knew he was straight, but a boy can dream."

"He sure can." Jesse smiled, too. "There's something else, isn't there, Rich?"

"Heather told me that Chris was her dealer. Everybody kind of knew that, but Heather said that Chris got his stuff from one of the teachers in school."

"How would she know that?" Jesse asked, his voice more serious. "Did he tell Heather?"

The kid shook his head. "No, but she said she caught Chris and her meeting a few times. Like by the lockers after practice and once in a classroom."

"Her?"

Rich nodded, his face reddening. "She saw them through the classroom window and . . . they . . . weren't talking."

"Who was it? Which teacher?"

He shrugged again. "She wouldn't tell me. I think she was afraid if I knew, I would try to save her by ratting out the teacher." He bowed his head. "It was the only secret she ever kept from me. I swear, Jesse, that's all I know. Maybe if I had said something . . ."

"If and maybe aren't places you want to go to, Rich," Jesse said, thinking of the circumstances surrounding Diana's murder. "You can't change the past, but you might have just helped stop anyone else from dying."

"How? I don't know which teacher."

"Believe me, it helps."

Jesse got up from behind his desk and came to stand in front of the kid. Rich stood as well.

"Thank you for coming to speak to me." He shook the kid's hand. "It was a brave thing to do. Sometimes the lines get blurry between right and wrong. Not this time. You did the right thing."

"I hope so."

When Rich got to the door, Jesse called after him. "My door's always open to you."

Fifty-one

She'd driven back home from the motel in a rage. Now she sat in her car, pounding her palms on the steering wheel and screaming. She understood the girl's panic, and on some intellectual level even empathized with it, but on a visceral level she just didn't really give a shit. Did Petra care about what would happen to her? Did that stupid little girl consider that the woman she said she ached for had degraded herself? She had risked everything—her career, her dignity, her life—to make sure she would always have that next dose. And now where was she? Nowhere. Worse than nowhere.

While she had been assured of a steady supply, she'd never given much thought to the jail time she was risking. The drugs weren't even the worst of it. Chris Grimm wasn't even sixteen when she seduced him and that was statutory rape. And now that Chris had been killed, she was part of a murder conspiracy. She took some deep breaths and looked over her right shoulder at the duffel bag containing the stash she'd taken from Petra's trunk. *She could run.*

There were enough pills in the bag to keep her going for a very long time, but not forever. *Forever.* She laughed an angry laugh at herself. Forever no longer had any meaning to her. For her, forever was the time between hits, and her tolerance was building up so that the duration of her high was shrinking. It took more and more Oxy to get her where she needed to be, never mind where she wanted to be. Simple want was a luxury she could no longer afford. Those days, the days of enjoying the high, were gone as gone could be.

Wasn't that the trap, the lie of it, the incredible euphoria of the initial high? How it made all the pain go away. Not just the physical pain, though that would have been enough. It was a magical thing, the way it was equally effective in vanquishing the little hurts of the day, the nasty remarks or people's simple rudeness, and the gaping wounds of a terrible childhood or a broken heart. When you were in as deep as she was, it wasn't the drug that chased those big and little hurts away. It was the desperation and panic about getting the drug that made everything else insignificant. Junkies don't need to search for or ponder the meaning of life. Life is about one thing and one thing only—chasing the next hit. But the cruelest irony was that once you were hooked, the physical hurt of not having it was worse than the pain that made you take it in the first place.

She had twice tried breaking free of the hold it had on her, and that had been enough to convince her that doing whatever she needed to do to get high was worth it. The cold sweats, vomiting, constant nausea, cramps, diarrhea, and the muscles that would not stop aching. Nothing was worth going through that again. Nothing!

She turned and looked once again at the stash bag in the backseat, stared at it, and decided to run. But just as she placed the key back in the ignition, her cell phone rang.

"Look across the street." It was a thickly accented man's voice. "Make a wave at the white van."

She waved. The headlights on a van parked across the street and facing her flashed on and off.

"You have something for Mr. Sarkassian?"

"Yes."

"Leave car doors open when you go."

"Okay."

"Do not fuck us around. You have seen the picture of the boy. We are doing this to him. To you, we would do much worse. We would pleasure ourselves with you and it would not be gentle like you do with the girl. Make sure the girl keeps her mouth shut. You understand."

She was so frightened she couldn't speak.

"Answer me, bitch."

"She'll be fine. I will take care of her."

"Good. You know the boy was calling your name when we hurt him. You must be good. The girl talks and we will find out just how good."

She was paralyzed with fear. Unable to speak or to move. When she said nothing, the man on the other end of the line laughed. His laugh was almost as frightening as anything he had said. The phone went dead.

She tried not to completely fall to pieces or to look again at the duffel bag behind her. She had removed some of the stash at the motel while she was hidden behind Petra's raised trunk lid. She knew she could always blame the girl for not keeping a good check on the inventory—they wouldn't go after Petra. But what she had taken wasn't going to keep her going for long. She got out of the car and walked as quickly as she could on legs that were weak from fear. She did not look back. When she turned the corner, she put her back against a wall and noticed she had sweated through her clothing. Fear did have a very particular smell. She stood frozen that way until she heard the van speed past. Even then, when she finally felt safe enough to move, she had to talk herself through the process of walking.

Fifty-two

It had been a long time since Jesse was awakened by both his cell phone and landline, and when it happened, it never meant anything good.

"Dad, Brian Lundquist is on the phone for you."

Dad. He hadn't yet gotten used to Cole calling him that. He wasn't sure he ever would. He certainly liked it. It was just that he didn't quite trust it yet. He didn't trust that it wouldn't disappear with a change of mood. But for the moment his concern was Lundquist's call.

Jesse reached over for his cell and dumped the incoming call. He stumbled into the kitchen. Cole was already dressed for work.

"I have to go," he said, handing the phone to Jesse. "Take care. See you tonight."

"See you." Then he put the phone to his ear and spoke. "What's up?"

"We got a John Doe outside of Helton. Fits your missing kid's description."

"Homicide?"

"From what I'm hearing from the locals, the vic looks like he could have been killed five times over. I'm heading that way. You want me to swing by and pick you up or you want to meet me there?"

"I'll meet you there. Text me the location." Jesse looked at his wall clock. "I'll be there as fast as I can."

"No worries. We won't move him until you arrive."

"Thanks."

THE SUN WAS COMING UP behind Jesse as he drove west to Helton. Helton was an old mill town, one Jesse was familiar with. Not for any reason he liked. It was a place of old redbrick buildings covered in soot that had once bellowed from its factory chimneys. Nowadays the only thing it manufactured was hopelessness. It was the sort of place that gets skipped over when times are good and suffers the most when they're not. But Jesse's unease had nothing to do with the economics or sociology of the place. It was the red line that began with the case that had brought him to Helton, a line of blood, geography, and time. It had begun with the murder of a teenage girl that resonated through time until it ended with a bullet ending the life of Diana, Jesse's fiancée. No, there was nothing about driving toward Helton to lift Jesse's spirits.

He turned off the four-lane road out of Helton and into a thickly wooded area that had been taped off by the state police. The usual collection of official vehicles was parked in a small clearing. Along with the Staties, the Helton PD, the office of the local medical examiner, and the local fire department ambulance corps were all represented. Jesse recognized Lundquist's car as well. He grabbed a file containing photos of Chris Grimm, some given to him by his mother, others generated from the security footage at Kennedy Park.

At the tape, Jesse showed his shield and gave the uniform his name. The uniform pointed the way. It was a scene befitting the kid's last name—Grimm. At some crime scenes, even at homicides, there'll be a smiling or disinterested face. That wasn't the case here. The sight of those faces told Jesse that Lundquist hadn't been exaggerating. Lundquist heard Jesse's approach, turned away from the body, and came to meet him.

Lundquist pointed at the file in Jesse's hand. "Photos of the Grimm kid?" Jesse handed the file to Lundquist who opened it up. Lundquist winced. "Good-looking boy." He nodded over his shoulder toward the body. "He doesn't look like this anymore. Whoever did this to him was either raging at him or enjoyed inflicting pain."

"Helton PD's case or yours?" Jesse asked.

"Mine."

"Good. I want to spend as little time in this town as possible."

Lundquist was going to ask why and then thought better of it. "Come on, let's have a look."

People say the anticipation of bad things is always worse than the real thing. Not always. And this was one of those "not always" occasions. Jesse, who had seen bodies in all manner of disrepair, was surprised at the level of brutality that showed on the kid's body.

"Are those entrance wounds?" Jesse asked the local ME, pointing to where dirt had caked around spots on the boy's hair and on his chest.

"Looks that way," the ME said.

Jesse said, "You think they were the COD?"

"If they were, they saved the boy from an incredible amount of pain. I haven't even had a very close look at him and I can tell you he was thoroughly tortured premortem." The ME pointed with his gloved finger. "There are visible burn marks on his neck, face, and hands. There are an array of broken bones. Teeth are missing, and some fingers. And if those bullets were postmortem, then the person or persons who did this to him were even more twisted than I would care to imagine."

Jesse walked around the body. "He wasn't murdered here."

"No," Lundquist answered. "And rigor has come and gone. He's been here several days."

The ME asked, "Is this your missing boy?"

Jesse asked Lundquist for the photos and handed them to the ME.

"I think so. It looks like him. His clothing is a match for the footage we took from cameras at a local park on the day he disappeared." Jesse waved at the ME and then pointed at a spot where no one was standing. The ME followed Jesse. "Doc, I noticed the kid's missing fingers look as if they were sawn off. Do you think he was mutilated in any other way?"

The ME was confused. Then, understanding the implication, nodded. "I see your point."

"Yeah, when I break the news to his mother and she comes to identify him, I need to prepare her. And God help us if she needs to see more than his face."

"I understand, Chief Stone. Give me a moment."

The ME went back to the body and asked everyone standing around the shallow grave to move away and to give him some privacy. A minute later, he came back to where Jesse was standing.

"Until I get him on the table I can't be one hundred percent sure, but I think he's . . . intact."

"Thanks, Doc."

Lundquist came over to Jesse as the ME went back to his business. "What was that about?"

"I needed to know some things before informing the mother."

"My case now, Jesse. My job, but if you want to come . . ."

"I think it would be a good idea. So tell me how he was found."

"Marathoner was training before dawn. She tripped over the hand. Used her cell phone flashlight to see what she tripped over. Called nine-one-one."

"And the Helton PD called you. Any ID on the body?"

"Nothing obvious. No wallet. No phone. When they get him to the morgue, they'll be able to do a more thorough search."

Jesse gave Lundquist the Walterses' address in Paradise and filled him in on the recent domestic abuse situation.

"We have to be careful when we enter. The husband is the kid's stepfather and he's a handful. We had him on an illegal weapons charge, but the wife claimed the gun was hers."

"Like that, huh?"

"Just like that."

Lundquist said, "I'll take her to identify the body. Maybe she'll let her guard down around me."

Jesse agreed. He went back to the shallow grave with Lundquist and took one more look at Chris Grimm. As far as he was concerned, Grimm was Paradise's second drug casualty. He may have been the one to supply Heather with the drugs, but Jesse believed not even Patti and Steve Mackey would have wanted the Grimm kid to die the way he had.

Fifty-three

Jesse got to the Walters house before Lundquist. As Lundquist had pointed out, it was his case, so Jesse waited in his Explorer for the state homicide man to arrive. Jesse had already called Molly and given her a heads-up about Chris Grimm's body.

"No official ID yet," he'd said. "But you can alert everyone to stop looking and asking. Until we notify the mother, nobody says a word."

"I got it, Jesse. Remember you told me to check for cases like Heather's?"

"I do."

"Well, I've come across several in and around Boston. I made a few calls and found two doctors whose names came up more times than made me comfortable."

"Good work, Molly. I'll have a look when I get back to the station."

Jesse decided to finally Google Swingline Sue's while he killed time waiting for Lundquist to show. He typed it into his phone, hit enter, and it popped right up. The first entry didn't show any-thing unusual. It was a bar restaurant in Tipton, a few towns north of Paradise. It had a pretty run-of-the-mill menu: wings, salads, burgers, cheesecake. The place featured live music, kara-oke, dancing, and cabaret. Jesse didn't get the point until the next entry.

Best LGBT Bar North of Boston

https://Swinglinesues.com/undergoundreviews321

Every night is ladies' night at this Tipton, Massachusetts, club. The 1940s-inspired décor is to die for and the place rocks. Rosie the Riveter, hang on to your hard hat. Whether it's karaoke, disco with tunes spun by DJ Femmebot, or a campy cabaret experience you're looking for, this is the venue. It's mostly a girls'-night-out kind of place, but all are welcome. Cover charge after 11:00.

Although Jesse wasn't getting the full picture of what the issue was between Maryglenn and Daisy, he had some idea of where whatever it was between them had its roots. But before he could get too invested in figuring it out, Lundquist rapped his knuckles against the glass of the driver's-side window. Jesse rolled the win-dow down.

"Let's get this over with," Lundquist said.

"Let's."

IT HAD BEEN JESSE'S EXPERIENCE that people understood what was going on even before a single syllable was uttered. When someone is missing and the police come to your door, there are a limited number of reasons for their presence. Although Jesse could not step outside himself to see the looks on his face and on Lundquist's, he knew what their expressions must've telegraphed to Kathy Walters. And he was right.

While she didn't collapse to the front hallway floor in hysterics, she took one look at Lundquist and Jesse and fell against the wall.

"He's dead, isn't he?" she said, hoping to be contradicted.

No one delivered on her hope.

"Kathy, this is Captain Brian Lundquist of the state police," Jesse said. "It's his case now."

"I'm very sorry to have to tell you this, Mrs. Walters, but we believe your son has been murdered."

Kathy Walters gasped and fell to her knees. There were no tears, not yet. Jesse got on his knees beside her. "Captain Lundquist has some important things to say to you. Try to listen."

"I know you have questions, Mrs. Walters, but I won't be able to answer them until the body has been officially identified. Are you up to it, or is there someone else, your husband—"

She glared at Lundquist. "Never!"

Jesse put his arm around her shoulders. "It's okay, but I have to warn you, he's in rough shape. Do you have anyone else?"

She was indignant. "I wasn't there for him much when he was alive. I'm not going to leave this to nobody else now."

Jesse helped stand her up. "Can I call anyone for you? Someone to be here for you when you get back?"

She shook her head.

Jesse handed her his card. "Captain Lundquist will take you. He'll explain everything on the way. If you need anything from me, all of my numbers are there."

She took the card, robotically, as if her arm was not a part of her. "Give me a minute, Captain."

Kathy Walters zombie-walked down the hall and up the stairs.

Lundquist stared at Jesse and said, "Never gets easier, does it, Jesse?"

Jesse nodded. "Hasn't yet. Doubt it ever will."

Fifty-four

At the stationhouse, Jesse was pounding the ball really hard into his new mitt. Molly could distinguish between his doing it out of habit or his doing it as meditation. When it was loud enough for her to hear through his office door and over any ambient noise in the station, it was meditation. Some men prayed the rosary, some chanted. Jesse pounded the ball. And as was his habit, he would do it while fixing his gaze on Stiles Island. It cleared his mind of clutter and helped him think straight. This routine used to be even more crucial to him when there was an office bottle in his desk drawer and his mind was clouded by alcohol.

Molly stuck her head into the office. "Jesse, sorry, but Lundquist's on line one."

He didn't turn to face her. "Thanks."

Jesse put the ball in the glove's pocket and placed them both on his desk. He gave an unhappy look at the glove. He wondered if he would ever get used to it.

"Brian," Jesse said, picking up.

"It's him, Chris Grimm. The mother positively IDed him."

"And how did that go?"

"About how you would expect. The kid was tough to look at with the dirt washed off him. The damage was more obvious. The mother went to pieces."

"She home?"

"She is. You should maybe have your sector car stop by, maybe keep an eye on her."

"Good idea. Anything else?" Jesse asked.

"One thing. Might mean something. Might not. We found a McDonald's burger wrapper stuffed into one of his jean pockets."

"Receipt?"

Lundquist said, "No such luck. No receipt."

"It's a place to start, anyway. I know it's your case, but I'll have my cops check with the local McDonald's to see if we can view their in-house security footage."

"I appreciate the help, Jesse. We'll do the same with every Mc-Donald's between your town limits and Helton. They fed the kid, then tortured him to death. Real sports."

"I can see it. The kid's running scared and his handler wants to keep him calm so they can get him out of town to a place they can deal with him."

"They dealt with him, all right." The building anger was evident in Lundquist's voice. "When I was there with the mother, the ME pulled me off to one side. Said the kid was even worse off than he imagined. They did everything except what you had asked him about. This was just from visual inspection after getting the kid's clothes off and washing him up. I know the kid was a dealer, but these guys are some coldhearted motherfu—bastards, Jesse. I'm going to enjoy putting them away."

"The drug case is still mine, so I better get over to the high school to let the principal know."

"I'll be in touch." Lundquist rang off.

ON HIS WAY out of the station, Jesse stopped to talk to Molly.

"The body was positively IDed. Who's in the Walterses' patrol sector?"

"Robbie."

"Have him stop over there to check on them, to see if we can help with the arrangements. Also, have someone go over to the McDonald's and see if we can't get parking-lot and in-store footage for the day of Heather Mackey's funeral. If we get it, check for that white van in the parking lot and drive-thru. In the store, look for the kid. You don't have to waste time going through the whole day. Only from—"

She interrupted him. "The time stamp on the footage from Kennedy Park forward. You know, I've done this once or twice before, Sherlock."

"Sorry. So what about these doctors?"

Molly shoved a pile of papers across the desk. She pointed at names she had in red in several places.

"These two doctors' names just kept coming up: Rajiv Laghari and Myron Wexler. Both of them have offices in Roxbury. Not many of the families of the deceased wanted to talk, but a few did. No one had very nice things to say. As far as I could tell from the people at the medical board, there are current ongoing state medical board investigations of both men, but they don't exactly give out information over the phone and they won't comment directly on ongoing investigations."

"I'll probably head down there tomorrow."

"You going to visit your buddy Vinnie Morris while you're in town?" Molly asked, sarcasm heavy in her voice.

Jesse didn't answer. He knew Molly disapproved of his relationship with the likes of Morris and the late Gino Fish. Jesse thought Molly was a great cop, believed she would have been a star detective in a big-city department if she had chosen that route. But because her beat was Paradise, she never understood how big-city policing often forced a good cop to associate with people on the other side of the law. Jesse knew how it must have looked to Molly. He could only imagine her reaction if she knew the whole truth about what had actually happened between Morris and him in the wake of Diana's murder.

"I'm going over to the high school to let Virginia Wester know what's going on. Heather Mackey's death was an accident, but not Chris Grimm's."

Molly noted he had changed subjects, but didn't push.

"One more thing, Molly. I may need you for a little overtime tonight. It can be after dinner. Are you up for it?"

"What do you need?"

"Steve Parkinson, Petra North, Sara York, Lidell Thomas, Carl Bedell, and Bob Mark."

Molly's expression wasn't a happy one. "We already talked about them."

"Time to stop talking about them and time to talk to them. Now it's murder."

"What do you want?"

"First, everything by the book. Wear civilian clothes, but let them know it's an official visit. Talk to the kids only in the presence of a parent. Offer the parents the opportunity to call a lawyer, but make it clear that you are there only to gather information and that it will be a casual talk. But if they choose to bring in a lawyer, make certain they understand the interview will be held in the station by me and it will be audio- and videotaped."

"What do you want me to ask?"

"Come on, Sherlock, you've done this once or twice. You know what to do."

Molly thought about arguing, but Jesse was right. She knew exactly what to do.

Fifty-five

The kids were loading onto the buses in front of the school as Jesse drove up. This visit wasn't meant as showtime for the students, so he parked around the back of the school in the teachers' lot and went in through the side entrance. On the way up to Principal Wester's office, he stopped at the art room. He needed to straighten things out with Maryglenn if they were going to salvage whatever it was they had.

Jesse looked through the door glass. Her back was to him. She seemed to be intently studying an array of line drawings taped to the wall. They were all of the same model—a boy dressed in his football team jacket, a pen or pencil dangling out of his mouth, a human skull in his right hand. Some of them were pretty good, but Jesse knew very little about art. He knocked and entered.

Maryglenn smiled in spite of herself.

"Some of them have talent," she said.

"Talent only gets you so far. Lots of people have lots of talent."

"Jesse Stone, philosopher."

"No, Jesse Stone, former professional baseball player. Everyone

I played with was the most talented baseball player in his town. Every one of them had been all-city, all-county, all-state. Not everyone makes it. Why is the kid holding a skull?"

"It's from Shakespeare, a scene from *Hamlet*. Do you know it?"

"To be or not to be, but that's about it. I know that it's about a kid who can't make up his mind."

"Most of the kids are reading that play in their English classes, and Hamlet would have been around their ages. Maybe a little bit older. It's a play about death, love, treachery, madness, and revenge. A lot about death. Teenagers are kind of obsessed with those things. What are you doing here, Jesse?"

"What I'm doing in your classroom is to ask you to dinner after my meeting tonight. I'd like to clear some things up."

"I'd like that."

"What I'm doing in the building is delivering bad news to Principal Wester. Chris Grimm has been murdered."

Maryglenn bent over, grabbing her midsection as if she'd been kicked in the stomach.

"I can't give you any details," he said, "but it will be out soon enough. I better go give her the news."

Freda was away from her desk, so Jesse walked to Virginia Wester's door and knocked.

"Damn it, Freda, how many times do I have to tell you, you don't have to knock when I'm in here alone?" Wester shouted.

Jesse opened the door, but Wester was looking down at papers on her desk.

"It's me, Virginia, not Freda."

Wester's face went from annoyed to worried.

"Jesse, I'm sorry."

"No need."

"What is it?"

He gave her the details, the few that he had, about Chris Grimm's murder.

"Oh my God!"

"It was pretty brutal, Virginia. I wanted to tell you myself so that you can inform the faculty and students. Have counselors here if you think you need them."

"Thank you, Jesse. What's going on? I know Paradise has had its share of crime. In this world, what place doesn't? But this, to torture a boy to death, even if he was a drug dealer . . . I can't fathom it."

Jesse said, "Drugs equals money, lots of it. And money can make people justify anything. It starts with legal prescriptions and ends with a dead girl and a murdered boy." He repeated the line about the war on drugs he'd read in a novel.

"Has the war on drugs really been going on for fifty years?" It was a rhetorical question. When Wester's eyes refocused on Jesse, she said, "I can see by your expression you have more to say."

"I have a confidential informant that claims one of your teachers is involved."

"Involved? Involved in what, the drugs?"

Jesse nodded. "And, by extension, the murder."

She pounded her fist on the desk. "Who? Who is it? I want to know."

"I don't know, Virginia. If I knew, they'd be in handcuffs. But I'll be back over the next several days to interview them. We can do this the hard way or the—"

"No, Jesse. No court orders. You'll have my full cooperation, the school board be damned. If they want my hide, they can have it. This has to stop. Now."

Jesse shook her hand. "Thank you."

He hadn't told her exactly what Rich Amitrano had said about the teacher being a woman. For one thing, he wasn't sure there wasn't more than one teacher involved. For another, it was always good for the police to have a piece of information that the public wasn't privy to.

Fifty-six

Molly had gone to Sara York's house first to get what she knew would be an incredibly uncomfortable situation out of the way. The Yorks lived around the corner from the Cranes. Molly's older girls had taken turns babysitting for Sara and her little brother and, as she had told Jesse, Sara played on the field hockey team with Molly's two youngest girls.

"Molly!" Toni, Sara's mom, said when she opened the door. When she saw Molly's expression, the enthusiasm drained out of her. "Come in. We've been expecting you or Jesse to knock since the day Heather died."

As Toni made Molly coffee, she explained that Frank had taken Frank Jr. to basketball practice.

Molly asked, "Sara?"

"At counseling."

After the coffee was served, they sat across the kitchen table from each other. Molly had learned about the power of silence from Jesse and used it. The story Toni eventually told Molly was eerily similar to what Patti Mackey and Moss Carpenter had told Jesse. There had been an injury, doctor visits, continued pain, a new prescription, and addiction. The difference was that Toni, an occupational therapist, wasn't going to play along or enable her daughter.

"I did my internship on a burn unit, Molly," Toni said. "As an OT on that unit, I witnessed what pain was like. Burns do terrible damage to more than the skin. They ruin muscles, ligaments, tendons. To get people to be able to grasp and hold things in their hands again or to range their limbs, I had to put them through hell. So when I found pills in Sara's room, I didn't believe her lies and we got her help. Remember that soccer camp we told you about last summer? There was no soccer camp."

Molly reached across the table and held Toni's hand.

"Sara now goes to group meetings twice a week and for private counseling," Toni said. "We get her tested every month. Sara says she did some things she's pretty ashamed of to get those pills." Silent tears poured out of her eyes as she spoke.

"Did any of those things involve Chris Grimm?"

Toni York's eyes narrowed with anger. "That son of a bitch. He made Sara—"

Molly squeezed Toni's hand, hard. "He's dead."

"Good."

"He was tortured to death and shot, left in a shallow grave outside Helton."

Toni paled but said, "You want me to feel sorry for him?"

"No. That's not why I'm here. I came to talk to Sara to see if she knew of anyone other than Chris involved in selling drugs at school. We're not looking to get the kids doing drugs in trouble. That never does any good. We want to get them help and we want the dealing to stop."

"As far as I know, it was only Chris Grimm, but I'll have Sara call you when she gets back. I promise."

Molly got up from the table and hugged Toni.

———

THINGS WENT VERY DIFFERENTLY at the North house. It was difficult enough for Molly to get in the house, let alone to talk directly to
Petra. Things got loud and heated in spite of Molly remaining calm.
There were threats of lawsuits, complaints about harassment . . . the
usual stuff. Even in a place like Paradise, police frequently heard
this kind of rhetoric. People hate the police until they need them.

"Tell Chief Stone we have had quite enough of this," said Ambrose North, returned from Boston. "Annette told me of Jesse's
unwelcome and unappreciated visit."

Molly caught sight of Petra listening at the top of the stairs, so
she raised her voice loud enough to make certain Petra heard
clearly what was going on.

"Mr. North, Jesse's visit was to inform you that we had recovered your missing watch from the room of a suspected drug dealer.
We were curious if you could tell us how your watch might've
found its way there."

"Preposterous! How would we know the answer to that?"

"Well, since the news will be out tomorrow, I can tell you that
the alleged drug dealer was Petra's classmate, Chris Grimm. His
body was found this morning after—"

That got Ambrose North's attention. "His body?"

"Yes, he disappeared on the day Heather Mackey was buried.
This morning his body was found in a shallow grave outside of
Helton. He had been tortured and shot to death."

"None of this has anything to do with anyone in this house. I
can assure you, Officer Crane."

"We would still like to speak with your daughter. As I said before, this was only going to be a casual conversation. But it's now
an official request for her to appear at the station for questioning

by Chief Stone in regards to any knowledge she may have concerning Heather Mackey's death and Chris Grimm's murder. We will be in touch to set a time that is convenient for you and to give you an opportunity to seek legal representation. Thank you."

Molly didn't wait to be shown out.

AT BOB MARK'S HOUSE and at Lidell Thomas's, it was the same story as at the Yorks'. They had been caught by their parents and sent to rehab. Bob Mark had had a slip, but was now back in rehab. Lidell was supposed to go to the University of Maryland, but his parents had kept him local. If he got through two years at the community college, he could pick the college of his choice at which to finish his degree. He was doing well, so far. He was on a program with group sessions and counseling much like Sara York's. He was also tested to make sure he didn't backslide.

When she got in her car to head over to the address she had for the Parkinsons, her cell phone rang.

"Mrs. Crane . . . Molly, it's me, Sara."

"Hi, Sara."

"My mom says you came by and you guys talked. She says I'm not going to get in trouble. Is that right?"

"We only want you to be healthy and safe, Sara. Did she tell you about Chris?"

"She did. There's some stuff I need to say to you about Chris, Mrs.—Molly." Sara's voice was strained and brittle. "I told my mom he forced me to do stuff, because I was ashamed. He never forced me to do anything I didn't want to do. Believe me, I would have done anything, much worse things than I did. He was a little weird, but he wasn't a bad person. I need you to know that."

"Okay."

"And I'm pretty sure he wasn't doing this by himself. There was a teacher, I think, who he had a thing for."

"A woman?"

"Yeah, but I don't know who. He never said, but he got calls from her when I was with him, and the way he talked to her . . . you could just tell it was a woman who was older than him and he'd say stuff like 'I'll see you tomorrow at school.' I guess he wasn't thinking I could hear him or that I would get it."

Molly tried to get more information about the teacher from Sara, but there was none to be had. She thanked the girl and hung up. She had to call Jesse.

Fifty-seven

Jesse had learned over the last several months that AA meetings were for self-maintenance as well as for the crises. Of course, when you were close to falling off the wagon, meetings were crucial. The thing was, since you could never be sure of what would set you off to want to drink again, you couldn't let yourself get lulled into going to meetings only when the thirst hit. The meetings weren't a Band-Aid to apply when the bleeding started. As Jesse had witnessed, it was often too late. How many stories of regret and guilt had he listened to from people who'd gotten complacent, returning to meetings only after they had fallen down and taken the dive back into the bottle? He wasn't judging them. Who was he to judge? But he took their backsliding seriously.

As he drove from Salem over to Maryglenn's he called in to the station to check with Suit to see if the kid's autopsy results were in or if there had been any developments.

"Nothing yet, Jesse," Suit said. "Molly told me to have the guys keep an eye on the Walterses' house. It's quiet."

"Good. Listen, Suit, unless it's an emergency, I'd like a few hours of peace."

"I got you, Jesse."

He parked around the corner from Maryglenn's as he always did and took the slow walk down Newton Alley. This time he wasn't so much haunted by the events of months past as he was by what seemed to be happening to his town at the moment. He had had experience with drug scourges in the past. First there was the wave of cocaine that had crashed over L.A. like high-tide waves during a nor'easter. Worse was the crack epidemic. Cheap and dirty, it was a drug of the poor. People already suffering at the bottom end of things had their lives and the lives of their families destroyed by little vials of rock. But it was more than that. It was the associated crime and violence that came with the epidemic that Jesse had been forced to deal with, first in uniform and then as a detective.

This thing with opioids had the same feel about it, like the heat coming at you from a fast-spreading wildfire. What disgusted Jesse most of all about these drug scourges was the complicity of the people at the top of the food chain. The same people who had lit the fire, the big pharma companies, their stockholders, doctors, drugstores, were now screaming for everyone else to put it out. He knew that the fire would claim many more victims before it would come under control. It was always the way.

As Jesse reached the door to the warehouse and Maryglenn's loft apartment, his cell buzzed. He saw that the call was from Molly and let it go to voicemail. If it was an emergency, she would get in touch with Suit and Suit would get in touch with him. Anything else would hold until morning.

"Hello, Jesse," Maryglenn said as she came to open the door.

She stepped out, closing the door behind her. She was not dressed in her usual black-on-black, paint-speckled uniform. Instead she wore a long peasant skirt of several shades of red, a white satiny blouse, and a red bolero jacket. As was always his reaction to her, Jesse thought how different she was from the women he was usually drawn to. Her looks, her dress, so different from Kayla, Jenn, and Diana. Although he loved how they had been so careful about their appearance and dress, he admired Maryglenn for her unique sense of style and for not letting her self-image be so bound up in those other things.

"The Gull," she said, grabbing his arm and looping hers through his elbow. "Dinner is on me. I insist." Noticing his expression, she asked, "What is it?"

He didn't quite know how to explain it so that it wouldn't sound insulting to her, so he punted. "Nothing."

She didn't believe him, but that was okay.

THEY SAT AT A TABLE at the rear of the Gull, one that afforded them a view of the marina, the ocean, and Stiles Island. He had sat at this table many times since his arrival in Paradise. The Gull had once been his go-to place, but in recent years the quality of the food had tailed off and it had pleased Jesse to do more of his drinking alone at his old house at the edge of town. Now he no longer drank at all and his house had been sold.

"What is it, Jesse?" Maryglenn asked again, as she noticed him gazing out the glass.

But this time, Jesse had something to say and it wasn't about Maryglenn's looks or her choice of restaurant.

"I couldn't help but notice the . . . I don't know, vibe, I guess, between you and Daisy. Even my son noticed it. Cole said he thought Daisy seemed jealous of me. I thought he was wrong, but now I'm not so sure."

Maryglenn squirmed a little in her chair but didn't turn away. "Did you ask Daisy about it?"

"Uh-huh."

"And?"

"She asked me if I'd heard of Swingline Sue's."

"Had you?"

Jesse said, "I have now. Google is magical."

"Do you have questions you want to ask?"

"No. But I would still like to know what it is with you two. Daisy's been a friend and ally for a long time, and we're . . . we're something to each other. I don't want that to change."

She held her lips tightly together as she thought. Then said, "I don't usually feel like I need to explain myself."

"That's fair. I don't, either."

"At art school, all of us used to go out partying together, dancing. No offense, but straight places suck for dancing. That hasn't changed since I got out of school. So when I feel like dancing, I head up to Tipton. One night I was there with an old girlfriend from school and Daisy asked me to dance. I didn't know who she was then. I danced with her. But when she kissed me, I backed her off by telling her I was already with my girlfriend. So you can imagine that she probably doesn't think too highly of me with the man in town she's closest to."

Jesse laughed, shaking his head. "Daisy's a pit bull to begin with. You sure pushed her buttons."

Between courses, he explained about why he and his cops had done what they did at the high school.

"I know we don't agree about some things, but I can't let it stop me from doing my job the way I feel I need to do it. We can argue about drugs like marijuana. My bet, it will be legal in this state in a few years. But opioids are a plague and it's not right."

Maryglenn didn't push back. What she did was pay the bill, grab Jesse by the hand, and make sure to have him speed back to her bed.

Fifty-eight

The next morning, while Maryglenn was just rousing, he noticed a scar on her right leg he hadn't seen before. Given the ferocity of their lovemaking, he wasn't sure he would have noticed it if they had been in full sunlight. It was a long vertical scar on the front of her shin that ran from the base of her knee to the top of her ankle. On either side of the scar were tiny, faint dots of faded pink scar tissue.

"I was riding my bike," she said, noticing him staring at her leg. "You're up."

"Yeah."

"What happened?"

"Car turned right into me. My leg was caught under the front tire. Compound fracture of my tibia, broken fibula, broken bones in my foot." She gathered the blanket around her, clutched herself, and rocked gently as if to calm herself. "I had three surgeries and they had me in all sorts of gadgets to hold the bones in place while I healed. The scarring actually used to be much worse, but I had some cosmetic work done. I'm a little self-conscious about it, Jesse, so if you could stop staring . . ."

He kissed the top of her head. "You must've been in a lot of pain."

"You can't imagine. It's a good thing we can't remember pain. We can remember having it, but not the pain itself."

Jesse realized he was rubbing his right shoulder. "Does it hurt anymore?"

"Sometimes, in damp weather," she said. "But nothing like when it happened. I was drugged up for months. I don't even like thinking about it."

Before Jesse could respond, his cell phone buzzed in his pants pocket. His pants were on the floor next to the bed and the wood amplified the buzzing. He grabbed his pants, retrieved the phone, and saw the call was from Molly. Unlike the night before, Molly was about to go on duty now. If she was calling him this early, he couldn't blow her off again.

"I've got to take this," he said, walked into the bathroom, and closed the door behind him.

"Molly, what's up?"

"Did you get my message last night?"

"No, sorry. What is it?"

Molly explained about her interviews and told Jesse that Ambrose North protested way too much.

"He didn't let me get within twenty yards of Petra, but I saw her listening at the top of the stairs. She heard everything. When do you want to speak with her?"

"Asap. Call them up and tell them I want her and her lawyer in tonight."

"You want me to call at this hour? It's six-fifteen."

"Time for polite manners is over," he said. "How did the other interviews go?"

Molly detailed the call she received from Sara York.

"She says that Chris Grimm was involved with a female teacher at the high school."

"That's what my source says Heather Mackey told him."

Molly was furious. "Why didn't you tell me about that, Jesse?"

"Think, Crane. I heard this secondhand from a kid. I didn't know if I could trust it. If it was true, we needed it to come out independently. I didn't want any of your questions to lead the kids to a false conclusion or to spook them into silence. I also didn't want to have them run back to the teacher to warn her. One of these kids knows who she is."

"Okay, Jesse."

"I'll be in by seven."

When he clicked off, he recalled the image of the scar on Maryglenn's leg, remembered her admission that she had been drugged up for months following the accident. The alarm bells were blaring in his head. She fit the profile.

When he came out of the bathroom a few minutes later, he began gathering up his clothing to get dressed. She got out of bed, letting the blankets fall away from her body. She pressed herself against him, kissed his neck. He kissed her back.

"Aren't you going to shower?" she asked when the kissing was done. "I can put up some coffee and join you."

"Won't you be late?"

"I'll call in."

"Sorry," he said, buttoning his shirt. "I can't. Duty calls. I'll shower at home and then I've got to get to work."

She looked at him sideways. "This about Chris Grimm?"

He half smiled at her, pulling on his pants. "I've already told you more than I should have."

"One of the perks of sleeping with the police chief."

Just now, Jesse didn't find that particularly funny.

Fifty-nine

Although Molly understood Jesse's reasoning for not sharing the information about the potential involvement of a female teacher in the drug distribution network at the school, she was still POed at him. But seeing the expression on Jesse's face as he walked through the stationhouse door changed that. Molly's wounded pride suddenly seemed less important. Reading a self-contained man like Jesse Stone was no mean feat. When he openly showed he was upset, as he did entering the station, it raised a red flag.

"What is it, Jesse? What's wrong?"

"My office in five," he said, blowing past her.

In the meantime, Jesse made a call Molly wouldn't have approved of.

Vinnie Morris picked up on the second ring. "Jesse Stone. What's up?"

"How would you like me to treat you to a meal? Lunch?"

"Today?"

"That's when I'll be in town."

"What's the catch? Not that I don't like your company, but this is short notice."

"Remember that pawn shop I—"

Vinnie said, "Precious Pawn and Loan. Like I told you, I know them."

"Should I ask how you know them?"

"Take a guess."

"I'd like to do more than use your name," Jesse said. "How about you meet me there at noon."

"You ask a lot. I getting anything out of this besides steak?"

"Creamed spinach."

Vinnie laughed. "Seriously, Jesse."

"I think the drug syndicate we were discussing might be using them," Jesse said, though he had proof that only Chris Grimm had actually done business with them. "You want your business tied to them if the DEA gets wind of things? They'll give you up in a second if it helps knock time off their sentence."

"Noon. Don't be late." Vinnie was off the line.

Jesse still had the phone pressed to his ear when Molly knocked and came into his office.

He put the phone down. "Sit."

"What is it, Jesse?"

"Call someone in to take the desk today."

"Do we have that kind of money for overtime in the budget?"

"Yeah, but for all the wrong reasons," Jesse said. "Since I was forced to let Alisha go, we're one officer down."

"But why do you need me to be off the desk?"

"I need you to do research without being interrupted."

"What kind of research?"

"Get the names of all the female teachers at the high school.

That should be easy enough to do. The names are public record. Then I want you to find out everything you can about them."

Molly stood. "Okay, I'll get to it."

"And, Molly," Jesse said, stopping her in her tracks. "Start with Maryglenn."

Now Molly understood the look on Jesse's face when he came into the station.

Sixty

Jesse caught rush-hour traffic on his way down to Boston, but still made it there by 8:45. He parked his Explorer partway down the block and across the street from the address he had for Dr. Laghari. The place was a storefront operation, literally. It had two large plate-glass windows on either side of a steel-and-glass door. The glass on either side of the door was covered in cheap black tint halfway up the windows. The door glass was completely covered in it so that it would be impossible for anyone on the street to see inside. To Jesse's eye, it looked as if it might once have been a Chinese takeout or a chain sandwich shop. The only thing missing was signage, any kind of signage. The only indication that the address was a doctor's office was the line of people waiting outside the door.

The people waiting for the doctor were a pretty shabby bunch. Many, if not all, looked homeless. Yet each of them was equipped with a cane, crutches, walkers, or some sort of joint brace. Knee braces seemed most popular. At nine sharp, the door opened and half the people waiting outside were let in. A big, brutal-looking man with a pale, pockmarked face stepped outside. He wore a black leather jacket, jeans, and motorcycle boots. He said something to the people outside. When he was done, he surveyed the street. His eyes seemed to lock on Jesse's Explorer, if only for a second. It wasn't as if the street was empty of other vehicles or that his SUV was particularly clean. Jesse shrugged it off when the brutal man stepped back inside through the door.

Ten minutes later, a beat-up yellow mini–school bus pulled up at the storefront. Its door opened at the same time as the storefront's door opened. About seven ragged people piled out of the bus and got on line. When they were out, the first batch of patients left the doctor's office and made their way into the bus. When the bus pulled away, the guy in the leather jacket repeated the routine. He let half of the waiters in and said something to the rest. He once again surveyed the street, his eyes hesitating at the sight of the Explorer. This time, Jesse wasn't prepared to shrug it off.

The issue was what to do about it. He was out of his jurisdiction and had no reason to march into Laghari's office. And what if he did walk in? He had no authority, no backup in case there was trouble. All he was armed with was his nine-millimeter and suspicions. And the Boston PD wasn't fond of small-town chiefs working their patch. It had been the same in L.A., so Jesse understood it from both points of view. What he did, instead, was take photos of what was going on. He watched three cycles of the bus loading and unloading. Each time, the brutal guy stared at his vehicle a little longer. It was pretty easy to figure out what was going on.

There was a knock on the glass next to Jesse's head. When he turned to look, an unshaven white man with a paper cup, begging for change, was standing there. Jesse wanted him gone, so he rolled down the window and held out a dollar bill. But the man didn't take it.

"Stone," the man said, "get the fuck out of here. You want to blow an operation that's been ongoing for six months?"

"You ran my plates."

"No wonder they made you chief," he said, finally snatching the dollar bill.

"Identify yourself."

The man's face turned red under his stubble. "I said, get the—"

"Uh-huh, and I said 'Identify yourself.'"

"Detective Hector, Joint Narcotics Task Force."

Jesse pressed the ignition button, rolled up his window, and pulled away.

THE ADDRESS MOLLY had gotten him for Dr. Wexler wasn't more than five miles away from Laghari's storefront, but it was a very different scene. The storefront here had a FOR RENT sign in the window and there wasn't any activity out on the side. Jesse Googled Wexler and came up with an address in Brookline. He still had plenty of time to get over to the South End to meet Vinnie, so he punched the address into his GPS and headed over.

WEXLER LIVED IN a big Tudor-style house on a tree-lined street not far from the Brookline Country Club. The house itself seemed sturdy and in good shape, but the lawn was shaggy, with patches of brown, and the hedges were overgrown. The driveway was in need of repaving and the mailbox was held to its post by a bungee cord and tape. There was a dusty, sun-bleached 1980 Mercedes parked in the driveway beside a light green Toyota Corolla.

Jesse had circled the block to make certain there were no surveillance vans parked anywhere or DEA agents in the trees with telephoto lenses. When he was sure he wasn't interfering with some major investigation, he pulled into the driveway and got out. He texted Molly a photo of the house and the address. "Wexler" was the sum total of the message accompanying the photo. He was tempted to ask how her investigation was going and thought it wiser not to ask.

He stepped out of his Explorer. He strode up to the front door, pieces of broken blacktop and crumbling concrete under his feet. Close up, the house looked less sturdy than it had from the curb. Though not quite in as bad a shape as the lawn or the driveway, it showed signs of neglect. Jesse pressed the bell but heard nothing ring inside the house. He knocked and waited.

Sixty-one

Arakel's phone rang, and somehow he knew the news wasn't good. Nothing had been right since the day the boy had called and told him about the dead girl in Paradise. Since then he'd become a murderer and a drunk. He had come this close to raping a woman. But he wasn't patting himself on the back for stopping himself, because he had, in turn, forced that woman to seduce a young girl into the trade. And even that had blown up nearly before it got started. He drank down one of his little vodka bottles and then picked up.

"Yes."

"We've got an issue," said the voice on the other end.

"An issue?"

"There was an out-of-town cop parked across from the clinic, and he wasn't there to get healthy."

"Cop. What cop?"

"Stone. Police chief in Paradise. We got rid of him today, but he'll be back. Now I've got to cover my ass with the brass in case they come back to me. I think you and the Shah better think about relocating and soon."

Arakel was fuming, but the man on the other end of the line clicked off before he had a chance to remind him about who worked for whom.

PETRA HAD SKIPPED HER second-period class to find her. The frightened girl made some lame excuse about another teacher needing to see her when she walked into the teachers' lounge. But now they were in the basement of the school in a room that not even the janitorial staff bothered with. It was full of old desks, worn shiny blackboards, and broken chairs.

She grabbed Petra's hair, pulling her head back and slamming her into the wall.

"How stupid can you be, letting other teachers see us together. This better be good."

Petra, already frightened, was now one little spark short of a total meltdown.

"Molly Crane came to the house last night to ask about Chris Grimm," she said, gasping for air as she spoke. "My dad didn't let her talk to me."

She relaxed her grip on the girl's hair. "So what's the problem?"

"Because my dad wouldn't let her talk to me, I am going to be questioned by Jesse Stone tonight at the station. My dad got me a lawyer and told me everything would be all right, but—"

She changed her approach to the girl. She was stroking her hair. "I'm sorry, Petra. I was just so frightened that it would spoil things between us if people saw us together. It's okay, I under-stand now."

"No matter what my dad says, I'm going to tell Jesse about the drugs. I can't take this anymore, all the lying and stealing and stuff. But I swear I won't say anything about us. I promise. I could never hurt you."

It was all she could do not to slap the girl and once again show her the photo of Chris Grimm's battered and lifeless body, but she couldn't afford to have Petra lose it completely.

"You can never tell anyone about me," she said before kissing the girl hard on the mouth. "You must never, never say you sold drugs to anyone. Never. They won't forgive that." She kissed her again and brushed her hand across the girl's breasts. "Tonight, no matter what your father and the lawyer tell you, don't say anything. Later on, you can admit to doing drugs, but please, for me, lover, not tonight. I need tonight to make sure we are both clear of this stuff." She kissed her again. "Promise me."

"I promise. I could never hurt you. I would rather die than hurt you."

"Shhh, lover. Now get back to class."

ARAKEL'S PHONE RANG AGAIN, and he was even less pleased when he heard the woman's voice.

"What now? I thought we had agreed you could handle the little girl."

"It's the local police, they are going to formally interview the girl tonight. She won't say anything, but I don't know how long that will last."

"We can have the men in the white van visit her. You have spoken with them, yes?"

She swallowed hard. "Yes."

"They have seen to the boy. They will see to the girl."

"No, don't you touch her! She disappears or gets hurt, all hell will break loose."

Arakel, fortified with more alcohol, said, "Or we can see to you. I think the men in the van would prefer that. One way or the other, this must be handled."

"Give me a few days," she said, "please."

"Handle it."

The click on the other end told her it wasn't up for debate. The image of Chris Grimm's body flashed before her eyes. She didn't actually care much for Petra as a lover and she was such a child, but she could never let those animals touch her. She would have to see to the girl herself, and she had an idea of how to do it.

ARAKEL KNOCKED ON Mehdi's door and entered his office.

"We have a problem in Paradise."

Mehdi laughed. "Yes, what a ridiculous name."

"It is quite a lovely place," Arakel said, feeling a pang of regret for what he had brought to the town.

"It tempts the fate to call a place on this earth Paradise."

Now it was Arakel who laughed. "I fear neither one of us will ever see true Paradise."

"Yes, let us concern ourselves with base, temporal things. You were saying."

"The teacher has called and the police are going to question the girl. She was warned to handle it or I said that I would have to have our men handle it. She will see to it. Also, the Paradise police chief showed up outside the clinic. We put him off for today, but he is a stubborn one and will return."

"Yes, Stojan called and reported to me. This policeman, he may be the bigger problem than the woman and the girl. We might have to see to him." When Arakel got to the door, Mehdi called after him. "But you must make certain that when one leak is closed that the other does not once again come open. All leaks will have to be sealed or what is the point? Do you understand my meaning?"

Arakel understood it, all right. He nodded at Mehdi and left. He understood that the woman and the girl would have to die and that he would be even farther away from paradise than the day he shot the boy to death.

Sixty-two

A gaunt white woman in green scrubs and running shoes opened the door.

"How may I help you?" she asked, an impatient look on her face.

"Is Dr. Wexler available?"

"Who's asking?"

Jesse was quick on the uptake. There were times when talk was best, but there were times when showing a shield helped cut through all the bullshit. This was one of those times. He flashed his shield in the woman's face and quickly put it away.

"Let me ask you this again," he said, giving her his best fish-eyed stare. "Is the doctor available?"

She twisted up her lips and shrugged, said, "He's inside the house, Detective, but he's not here."

Jesse wasn't in the mood. "Do I look like I'm in the mood for games?"

"Alzheimer's," she said. "Come have a look for yourself."

Jesse followed the nurse into the house. The place had that peculiar odor that wasn't quite home and wasn't quite hospital but a little bit of both. It was the scent of pine, ammonia, and human decay mixed up with cooking smells like fried onions, burnt coffee, and eggs.

"He's in there," the nurse said, pointing at a door near the kitchen. "The stairs are blocked off. He's taken a few falls when he gets confused and wanders. He's safer this way."

Jesse asked, "What's your name?"

"Millie."

She was testing Jesse's patience. "Millie what?"

"Millie Lutz. I'm an RN and the family pays me and a few other nurses to watch the doctor."

"If his Alzheimer's is that bad, shouldn't he be in assisted living?"

"Above my paygrade, Detective."

Jesse walked into the room off the kitchen. Sitting in a brown leather recliner was a hunched, bald-headed man with a freckled scalp. He was dressed in expensive blue pajamas and slippers. He was staring out the window and didn't seem to notice Jesse had come into the room. Next to the recliner was a hospital bed. In front of the bed was a wide-screen TV on a stand. Jesse moved around by the window so that the doctor could not help but notice there was someone standing there. Only he didn't seem to notice. Dr. Wexler wore an expression that Jesse had seen many times before on the faces of those suffering from severe dementia. It was what he thought of as a sad, confused smile. Jesse could only imagine what could produce such an expression and had no desire to ever find out. As he had once confided to Molly, he preferred cancer to Alzheimer's.

"Dr. Wexler," he said.

The old man blinked, but that was his only concession to Jesse's presence. The nurse had been correct. The doctor was in the house, but he wasn't home. Jesse put a hand on the doctor's shoulder. He wasn't sure why he did it. This time, Wexler turned his head and looked up at Jesse. Unfortunately, his expression was unchanged. Jesse stayed with him a few moments and then left.

"I told you," Nurse Lutz said when Jesse stepped out of the room.

"Do you know if Dr. Wexler's medical license is still active?"

She blew air through her lips and made a sarcastic face. "As if it mattered."

Jesse thought about giving her a hard time about her attitude, but he thanked her for her time instead.

"There a bathroom I can use?" he asked.

"Sure. Down the hall, past his study, on the right."

Jesse wasn't really interested in the bathroom. He was curious to have a quick look around. When he walked by the study, he noticed prescription pads on the desk. When he passed the study again on his way back from the bathroom, the pads were gone. But again, this wasn't his jurisdiction, and all he had at the moment were suppositions. They were strong ones, but knowing something in your guts didn't stand up in court. On the way out, he stopped to deliver a message to Nurse Lutz.

"When your bosses ask who was here, tell them Jesse Stone."

He left without bothering to wait for her denial.

Nurse Lutz watched out the front window and waited a few moments after Jesse pulled out of the driveway to punch in Mr. Sarkassian's number.

Sixty-three

Vinnie Morris was well turned out, but that was no surprise to Jesse Stone. Except for a brief period several years back when he had taken to wearing track suits, Vinnie's wardrobe on any given day tended to surpass the value of Jesse's weekly paycheck, before taxes. Today was no exception. Morris was dressed in a light gray wool box-check two-piece suit. The creases on the front of the pants were knife-sharp. Beneath the suit jacket was a custom-made light blue shirt and a slightly darker silk tie. The shirt cuffs extended a perfect inch below the jacket sleeves.

Vinnie shook his head at the sight of Jesse in his rumpled navy blazer, white shirt, jeans, and running shoes.

"Who dresses you? Let me send you to my tailor."

"No, thanks," Jesse said. "One day's outfit would bankrupt me."

"What's the plan?" Vinnie nodded at the pawnshop.

"I want to rattle them."

Vinnie smiled. "Easy enough."

"Good."

"You want me to say anything?"

Jesse said, "You'll know what to say and when to say it."

"Better be a good steak for lunch."

Vinnie followed Jesse through the door. Jolene was helping another customer but noticed the two men enter. She didn't make a happy face at the sight of Jesse, but it wasn't a frightened expression. If she knew who Vinnie Morris was, Jesse was certain the look on her face would have been quite different. And if Molly had seen the two of them together here like this, Jesse could only imagine the look on her face.

Jesse made certain to place himself in front of the display case containing the Western novels he'd been looking at the last time he was there.

"Hello, Jolene," Jesse said, as the woman came up to them.

Vinnie Morris stood next to Jesse, not saying a word. Jolene turned to Vinnie and was effusive about his clothing. Jesse was certain that she had made Vinnie's day. Then she turned back to Jesse.

"Yes, I'm so sorry we weren't able to help you during your last visit. But I see you are still interested in these novels."

"I am, but could you please ask Jerry to come out here."

She said, "I'm not certain he's in."

It was a familiar stall that Vinnie took as his cue. "Tell him I'd like to speak with him."

Jolene rolled her eyes. "And you are?"

"Vinnie Morris."

Jolene suddenly seemed to need the display case to hold her up. When she recovered, she turned and headed straight to the door she had disappeared through during Jesse's last visit. But this time, Jerry was already coming through the door. He had no need of Jolene to deliver the message.

"Hello, Mr. Morris."

"Hello, Jerry. How are you?"

"Fine, Mr. Morris. Good."

"Really? You seem to be sweating a little there." Vinnie offered him a pristine white handkerchief.

"Thanks," Jerry said, waving the hankie off. "I'm fine. It's nothing."

"My friend, here," Vinnie said, putting his hand on Jesse's shoulder, "says you sold something that he had a receipt for. Normally, I wouldn't care, but I like having good relations with the police."

Jerry's eyes got big, and he was sweating more heavily. "The police?"

Jesse took that as his cue and showed Jerry his Paradise police chief's shield. Jerry seemed afflicted with the same weak legs that Jolene had experienced and put his hands on the display case for support as she had.

"Chief Stone has some pretty crazy notions about you, Jerry. He thinks you've been moving merch through here that is connected with a drug syndicate. You know how I feel about drugs. I told him you would never do anything that stupid, something that might blow back on me and my business. I told him you knew how angry I would be if you did such a thing. Tell him he's crazy, Jerry."

"Chief Stone, I can assure you we would never do anything to risk Mr. Morris's concerns. Never." Jerry was unconvincing.

Vinnie Morris reached across the counter and patted Jerry on the biceps. "Good man." He turned to Jesse. "See, Chief Stone, what did I tell you?"

Jesse said nothing. He was sure Vinnie had sufficiently rattled Jerry's cage. He shrugged, and after taking one last look at the

Western novels, he left. Vinnie Morris stayed behind to say a few parting words to Jerry.

Just as Nurse Lutz had waited for Jesse's Explorer to pull away before punching in Arakel Sarkassian's number, Jerry did the same.

Sixty-four

Ambrose North strolled into the stationhouse as if he owned the place. Ambrose North was the kind of man who would stroll into the White House or St. Peter's and act the same way. Annette North looked slightly embarrassed and not a little bit wary. Petra North appeared about ready to jump out of her own skin. Jesse didn't recognize the attorney who accompanied them, but was certain he was a high-priced Boston criminal lawyer bound to underestimate Jesse.

"This is William Clark," Ambrose North said, pointing at the attorney. "He is our daughter's legal counsel."

Jesse nodded. "Counselor."

They shook hands, but it was perfunctory. Clark was conservatively dressed in a dark blue suit. He was a small, tidy man with a receding hairline and a serious demeanor.

"Chief Stone," Clark said, "will you please explain to me why my client has been summoned?"

"Officer Crane went to the North household to have a casual conversation with your client about the opioid issues at our local high school. As is their right, Mr. and Mrs. Ambrose refused to

give the officer access to their daughter. We have therefore re-
quested a more formal interview. Your client is not under arrest,
nor do we anticipate arresting or charging her, but we do have
credible information that she has knowledge of a drug ring operating at the high school. The interview will be digitally and audio
recorded."

"May her parents join us in the interview room?"

"One parent, yes," Jesse said.

Petra looked more and more nervous as her parents huddled
with Clark. Jesse heard the lawyer advising the parents to leave it
to him and not to come into the interview room. It was sound advice. It was Jesse's experience that parents, even ones with law
degrees, could not help but react emotionally when their child was
involved or when questions touched a nerve. But, as Jesse had
anticipated, Ambrose North insisted on accompanying Clark and
Petra during the interview.

"Let us proceed, Chief Stone," said Clark, gesturing for Jesse to
lead the way.

MEHDI, ARAKEL, STOJAN, and Georgi sat in the back room of a local Italian restaurant. The two thugs had stuffed their faces,
seemingly without any sense of what they were there to discuss.
Once their coffees had been served, Mehdi gave the waitress an
extra twenty-dollar bill on top of the tip and asked her not to re-
enter the room for at least another fifteen minutes. She was happy
to oblige.

Mehdi began when the waitress slid the door shut behind her.
"Gentlemen, we have a serious problem."

Stojan said, "Not to worry. We will be taking care from the girl
and the teacher. We will enjoy, no, Georgi?"

Georgi smiled a gap-toothed smile and nodded. "Enjoy very much, yes."

"At the moment, the girl and the teacher are mosquitoes on the ass of two elephants. First we must concern ourselves with the elephants. The mosquitoes can wait. Arakel, explain to them."

"Today, the police chief from Paradise, this Jesse Stone, came to the block of the clinic and exposed our police protection to scrutiny. He visited the old doctor's home and he came to the pawnshop with—"

Stojan interrupted. "We have already made move to the other location with clinic and Laghari says nothing. The old doctor is saying nothing."

Mehdi exploded. He slammed his fist onto the table, rattling the silverware and spilling his coffee on the tablecloth. "Shut up, you stupid gargoyle, and listen. Do not talk. Do not think. Listen!"

Stojan glared at him but kept his mouth shut.

Arakel went on. "Stone showed up at the pawn shop with Vinnie Morris at his side."

That got the thugs' attention. Like everyone else in the Boston area, they knew of Vinnie Morris and were aware of his reputation.

Mehdi said, "I see now that Arakel has gotten your attention."

"This cop is being paid by Morris?" asked Stojan.

"I do not think so. I hear they are . . . friends." Arakel turned his palms up. "They go back to a relationship with the late Gino Fish. At the pawn shop Morris tells Jerry the pawn man that he is aware he is doing business with us. Jerry is frightened."

Stojan had had it. "Enough talk. Who are we to kill? Morris?"

"Not Morris," Mehdi said. "We are not yet powerful enough to win a war we start. Not only would Morris's people come at us, but the other families and gangs would worry they would be next.

Morris, for now, is untouchable. We will deal with Jerry, along with the girl and the teacher. First—"

"The cop," Georgi said. "We kill the policeman."

Mehdi nodded. "With him gone, it will buy us the time to do the rest of what must be done. But it has to be done neatly and soon, not like the boy. An accident is best. Do you understand?"

JESSE SAT ACROSS THE TABLE from Petra. He'd done all the pre-liminaries: given her a can of soda, reassured her, and explained about the camera and the recorder.

In conclusion, Jesse said, "You have to give me verbal answers, Petra. Nodding or shaking your head doesn't count, okay?"

Naturally, she nodded yes. Everyone in the room, even Petra, laughed at that. Jesse had set her up for that in order to try to put her at ease. It did, for about five seconds. Then the near panic set back in. Jesse switched the equipment on, introduced himself, the others in the room, and stated the purpose of the interview. The first few questions were easy ones: What is your full name? What is your date of birth? Where do you attend school? Like that.

"Petra, are you aware of drug dealing, specifically Vicodin, Oxycontin, and heroin, at Paradise High School?"

"No."

"Have you ever used or been addicted to any of the drugs I just mentioned?"

"No."

Jesse reached under the table and produced an evidence bag. "Did you steal and barter your father's Rolex Submariner, now con-tained in the evidence bag, for drugs?"

The girl looked ready to crack, but her father lost it, screaming at Jesse and threatening to end the session. Jesse ignored North's threats. Clark, noticing the panic in the girl, seemed almost relieved by North's outburst. He turned and advised North to calm down, but only after the girl had collected herself.

"Petra, do you need me to repeat—"

"No," she said, calmly. "The answer is also no to your question."

She was asked if she knew about locker 113. Asked about Chris Grimm. Asked if she knew anyone else in the school doing drugs. Asked about Heather Mackey. The answer was always no. Although Jesse had been a shortstop and not a pitcher, he was preparing to throw the girl a curveball.

"Okay, Petra, we're almost done. One more question. Are you aware of the involvement of a female teacher at the high school connected to Chris Grimm and—"

Both father and lawyer saw the change in the girl's body language and the horrified look on her face.

"My client won't be answering that," Clark said, standing as he did and pulling Petra up by the arm. "This interview is at an end. My client has given you your answers, Chief Stone. She has, as the recordings will show, denied having any connection to or knowledge of the drugs and how they are distributed. Therefore, the answer to your last question is obvious."

Jesse did not object. It was answer enough. "Thank you for coming in, Petra. You can go." But as they were leaving, Jesse held the lawyer back. "You realize your client didn't give a single truthful answer."

"Do I?"

"Remember this, Counselor. Today was a free-pass day. That's two chances I've given her to tell me what she knows. I like the girl and want her to have a happy life, but if another kid ODs and I find your client lied here tonight, trust me when I tell you you will be earning every cent of your hourly fee."

"Threats?"

Jesse stared hard at the lawyer. "I don't make threats, Mr. Clark. Have a good night."

Sixty-five

The next morning Jesse pulled a chair up alongside Molly's and had her run the video of his interview with Petra North. They sat and watched in silence. When the video of the interview was finished, Molly spoke first.

"She's lying."

"I think so."

"She was coached to give one-word answers and not to give a single syllable extra."

Jesse agreed. "Just like we're taught to testify. No embellishments, no information beyond answering exactly what's asked."

"She knows who the teacher is, doesn't she?" Molly said. "When you asked her that, she looked like she was going to melt down."

"She knows. That girl is barely treading water, and I think her parents are going to let her go under rather than have their reputations dirtied."

He told her about what he had discovered in Boston, omitting Vinnie Morris's presence at Precious Pawn and Loan and their lunch together. For the most part, Jesse didn't care what other people thought of him, but Molly's disapproval was an exception.

"I need you to find out if Dr. Wexler has stopped writing prescriptions or whether he is still at it. If he is, it's a miracle. Severe Alzheimer's."

"Do you want me to do that before or after I finish the research on the teachers?" Molly asked, even as she handed Jesse a file. "That's hers, Maryglenn's."

Jesse understood. "Do it before, then get back to the teacher research. I'm going to go over to the high school later to let Principal Wester know we intend to interview all the women teachers sometime in the next few days. Now that I tipped my hand by asking Petra about the teacher, word will spread."

"Maybe not, Jesse. She might only warn the one teacher."

"We'll see. Can you get Lundquist on the phone?"

"Please would be nice."

"Would it?"

"Jesse Stone!"

"Please."

THIS TIME *she* went looking for the girl between classes and found her by her locker. As she walked by she whispered to the girl to meet her downstairs in the room with the discarded desks and blackboards.

It was all Petra could do not to fall apart right there in the hall, but she held it together long enough not to follow immediately.

Things in the dank, dimly lit room were very different from the last time they were there. Petra's book bag was thrown to the floor, her lover grabbed her, pushed her gently onto one of the discarded teacher's desks, and climbed atop her. Several minutes went by before a word passed between them.

"I'm so sorry about how I treated you the last time we were here," she said, brushing the back of her hand along the girl's cheek. "I want to make it up to you. Please let me make it up to you."

But unlike in the past, when those words would have made Petra glow with excitement and vow eternal loyalty, she began sobbing.

"What is it, lover? Don't cry. Was it the interview?"

Petra said, "They know."

It was all the older woman could do not to slap the girl and demand straight answers, but she knew she couldn't play it the hard way. No, this performance had to be her best, because it was all about one thing—survival, her survival.

"It's okay, darling." She kissed her eyes. "It's okay. We'll get through this. Just tell me."

"Jesse knows about you . . . not your name. I would never, ever tell him your name. I would die first, but he asked me if I knew about a female teacher at the high school being involved with the drugs."

"It's okay. It's okay. As long as he doesn't know my name and we're sure you will never betray me. You know I would never betray you."

"I know that. But things are . . . bad at home. My folks know I've been using and they knew I was lying when I told Jesse that I didn't know anything about you. They pushed me to give them your name. My dad said we could use it as leverage in case the police charged me with anything, that they would drop charges against me if I could give up the teacher."

She kissed the girl. "But you didn't."

"Never. I couldn't. I love you."

"And I love you and I have a gift for you to prove it." She climbed off the girl, retrieved her own bag, and pulled out a vial. She placed the vial in the girl's right palm and closed her fingers around it. "I crushed up some pills for you from my stash. Snort a line or two of the powder and you will get a jolt and everything will be better. I promise. It will make it all go away for a while." She kissed the girl softly on the lips.

"I needed this," Petra said. "Thank you. I've never snorted it before, so I'm a little nervous."

"Don't be afraid, lover. It's easy."

The girl began to twist open the vial.

"No, no, darling, not here. It will be too much the first time to be in public. At home, in your room first, where no one can see you. Here, this is for now." She handed Petra a little green pill.

The girl swallowed it without hesitation. "Can we be together soon?"

"Together, yes. Very soon. I have to go." She kissed the girl and left.

JESSE STARED AT the open file on his desk. He rarely felt dirty about his job. Sure, being a cop meant you sometimes had to look at people's lives under a microscope and that you often wouldn't like what you found there. But this was different. He wasn't looking at just anyone under the lens, but a woman he had twice spent the night with and for whom he had a growing affection, a woman he now suspected of possibly being at the center of a high school drug ring and having seduced a teenage boy.

Molly stuck her head in. "Lundquist on line one. I have a call in to the state medical board, but they work at their own pace." She didn't bother waiting for Jesse to say anything and left.

Lundquist asked, "What's up, Jesse?"

"I may have found something bigger than a drug ring at Paradise High School."

"What's that?"

"First, are you in good with the Narcotics Division?"

"I have some friends over there, yeah. Why?"

"I need a favor before I say for certain."

"Okay, ask."

"Find out how many prescriptions Drs. Rajiv Laghari and Myron Wexler have written over the last month and what they were for." He spelled the doctors' names for Lundquist. "Also, can you see if the Boston PD is working a Joint Narcotics Task Force? If so, are your people involved? When you come back to me with that, we'll talk. Any progress on the Grimm homicide?"

"I'm going over to Helton later today to look at some surveillance-camera footage."

"Keep me posted."

Lundquist was off the line and Jesse went back to reading the file on Maryglenn.

Sixty-six

Cole walked into the stationhouse. He hadn't been there since his first weeks in Paradise. The chip on his shoulder in those days was enormous. His misunderstanding of what had actually happened between Jesse and his mother had eaten at him for years. He had finally come to Paradise to see and take the measure of the man he thought had abandoned him and turned his back on his mother. Jesse was in the final stages of rehab when he came to town and Cole's frustration at Jesse yet again being absent pushed him over the edge. He had twice been brought into the jail for drunk and disorderly behavior but had never been charged. That was department policy. As Jesse told his cops, he'd seen too many people's lives ruined by getting fed into the system for no good reason. Cole didn't know it then, but that policy had saved him. He knew it now.

"Molly," he said, getting her attention.

Molly looked away from her computer screen. "Cole!" She stood up and came out from behind her desk. She thrust out her right hand. "I hear congratulations are in order, though there aren't but two Staties I can stand being around. I guess you'll be the third."

"Thanks, Molly." He shook her hand and smiled.

"What are you doing here?"

"Is my dad around?"

She tilted her head toward his office. "Go on in."

"Thanks."

JESSE WAS FACING OUT the window behind his desk, his eyes not focused on anything in particular. He heard the door open and shut but didn't turn around.

"What is it, Crane?"

"You always speak to Molly like that?"

When Jesse turned around he saw Cole standing by the door, shaking his head.

"Not always." Jesse pointed to a chair in front of his desk. "C'mon, sit for a minute."

Cole sat. "I haven't been here long, but I can tell you'd be in trouble without Molly."

"I know."

"Does she?"

"Believe me, she does. She reminds me of it every five minutes."

Cole smirked. "I doubt that. When you were staring out the window, what were you thinking about?"

"The drug case. Forget that. Why the visit?"

"I need to borrow your Explorer. I've got to go to the academy and do some final paperwork. And now, since you know about it and Daisy knows you know, I can't really keep borrowing her car."

Jesse threw his keys to his son.

"You sure?"

"Uh-huh. I'll see you later."

Cole stood up, waved bye, and left.

———

PETRA, STILL FREAKED about the cops and her parents breathing down her neck, and excited by the prospect of another night in the motel, cut her last two classes and drove home. The dose from that morning was wearing off and she was beginning to feel the sick, the kind of sick that had nothing to do with tender loving care or a nice long nap. It was the kind of sick with only a singular magical cure. And that cure was in a vial in her bag. She had been tempted to do a line in school or in her car, but she was pretty paranoid about the cops watching her and forced herself to wait. Besides, she knew that some of the sick was just worry.

Although she had the vial and had taken some pills out of the duffel bag before giving it back, the worry and fear always came with the sick. It came with it because she knew that eventually the day would come when there wouldn't be a vial from her lover, or stolen pills or any more watches to trade, or another doctor to write a phony script. That someday she would have to turn to heroin and that she was much closer to that day than she was far away from the first time she felt the sick.

She had also come home to escape and be alone. She had put on a brave face for her lover and made promises she wanted to keep, meant to keep, but knew that she couldn't keep forever. Petra understood she was weak and that even if she were strong, she had a soft spot. All her parents or the cops had to do was keep her away from her drugs for a few days. Petra knew if she got hungry enough for a dose she would say or do anything to get healthy. All addicts knew that about one another. Strength, bravery, and resolve could be measured by the milligram.

So up in her room, Petra laid out a very thin and short little line because she wasn't sure of the ratio of the drugs crushed up into a powder and a pill. She was sure she was being too cautious, but that didn't matter. There was no one there to call her chicken or say she was scared and weak. No one but herself. She didn't bother with a chopped straw or a rolled-up bill. She put her left nostril onto the dresser top and inhaled.

ON THE ROAD OUT OF PARADISE, Cole was blasting a hip-hop station from Boston. He was spitting out the rhymes along with the rapper, bobbing his head, moving his shoulders, thinking about how proud his mom would be of him in uniform. He was so into the music, so lost in his thoughts, that he didn't notice the white van coming up alongside his father's Explorer.

Sixty-seven

At first, the buzz was incredible. Petra had never felt anything like it, but after the first few seconds of absolute ecstasy, she knew it was all wrong. Her arms ached and her legs felt like they couldn't hold her. She grabbed onto her dresser. She was dizzy and disoriented. *I'm in my room. Am I in my room? Am I standing?* And then she wasn't standing. Her dresser came down on top of her.

In the distance she heard someone calling to her. "Petra, Petra, are you all right? What was that?"

But Petra's voice didn't work and the other voice had come from too far away. All Petra wanted to do was sleep. She wanted to sleep forever and never have to worry again about where the next pill would come from. Her eyes fluttered and her last thought before sleep was that her lover hadn't lied. It was going to be all right.

BANG!

Cole wasn't quite sure what happened. His first instinct was that the Explorer's left rear tire had blown, but when he looked in his side-view mirror he noticed a white van had turned its right front fender into his left rear wheel well and was nosing it hard. His heart was pounding, his mouth dry; the hip-hop blasting through the speakers sounded tinny and a million miles away. His vision had never been so acute. He soaked through his shirt. He tried oversteering to the right in the opposite direction to try to fight against the force pushing against that tire. It didn't work and set the Explorer spinning in circles.

When the big Ford was sent spinning, he switched strategies. Instead of steering against the force, he steered with the spin. The Explorer almost righted itself. However, as it crossed over into the oncoming traffic lane, the SUV's tires hit something, a curb. The Explorer slid back across the road and flipped over once, then again over the guardrail, down a gully, and into some trees at the side of the road.

The white van stopped, went into reverse, and stopped again at the point where the Explorer had gone over the rail and into the gully. Georgi got out of the van, hopped over the guardrail. The plan was to make certain that if Stone wasn't killed by the "accident," to ensure his neck got broken one way or the other. The Explorer was lying on the driver's side, its front end crumpled by the trees, engine whining. Georgi got about halfway to the SUV when he heard the siren screaming. It was close. He had to get this done quickly. He ran, slipped, slid down, tumbled, and banged into the Ford. He got up, went around to look through the windshield, and froze.

"*Luyno!*" he said to himself in Bulgarian. *Shit!*

He began to claw his way up the embankment, but it was too late. A state trooper was working his way down toward him.

———

ANNETTE NORTH OPENED THE DOOR and saw Petra, her arms flung over her head, underneath her dresser.

"Oh my God. Petra! Petra!"

She knelt down by her daughter, tried to rouse her, but it was as if her daughter was beyond reaching. Then she noticed the vial and the powder, saw the grains of powder on Petra's nostril. She didn't panic. People like her didn't panic. That's what she told herself even as she was immobile, lost as to what to do next.

The rumble of a passing truck seemed to snap her out of her frenzied stupor, and she ran to the phone.

JESSE DROVE ONE of the spare cruisers to the North house. Molly had called the fire department to send an ambulance, but Jesse got there first. He rushed through the door and didn't bother to wait to hear Annette's explanation of what had happened.

He shoved the dresser off the girl, tried unsuccessfully to rouse her, but didn't want to pull her up for fear that the fall and/or the dresser coming down on her might have done spinal damage. He, too, saw the powder and the vial, saw the grains on Petra's nose. He pulled the naloxone out of his jacket pocket but had a decision to make that might either save the girl or kill her. Naloxone used incorrectly or for the wrong substance could induce severe reactions, including death. He dabbed his finger into the spilled powder, rubbed it between his fingers. Before fentanyl was introduced as a way to boost heroin's potency, he might have tasted the powder to make sure of what it was. He couldn't risk that now.

He ripped open the package of naloxone, placed the nozzle deep into the girl's right nostril, and pressed the plunger. Just as he finished, Tommy and Ralphy, two fire department EMTs, came up the stairs and into the girl's room.

"I just finished giving her a dose of naloxone," Jesse said. "Be careful when you move her, the dresser fell on top of her, and try not to disturb the vial on the floor."

Tommy, a big man, put his hand on Jesse's shoulder. "We'll do our best, Chief. Let us take over from here." Tommy knelt down where Jesse had been.

"Chief," Ralphy said, "Pete Perkins is downstairs. He says he's got an urgent message for you."

"Thanks."

When Jesse saw the look on Peter Perkins's face, he knew the message to be delivered wasn't a good one. "Cole had an accident just outside of town."

"Bad?"

"They're bringing him to Paradise General. He's probably there already."

"Peter, there's evidence in the room. Particularly a vial of drugs. Try and bag it before the EMTs do too much damage." Jesse stopped talking. He didn't think he could take losing the son he had barely gotten to know.

Sixty-eight

Jesse parked by the ER entrance and ran into the hospital, blind to the world around him. A strong hand grabbed him around his left biceps and stopped Jesse's unseeing momentum. Jesse came back into the moment, seeing the stocky man in the black leather jacket, gray/blue uniform shirt, yellow-striped dark blue pants, and tall, black boots.

"Chief Stone, I'm Trooper Quinton."

"What happened?"

"I only witnessed the very end of the incident as the vehicle driven by Mr. Slayton flipped over the guardrail. Lucky thing I got there when I did. There was already a man down in the gully. We got him out of the vehicle."

"How is he?"

"I understand he is your son. Is that right?"

Jesse was losing patience. "How is he?"

"Sorry, Chief. He's banged around pretty good. Probable concussion, but unless there's internal damage or something I didn't see, he'll be fine."

Jesse shook the trooper's hand and thanked him. "I'm going to check on my son, but will you please wait for me?"

"Sure thing."

Jesse stopped and about-faced. "You saved one of your own, Trooper. My son's going into the academy next month."

Quinton smiled. "Then go see about him."

JESSE WAS SURPRISED to see Dr. Nour in the examination room standing next to Dr. Marx. Unfortunately, Jesse had had many dealings with Dr. Marx over the years. Unfortunately, not because he disliked Marx, but because cops and doctors rarely meet for good reasons in ER examination rooms.

Nour, her all-business expression on full display, looked up at Jesse. "We're going to do some X-rays on him, but I think Mr. Slayton will be fine."

"He's got a concussion," Marx said. "But there are no internal injuries."

Dr. Nour nodded. "I concur with Dr. Marx. He is badly bruised but otherwise intact, Chief Stone. He is your son?"

"I am," Cole said. "Stop talking about me like I'm not here. It's creepy."

"Dr. Nour, after I speak to my son, can I have a moment?"

She looked at her watch. "A moment, yes." She stepped out.

Jesse put a hand on Cole's shoulder. "What happened?"

"I don't remember much. There was a white van."

"What about a white van?" Jesse asked.

"I don't know, Dad. I remember a white van next to me and then I don't remember anything. I'm sorry."

"That's okay." Jesse looked at Dr. Marx. "You keeping him?"

"Just overnight. If he shows no other symptoms, he'll be free to go home tomorrow."

Jesse said, "Rest up, Cole. I'll be back to see you tonight."

"Okay, Dad. I'm sorry about the Explorer."

"Seems like I get a new one every few months. Forget it."

Jesse pulled Marx over to one corner. "Petra North."

Marx's optimistic smile vanished. "I don't know. We sent some to the lab so we knew what we were dealing with. Fentanyl, heroin, and Oxy ground up into a pretty lethal mix. Probably would have killed anyone without some tolerance for opioids. Good thing you got to her when you did. Prognosis?" He shrugged. "We'll know more tomorrow. At least there's brain function."

Dr. Nour was pacing outside the examination room door.

"Thank you, Dr. Nour."

"It is my job to consult on these sorts of things, but you are welcome. Is there anything else, Chief Stone?"

"Rajiv Laghari and Myron Wexler."

Dr. Nour took her dour expression to a new level. "What of them?"

"Yes, what of them?"

"Rajiv is a good doctor, but the high life brought him low. Lost his family, privileges at two hospitals, and his practice. I haven't seen or heard of him for a year now. Dr. Wexler was my supervising physician when I came to the Boston area. A very good man and an excellent orthopedist. I heard he had to resign because he was losing his faculties, but that was many years ago. Will that be all, Chief Stone?"

"It will. Thanks again."

TROOPER QUINTON WAS chatting up the triage nurse when Jesse returned. Nurses and cops: So it ever was, so it would ever be. Jesse cleared his throat.

"Chief, how's your boy?" Quinton asked.

"Your diagnosis was a good one. Thanks for getting him out of there. You mentioned there was a man down in the gully already when you arrived on scene."

Quinton nodded. "A Russian, I think. Guy had a thick accent, but he helped me get your boy out of the car."

"When you arrived, was this Russian guy heading down the embankment or up?"

Quinton tilted his head at Jesse. "That's a funny question, but now that you ask, he was heading up. I guessed he was going to get something from his van, a tool or a pry bar to get into the van."

"A white cargo van?"

Quinton's eyes got wide. "Yeah, how'd you know?"

"My son mentioned it." It was only half a lie. Cole had mentioned a white van but hadn't mentioned that it was a cargo van. "If you saw the van again, would you recognize it?"

"Probably."

"Good. When we're done, can you go over to our stationhouse? I'll have my officer, Molly Crane, pull up some footage for you."

"I've got to clear it with my commander. He says yes, sure thing."

"Do that. I'll call Officer Crane."

They both got off their phones at the same time.

"My commander told me to give you whatever you needed."

"This Russian guy, did he give you a name?"

"Nah. After the ambulance came, I lost track of him, and the van was gone."

They shook hands. Jesse gave him directions to the station. When the trooper was out of sight, Jesse set out to find Petra North's room.

Sixty-nine

Things could not have gone worse for Mehdi, Arakel, Stojan, and Georgi.

Mehdi was livid. "Idiots! You know the expression 'If you try to kill the king, you had better not miss'?"

Stojan opened his mouth to answer, but the look on Mehdi's face closed it.

"That was not a real question. Not only did you miss the king, you did not even kill the prince. If we thought the heat was on beforehand, now it is about survival. We must clean up the loose ends not in Paradise, but on this end. Do you understand me?"

Arakel said, "But if we produce no profit, we will have nothing to kick upstairs."

"For now, we empty our accounts to kick upstairs. We must buy ourselves some time with those who might choose to replace us."

Arakel wanted to argue with him, but for once he was in lockstep with Mehdi. The bosses wanted their money. They would not care from where it came, and in the meantime they would make alternative arrangements with other doctors, other teachers, other students, and other cops.

Mehdi said, "What are you waiting for? Begone. And do your worst without pleasure, you animals. We want the loose ends to be ends, not to create more questions and anger."

Stojan and Georgi got up from their seats and proceeded to the van. They drove into Boston, but not to Dr. Wexler's home or to Dr. Laghari's.

THE WOMAN AT the hospital switchboard fielded the call.

"Paradise General. How may I help you?"

"I need to know Petra North's condition."

"I'm sorry, miss," she said. "I don't have that information."

"Then please transfer me to someone who does."

"Are you an immediate relative?"

"I am her sister."

"Well, then I suggest you call your parents for an update. It's hospital policy not to give information regarding a patient's condition over the phone."

"Can you connect me to her room, then?"

"I can't. I'm sorry, but I can connect you with the nurses' station on that floor. Please hold."

She waited, pacing, listening to a distorted elevator-music version of "Norwegian Wood."

A woman answered the phone in a hushed voice. "ICU."

"Can you give me an update on Petra North's condition?"

"One moment, please."

More "Norwegian Wood."

"Hello, this is Officer Weathers of the Paradise Police Department. Who is—"

She clicked off and dropped the phone to the floor as if it were a piece of white-hot metal.

Now she was faced with that same dilemma she had been faced with before: to run or not to run. Those threats of violence against her now seemed less frightening than the prospect of a life in prison. The police were close, knew a teacher was involved, and if the girl recovered there would be no counting on her to keep her secret. There was only one other option, but she had to be smart about it and careful.

JESSE STOPPED BY Cole's room, but he was asleep. The nurse at the station reassured him that his son was doing well. Still, he asked to speak to the doctor.

"He's been called to the ER. Come back in a little while, or I can have him call you."

Jesse said he'd be back up. That he had to stop by the ICU.

Annette and Ambrose North were seated in the visitors' lounge down the hall from the ICU. Both looked exhausted and lost. It was amazing, Jesse thought, how violence and tragedy can strip away the veneer and masks people show to the world. He suspected that the Norths had been showing them to the world for so long that they had come to believe their façades were actually who they were.

Annette looked up. "Jesse."

"Any change?"

"None," Ambrose said. "You saved her life. Thank you."

"If you really want to thank me, a little truth would be nice."

"Anything," Annette said, glaring at her husband. "Anything."

"Yes, Chief Stone. As my wife says, anything. Ask your questions."

He asked and they answered. They had known about Petra's drug use. They had made the same mistakes that Patti Mackey and Etta Carpenter had made by trying to wean their kid off the drugs and then by being willingly fooled by Petra's lies. They had figured out it was Petra who had stolen the watch, but by then it was too late to take things back. They had gotten Petra counseling. She had detoxed. But it was no good.

"The drugs she snorted to put her in here," Jesse said. "I think someone was trying to kill her."

Annette gasped and Ambrose North's face twisted in fury.

Jesse continued, "I've got her under police guard and I don't think the person who did this is stupid enough to try something in the hospital. It was an act of desperation."

Ambrose said, "You think it was the teacher."

"I do."

"After the interview at the station," Ambrose said, "we pleaded with her to give us the name. We explained that it might be used as leverage if you pursued criminal charges against her. But she denied knowing. She is definitely protecting someone."

"Do you think she wouldn't tell you because she was afraid?"

Annette spoke up. "No . . . Well, maybe a little. But it wasn't that. I'm sure of it. It was as if she was protecting a loved one."

Ambrose started to speak and then decided the time for pretense had ended several hours ago.

Before heading back to Cole's room to speak with his doctor, Jesse checked in with Gabe Weathers.

"Boss, good thing you're here. Saves me the trouble of calling you."

Jesse was curious. "Call me about what?"

"A little while ago, a woman called up to ICU to check on the girl's condition. But when the nurse put me on the phone, the phone went dead. I called the front desk. The woman didn't leave a name but claimed to be the North girl's sister."

"How old did this 'sister' sound to you, Gabe?"

"In the thirty-to-forty range, but it's hard to tell with voices over the phone."

Jesse told Gabe he'd have some food and coffee sent up for him and that he would send someone up to relieve him as soon as he could.

"Was it a sister, Jesse?"

"The teacher," he said. "She's scared."

"Is that good, her being scared?"

"Good, but dangerous."

"You think she'll try for the girl again?"

"No, Gabe. She tried to kill the girl and failed. Now she'll have to try something else."

"Like what?"

"I don't know," Jesse said. "That's what makes her dangerous."

Seventy

Millie Lutz was exhausted. Taking care of Wexler was a lot of work, and it wasn't the kind of work she liked. She had been trained as a surgical nurse and had worked with some of the top surgeons at the best hospitals in Boston. She'd seen hearts, kidneys, and lungs transplanted. She'd seen twins conjoined skull-to-skull separated and made healthy. And she had been reduced to changing the diapers of an old man who was lost inside his own head. Worse, she was risking a lifetime in jail for forging scripts.

She gave the relief nurse instructions about Wexler, who had finally gone to bed after hours of unintelligible babbling and roaming about the house. As she looked in the hallway mirror, she thought about the young doctor who had first turned her on to Oxy. How stupid she had been to believe the bastard was going to leave his wife for her. She hoped he was dead but could not deny the rush of excitement she got thinking about him inside her. The hollow-cheeked zombie who looked back at her from the mirror knew that she would never feel that type of excitement again. That she would have but one love for the rest of her miserable life.

She stepped out into the purplish dawn light, a chill in the air that was a welcome change from the stale air and stink of the old doctor's house. She noticed the birds singing to one another and realized she hadn't been conscious of them for many months. She took the paper at the end of the driveway and tossed it toward the front door, then got in her Corolla, backed out of the driveway, and headed past the little guardhouse at the entrance to Brookline Country Club.

About a half-mile from there, a motorcycle rode up behind her, the glare of its headlight in her rearview, blinding her. She slowed, pulled to the side of the road, stopped, and waved for him to pass. But he did not pass. He drove up next to her window. The motorcyclist stared at her through an opaque visor. He raised his right hand. In it was a pistol with a thick metal sound suppressor on its muzzle. There were five flashes, a cloud of gray smoke, and five muted barks. Millie's brake foot, now lax, fell away from the pedal, and her Corolla rolled into a thicket of trees along the road.

THAT MORNING, Molly greeted Jesse by tilting her head at his office door.

"Brian Lundquist is in there waiting for you."

"He's up bright and early."

"How's Cole?"

"Banged up. Concussion, but they're probably releasing him from the hospital later. Any change with Petra North?"

"She stirred a little. Not conscious, but the doctors are encouraged."

"Who's got ICU duty?"

"Peter."

"Your girls know about Petra?"

Molly laughed a sad laugh. "I think it was on Twitter before you left the house. There are no secrets anymore, Jesse. No privacy. I'm glad I wasn't raised in the world my girls have grown up in. A girl needs a safe place for herself where she can live with the little embarrassments and mistakes she makes and grow from them. I would hate to think of the world as a stage I would be forced to live on for everyone to see. It was one thing when I was a girl and came out of the bathroom trailing some toilet paper and having the other girls laugh at me. Now someone would take a photo of it or video with their phone and post it."

That gave Jesse an idea, but one he wasn't yet willing to share.

"Your girls will be fine, Molly. Their dad is a good man and they have you for a mom."

IT WAS STRANGE to see Lundquist standing where Jesse often stood, staring out the window behind his desk and gazing out at Stiles Island or the ocean beyond. It was stranger still when the state Homicide captain spoke without turning to face Jesse.

"There *is* a Joint Narcotics Task Force," Lundquist said. "DEA, Boston PD, and my team. They're working specifically on opioids. Last time we spoke, you mentioned you had something bigger than just the drug ring at the high school. You want to explain that to me now?"

Jesse sat in the seat Cole had sat in the day before, one of the two that faced his desk. "Sit in my seat," he said. "We need to look each other in the eye for this conversation."

Lundquist sat behind Jesse's desk. "Okay, I'm sitting and facing you."

"One more thing. Drs. Laghari and Wexler. What about their prescription writing?"

The corners of Lundquist's lips turned down. "They've been busy little beavers, those two. I imagine they must have writer's cramp from all the Vicodin and Oxycontin scripts they've been writing."

"Fascinating. Dr. Wexler is suffering from severe Alzheimer's and doesn't know where he is or who he was. Laghari, he's something else."

"What's the bigger thing, Jesse?"

"The other day, I parked across the street from a storefront in Roxbury. Nominally, it is Dr. Laghari's office or clinic. What it really is is a script mill. People, probably opioid addicts themselves, are getting paid to get the scripts written by Laghari filled at 'friendly' pharmacies. A bus drops them off at the clinic, then drives them to various pharmacies they know will fill the scripts. Those pills wind up in towns like Paradise, Salem, and Swan Harbor, where the dealers know they will get top dollar for each pill. And when the addicts can't afford the pills anymore, they turn them on to heroin. Helluva business model."

"But what's this got to do with the task force?"

"I was approached by a Detective Hector of the BPD. Told me to scoot."

"So?"

"Truth?"

"I asked, didn't I, Jesse?"

"Hector was protecting the clinic."

"How can you know that?"

"Know it?" Jesse said. "I can't know it, but I do. The guy guarding the door at the clinic made my Explorer. Probably knows every car on the block. He called his man on the task force and his man came and chased me."

"Maybe it was legit and the task force spotted you."

"I don't like the idea of dirty cops any more than you do, Brian. What you do with this info is up to you. But I can tell you this, put someone on a registered nurse named Millie Lutz. She's the one writing Wexler's scripts. She's part of a rotating crew of caretakers for Wexler. Also put one on Laghari. If they're not already dead, they will be soon."

DR. RAJIV LAGHARI did not like or trust the crude men who had coerced him into being their boy. He had himself to blame for that, but he had taken responsibility for very little in his life except the successful parts. That morning he was very pleased that his escort to the new location would not be that animal Stojan or his silent sidekick, Georgi. Detective Hector was a reasonable fellow who enjoyed talking about the things that interested Laghari: women and other women. So when the bell rang, he answered it without question. Detective Hector was there, but behind him was another man, an addict he recognized as a patient from the clinic.

"What is he doing here?" Laghari asked, as if the other man wasn't there.

Detective Hector didn't answer. Instead he stuck a six-inch blade into Laghari's liver, pulled it out, and sliced through the doctor's left femoral artery. Then he stepped back, shoved the junkie in front of him, drew his weapon, and screamed loudly enough to be heard on the street and in the condo next door, "Drop the knife now!"

Hector emptied half his clip into the clinic patient's back. He died of his gunshot wounds even before Dr. Laghari bled out. Hector gloved up, wiped the hilt of the knife, and wrapped the dead man's hand around it. He then removed several scripts written by Laghari out of his own pocket and carefully placed them in the patient's front pocket. When he was sure the scene was believable, he called it in.

WHEN JERRY OPENED Precious Pawn and Loan, he held the door for Jolene and hurried to shut the alarm. The second the alarm was disarmed, a man in a Patriots ski mask grabbed Jolene around her throat and pressed a Glock to her temple.

"Do what I tell you and she doesn't die."

Jerry held his hands up and promised to do as he was told.

"The cash. Now!"

Jerry hurried to the back room.

"Faster! Faster!"

But he wasn't fast enough. As Jerry ran toward the back room door, the masked man shot him twice, once through his left shoulder blade and then the back of his head. Jolene screamed as Jerry went down face-first. The gunman released Jolene, who knelt by Jerry. When she turned to look back, a bullet ripped through the top of her left breast. She was already dead when the second bullet made certain she wouldn't be nearly as pretty in death as she had been in life.

On the way out, the gunman smashed one of the display cases with the butt of his gun and grabbed a fistful of jewelry with a gloved hand. It would all look good for the cameras, like a robbery gone wrong at the hands of a nervous junkie. A nervous junkie who was an expert shot and who would eventually throw the stolen jewelry into the Charles River.

Seventy-one

After Lundquist left, Jesse headed to the high school in a cruiser. What he had to tell Virginia Wester was not the type of thing you did over the phone if it could be avoided. Although telling Wester he had to investigate every female teacher in her school was tough, it was nowhere near as difficult to do as a next-of-kin notification. That was the worst thing to do over the phone, and he had been forced to do it more than once, both in L.A. and in Paradise. The hardest call he had ever had to make was several years back, when a college freshman from California had been murdered in the Salter mansion up on the Bluffs. That call to the girl's parents would haunt Jesse.

When Jesse entered the high school, he drew stares and sideways glances. Heather Mackey's death was one thing, but the drug locker display, and now Petra North's OD . . . There was a cloud that had settled over the school, a veil of guilt and suspicion. It hung in the air in the hallways and classrooms so that even the innocent and naïve were touched by it.

As he climbed the stairs, Brandy Lawton came down.

"Hi, Jesse."

"Brandy."

"On the way to see Virginia?"

He nodded.

"How is Petra North?"

"You've heard?"

"Everybody's heard. How is she?"

"Alive," Jesse said, being purposely vague. If he was going to interview these people, he wanted them as uninformed and on edge as possible.

"That's something, at least. Was it like Heather? I mean . . . you know."

"I've got to go, Brandy. Excuse me."

But as he tried to move past her, she asked if he would be willing to do his talk to the softball team again this spring. He agreed more out of expediency than a desire to give a motivational talk. He had never found those talks very helpful during his baseball career. Then again, Jesse was old-school and thought a kick in the ass often worked better than talk.

JUST AS BRANDY LAWTON had asked about Petra, so, too, did Freda and Principal Wester. He was a little less vague with these two women than he had been with Lawton.

"She's in a coma," he said. "There is brain activity and there's a chance she will recover, but I'd prefer it if you would not share that information with the faculty."

Principal Wester didn't like that. "And why wouldn't I share that with my people? They are all concerned about Petra's recovery."

"Most, not all."

"What?"

"Virginia, it's my belief that one of your teachers tried to kill Petra. That's why I'm here."

"To make an arrest?"

"No, to tell you that I need to set up interviews with all your female faculty members and employees. We'll talk to everyone, from the teachers to the lunch ladies and the bus drivers."

"Jesse, I've bent over backward for you, but you're going to have to give me something more than your word on this, and I will have to alert the school board."

Before Jesse could answer, his cell vibrated. The screen said the call was from Lundquist, but he declined the call and let it go to voicemail.

"What I tell you, I say in the strictest confidence. Do you agree not to share this and to keep the students' names out of your discussion with the faculty and the school board?"

"I do."

"Independently of one another, Rich Amitrano and Sara York have given my department credible information that a female teacher on staff here had an intimate relationship with Chris Grimm and that relationship extended beyond romance to include the distribution of drugs on school grounds."

She said, "Some of them will refuse and want a union rep or lawyer."

"We'll invite them to bring their reps and lawyers to the station."

"Then I had better call the president of the school board."

"I doubt this will make you feel any better, but I think this is almost over."

"You're right, Jesse. It doesn't."

———

AS WAS HIS PATTERN OF LATE, Jesse stopped by the art rooms on his way out of the building. This time, however, there was no joy in him at the prospect of seeing Maryglenn. He did his usual peeking through the door glass and waiting for a pause in her lesson. When she spotted him lurking, she stepped out to join him in the hall.

"You look terrible," she said. "Is it Cole? Petra North? Has she—"

"Cole will be fine. I'm going to pick him up now. Petra's condition is unchanged."

"Then what?"

"We have to talk . . . tonight."

"That sounds ominous."

He didn't deny it but said, "After my meeting, but if that doesn't work for you—"

"That's fine."

"Tonight."

He turned and walked down the hallway without looking back.

Seventy-two

He listened to Lundquist's voicemail as he strode to the car. He didn't say much, but there was something foreboding in Lundquist's voice.

Jesse sat in the front seat of the cruiser and returned the call.

"You ever think about taking your act on the road or handicapping at the track?" Lundquist asked.

"No riddles, Brian. I'm not in the mood."

"Boston Homicide is having a busy day. You called it. Millie Lutz and Rajiv Laghari, both murdered. Lutz was shot to death early this morning driving away from Wexler's house. Pro hitter, all the way. Motorcycle drive-by. Laghari's death is more interesting. A junkie allegedly stabbed the good doctor to death in the vestibule of his condo. Want to guess what Boston PD Joint Task Force detective was there to arrest the doctor, showed up just two seconds too late to save Laghari, but was Johnny-on-the-spot to shoot the perpetrator to death?"

"Detective Hector."

"Bingo."

"Loose ends no more."

"Looks that way."

"Any other predictions, Nostradamus?"

"If I worked at Precious Pawn and Loan on Washington Street in the South End, I might watch out. And a guy named Arakel Sarkassian might want to start wearing a Kevlar vest."

"You're a little late on the pawn shop."

"Two victims?" Jesse asked. "Man and a woman?"

"Nice recovery, Kreskin. Yes. A robbery gone wrong."

"You still believe in the tooth fairy and Santa?"

"Santa. I never believed in the tooth fairy. But I hear what you're saying. More loose ends taken care of. Who is this Sarkassian guy?"

"Maybe no one, but he had a connection to Chris Grimm. I'll text you what I have on him."

Lundquist cleared his throat. "Far as I can tell, Sarkassian is still drawing breath. How's your boy?"

"I'm headed over to the hospital to pick him up."

"Good—oh, Jesse, one more thing."

"Uh-huh."

"The white van, we got it on video in Helton and coming out of Helton."

"You think the Grimm kid was killed in Helton and dumped on the way out of town?"

"Maybe so. That's how I'm looking at the case, working back from where the body was discovered into Helton."

Jesse wanted to know. "Any hits on the McDonald's angle?"

"None in or near Helton."

"Okay, Brian. Thanks. Can you send me the surveillance camera footage?"

"Will do."

———

BEFORE HEADING TO THE HOSPITAL, Jesse drove into the Swap. Jesse's Explorer had been flatbed-towed over to Galliano's Auto Body Shop on Trench Alley. Over the last several years, Jesse and Tony Galliano had become well acquainted. Jesse's old Explorer, the one he'd had since L.A., had been shot to hell and wrecked during a wild car chase that had ended in a fiery explosion not far from the body shop, and a few months ago his new Explorer was deliberately rammed off the Bluffs and destroyed.

"Hey, Chief, you ever think maybe you might try a surplus tank or something?" Tony said, as he walked to greet Jesse. "You're freakin' murder on Explorers."

"Totaled?"

Tony shrugged. "That's up to your insurance adjuster. All I know is the replacement airbags alone will cost a fortune, never mind the body work. Jeez, Jesse, you think you can manage not to roll the next one over? That's two outta three."

"My son was driving."

Tony's cheery face became confused. "Son? You got a son? Runs in the family, then."

"Long story for another time."

"Yeah, sure."

"You think I can have a look at it?"

"You own it . . . at least until the adjuster gets here. C'mon with me."

Tony walked Jesse around behind the shop to the small lot where he kept the cars waiting to be worked on. When Jesse saw his SUV, he knew that totaling the thing would be a formality. It was damaged in a way only a rollover accident can damage a vehicle. But remembering what Cole had said about the van, he stepped to look at the driver's side of the Explorer.

Tony spoke before Jesse had the chance. "Kid's lucky. Looks like a vehicle wedged into the driver's-side rear wheel well. Look how the quarter panel is pushed in. And you see how it's sitting leaning over like that? That whole side of the suspension is bent up. So you want to take your stuff out of it?"

"I'll send someone over for that. Thanks. I've got to go."

Tony slapped Jesse on the shoulder. "Okay. In the meantime, I'll get you some prices on a used Abrams tank."

But Jesse wasn't listening. He realized that he'd been meant to be the first loose end to be tied up.

Seventy-three

When she answered the door, it was obvious on her face. She feared Jesse had found her out, he knew her secret. Or, if not the secret itself, that she had one. And it was a secret she thought was safe in a place like Paradise. She had thought, she hoped, foolishly, that living in a small town above a warehouse on a dead-end street and doing her art was cover enough. But experience should have taught her that circumstance could lay you bare, no matter how carefully you planned your moves or how small you made your life. When she saw the file in Jesse's hand, it confirmed her fears.

"Come on up," she said.

In her apartment, there was a half-empty open bottle of Malbec and a lipstick-smeared glass next to it on the kitchen table. There were only a few purple drops at the bottom of the stemmed, bell-shaped wineglass. Before she sat down or offered Jesse a seat, she poured more wine into her glass and took a swig. Jesse had never seen this version of Maryglenn before. As he now understood, there were several versions of Maryglenn, seen and unseen.

As he walked past her, Jesse placed the file on the table next to the bottle. He sat on a beat-into-submission leather chair that looked like it had begun life a decade or two before in a doctor's waiting room. Still, it was a comfortable chair that suited Jesse, given how uncomfortable their conversation was bound to be. Like almost everything else in the apartment, the chair was flecked with paint.

Maryglenn flipped open the file, thumbed through the pages, and finished her wine.

"Do you so thoroughly investigate all the women you sleep with?" She laughed in a joyless way. "Must be quite a collection of files you have."

"I hope you know better than that."

She poured herself another glass. "Then why?"

"I can't tell you that, but you'll know why tomorrow."

"The drugs." She fixed her lips into a pained smile. "The reason you've been around school so frequently. You think I'm involved somehow."

"Are you?" Jesse stood. Walked to the large window that looked out at the yacht club, Stiles Island, and the Atlantic. "All that file tells me is you've got something to hide, but it doesn't tell me what it is or why."

"Don't you have things to hide, Jesse?"

"Of course, but none of them worthy of name changes and false histories. I always wondered why we never talked about your past. I know you are from around Nashville. At least that's what your accent tells me. You say you went to art school, but I don't know which one. You call yourself Maryglenn, but—"

"We don't talk much about my past because we're often preoccupied."

Now it was his turn for a joyless laugh. "True."

"There were no lies in there, Jesse." She pointed to her bed and then to her heart. "Or in here. No, my name isn't Maryglenn, but it's the name I gave myself. I like it. Better to have a name that draws attention than one that is plain as a sheet of white paper. People who try too hard to hide make it obvious they're hiding. Besides, Maryglenn is a good name for a painter."

"Witness protection?"

"I can't say."

He asked, "That story about your leg."

"A lie. The injuries and the pain were real enough, though."

Jesse pointed at the bed. "A lie told in bed. Just contradicted yourself."

"You know what I meant."

"I would know what most women meant, but you aren't most women."

"How I sometimes wish I were. Who else knows?"

Jesse shook his head. "Knows what? All I know is what I don't know."

"That's beneath you, Jesse."

Jesse changed subjects. "You know about my fiancée, don't you?"

"Diana. I know what I've heard. That she was murdered and the killer escaped."

"She had a secret, too. When we met, she was an FBI special agent using an alias and working undercover."

"What does that say about you, do you think?"

"I'm not sure, but I'm not here about me."

She laughed. "You think not? Jesse Stone, police chief, homicide detective, blind man."

"Maybe." Jesse picked up the file and went to the door. "I gave you a chance to explain and you didn't. Don't run and don't be absent from school tomorrow."

He let himself out without saying goodbye.

Seventy-four

He had resisted making the call, but now felt he had no choice. He had hoped that by confronting her she would explain herself. But Jesse was a realist, if nothing else. Anyone who had worked so hard to cover her tracks was unlikely to just cop to the facts because someone, even her lover, asked her to remove the veil from her past.

Molly had picked up on it almost immediately; something wasn't right with Maryglenn's background. When she had asked for yearbook photos from the schools Maryglenn was alleged to have attended, there were none. None of the administrators at those schools remembered her. She had gotten contact info for some of the faculty alleged to have taught her. None remembered her. Molly was a bulldog that way. That's why Jesse had always been convinced she would have been a great detective. She had the instinct, the skepticism, and the drive. Once she had found those inconsistencies in Maryglenn's past, she found others.

Jesse might have been inclined to let things be, were he not aware of some of the abuses by people covered by programs like witness protection. For one thing, most of the people involved in such programs were usually criminals themselves, protected only because they could give up other criminals, ones even worse than themselves. And he knew that the branches of law enforcement administering these types of programs often went out of their way to shield their witnesses from prosecution for other local or unrelated crimes. There had been cases of protected witnesses dealing drugs, robbing banks, raping, committing murder. For all Jesse knew, Maryglenn could have been guilty of anything. He had hoped, if not to get the whole story, at least enough of it to eliminate Maryglenn as a suspect in the drug ring. What he got instead were his own suspicions reinforced.

He scrolled to the name Abe Rosen and pressed the number.

Abraham Rosen had been a colleague of Diana's at the FBI. Like most straight men who knew her, Abe had been a little bit in love with Diana. More than a little bit, but Abe was different from those others. He had understood Diana, understood why she had undertaken the mission that led to her being forced out of the Bureau. He understood her frustration at never being taken seriously because of her looks. Even understood why she had fallen for a man like Jesse Stone.

Although Jesse had tried to throw himself between the gunman and the bullet that had taken her life, Diana's parents and just about everyone else from Diana's old life blamed Jesse for her murder. The perception that Jesse had allowed her killer to escape made their pain that much worse. The facts of what had actually happened in the wake of Diana's murder was his and Vinnie Morris's secret to bear. So furious and grief-stricken were her parents, they had refused to let him attend her funeral. If there was anyone

Jesse was tempted to share the truth with, it was Abe, but that could never happen. Jesse had already traded once or twice on Abe's enduring affection for Diana. He was going to that well again.

"Jesse Stone," Rosen said. There was little enthusiasm in his voice. "Another favor?"

"Uh-huh."

"What is it this time?"

"I will email a file to you. You'll understand when you get it. I need an answer asap."

"Always. Am I risking my career this time?"

"Doubt it."

"You know, Stone, my having been in love with Diana doesn't give you carte blanche with me."

"Never thought it did. But Diana always said you believed in right and wrong."

Rosen cleared his throat, said, "Things were rough there a few months back. Big news. We had people inside that racist bastard's organization, and you did more to damage it than we ever could."

"They were never going to win, but they came pretty close to killing a lot of people."

"Diana would have been proud of you." Abe's voice was brittle.

"I'd like to think so."

"I miss her."

"Hard woman not to miss."

"Send me the file and I'll see what I can do."

Rosen was off the phone.

Jesse sat there for a few minutes, thinking about Diana. He had forgiven her for lying to him because he understood why she had lied. He hoped he could do the same for Maryglenn or whatever her name was, but it was going to be impossible if she stood by her lies. Sometimes he still missed drinking. Although he had walked out of an AA meeting less than an hour ago, tonight was one of those times.

Seventy-five

When Jesse got in the night before, Cole had been sleeping. He was still asleep when Jesse left for work. But the sun and most of Paradise were still sleeping, too. As he drove to the station from his condo, he stared at the brightening skies over the Atlantic.

There was a certain quality of light to the sunsets in L.A. that was like no other. He was not a man capable of the poetry it would have required to do justice to the dusk in L.A. Not even sundown in Tucson could compare. Here in the East, it was sunrise for Jesse. In L.A., sunrise often meant the ground-hugging clouds of the marine layer and a leap of faith that the sun was out there somewhere. Not here. Here the mornings were so beautifully blue that they almost hurt. Jesse, though, enjoyed the dangerous pink dawns—*Pink sky at dawn, sailors be warned*—even more than the severe blue ones. Today, there was no joy in the pink morning skies for Jesse Stone.

He had emailed the file to Rosen as promised, but there had been no response. Of course there hadn't been. Jesse had sent it after hours, and it was before hours now. When he got in to work, Suit was at the desk, reading a Boston paper. Jesse noted the headline:

Bloody, Bloody Boston

He saw the photos beneath: Millie Lutz's Corolla, a string of crime scene tape stretched across the front of Precious Pawn and Loan, and the ME's men with a body bag slung between them at Rajiv Laghari's condo.

"Reading about the murders?" Jesse said.

"Bad day for BPD."

"Say anything about the homicides being connected?"

"Wait a second. Where was it? Here." Suit folded the paper and pointed with his finger. "'*Millie Lutz was ambushed as she was returning home from work. She was a caretaker for once prominent orthopedist Dr. Myron Wexler. When reached for comment, two of Dr. Wexler's colleagues noted that the doctor had been suffering with severe Alzheimer's disease for the past several years. Dr. Rajiv Laghari, also an orthopedist, was slain by an as-yet-unidentified man who police speculate had been a patient of the doctor's. The assailant was in turn slain by an unidentified member of the Boston Police Department. Unnamed sources confirm that both men were under investigation by state regulatory agencies and law enforcement. Spokespersons for both the regulatory agencies and law enforcement refused comment . . . '* You know something about this, Jesse?"

"Remember I went down to Boston?"

"Yeah."

"I spoke with Millie Lutz inside Dr. Wexler's house. That pawn receipt we found in Chris Grimm's room was from Precious Pawn and Loan, and I sat outside a clinic run by Dr. Laghari. I think we can draw a straight line from Heather Mackey's OD to Chris

Grimm's murder to Petra North's OD to these killings and to Cole's accident."

Suit sat sharply back in his chair, as if avoiding something thrown at his head. "What?"

"That was no accident. They thought I was driving the Explorer. Everybody is playing for keeps now. Us, too."

Jesse walked into his office, picked up his new glove, and pounded the ball.

SHE HAD COME TO SCHOOL EARLY, but not to work on schedules or lesson plans. It was to work on her own survival. She had been planning to do this anyway, but after she crushed up and snorted her wake-up hit, and listened to the news as she dressed, the level of urgency was in the red. She would cry no tears for Rajiv Laghari, the doctor she had been "referred" to. He had been pleasant and accommodating on her first script visit. That had changed on her subsequent trips to his storefront clinic. The extorted sex was sickening and reason enough to detest the man, but it was Laghari who had introduced her to Arakel Sarkassian and turned her into the desperate, manipulative whore looking back at her from her bedroom mirror.

There was a time a million years ago that the high from her morning hit coursing through her veins would have made it all feel all right. That was the amazing power of the drug, the euphoria and untouchability it gave her. She had been a bulletproof goddess in her own heaven. Now there were bullets everywhere, nothing to keep them out, and heaven was barren of goddesses.

She didn't fool herself that this would be her final act of debasement or treachery, but she had learned not to think too far ahead or to assume there was a bottom to hit or how low it would be. She would do this thing, and when everyone was sure they had who they were looking for, she would vanish. She had done things like this before and didn't think this would be especially hard to pull off. A careless whisper, a note, and it would be done.

JESSE STOPPED THE POUNDING. It was no good. He would never get used to this style of glove. He was an old dog who had learned some new tricks, but there were some he didn't choose to learn. He put the glove down and booted up his computer. He spotted the email from Lundquist that came with an attachment. Jesse clicked open the attachment. It was a series of time- and date-stamped still shots gleaned from Helton CCTV footage. The white van that had shown up on footage from Kennedy Park was prominently featured in these shots from Helton. They showed the van both entering and leaving town. It had also appeared on street cameras. The one shot that got Jesse's attention was a photo taken by a red-light camera. The license plate was obscured, but the face of the driver was clear. It was a face Jesse recognized, a brutal one. It was the face of the man who had guarded the door at the storefront clinic in Roxbury.

Seventy-six

By the time Jesse emerged from his office, Gabe Weathers had replaced Suit at the desk. Molly was off the desk for the day, as she was going to accompany Jesse to the high school. It was a sad commentary on the state of things, but Jesse made sure to have a female officer with him whenever questioning a female subject or suspect. With Alisha fired, that duty always fell to Molly.

"You ready, Molly?"

She nodded. "The files are in the car."

"Gabe, anything comes up . . ."

"I know where to find you, Jesse."

At first, they made small talk. It didn't last. Jesse reiterated that the people to be interviewed had the right to refuse or to be accompanied by a union rep or lawyer.

"Just remind them that if they refuse this interview, we'll do what we did with Petra North. We'll make it formal and do it in the interview room at the station."

"I know, Jesse." Molly then broached the inevitable question. "So, did you discuss it with her?"

Jesse understood who Molly was talking about. "I did."

"Anything? Did Maryglenn explain herself at all?"

"No."

Seeing the look on Jesse's face, Molly dropped it. Even aside from interrogating Maryglenn, neither of them looked forward to this exercise. While there was a chance more than one teacher was involved in the drug supply chain or that their intel was wrong, they both thought either unlikely. And this sort of mass interview was a clunky way to go about it, but until there was more specific information or until they caught a break, it seemed like their only option. When they got to the school, Molly reminded Jesse of something that had almost slipped her mind.

"Chris Grimm's burial is this afternoon, but we won't have time."

"We'll make time. We need to be there."

With that, they got out of the car and headed to Principal Wester's office.

VIRGINIA WESTER WAS no happier about this approach to finding the suspect than Jesse and Molly were, nor any more enthused than she had been when it was proposed.

"Jesse, this is causing real turmoil. The school board is furious, and all the union reps . . . you can imagine."

"If another student dies," he said, "that will be real turmoil."

Wester had Freda walk Molly and Jesse to an empty office in the administrative suite, in which there was a desk and several chairs.

Freda said, "Virginia has instructed me to help you any way I can."

Jesse smiled. "Thank you, Freda. You will escort Molly to get each person we want to interview, and you can escort them back here. Between interviews, you can do your work. We want to interfere as little as possible." He pulled a file out of the stack. "Let's start with Joan Grace."

THE INTERVIEWS WITH JOAN GRACE, Tricia Allen, Ellen Schare, Marla Bayles, Jaqueline Goodwin, and Ming Parson were all of a type. They were unsettled to begin with, and when they sat across from a silent, blank-faced Jesse Stone, their levels of anxiety rose considerably. They all babbled nervously at first, just like their male counterparts would have. Most expressed a dislike of being suspected and claimed no knowledge of the drug problem in school. They all denied any involvement. Jesse believed them. He thanked them for their time, apologized for upsetting them, and wished them well.

It wasn't until Molly and Freda escorted Wendy Sherman into the office that things changed.

Wendy, a history teacher, was in her mid-thirties, with shoulder-length dark auburn hair, bright brown eyes, and a normally white and cheery smile. She wasn't smiling when she sat down across from Jesse and seemed much edgier than the other women had been. She kept looking over her shoulder at Freda, as if she was more unnerved by the principal's administrative assistant than she was by Jesse and Molly.

Jesse picked up on the cue, and while still standing to greet Wendy, said, "Thank you, Freda."

Even after Freda had left, Wendy kept checking over her shoulder. Molly had noticed, too, and said, "What is it, Wendy? What's wrong?"

"I swear someone just left this for me on my desk." The teacher reached into her bag and handed Jesse a computer-generated note.

Jesse, holding the paper at the edge between the nails of his left thumb and index finger, read the note. He wagged his finger at Molly to come read the note as well. Without having to be told, Molly left the office.

"How many people have seen this note and how many people have touched it?" Jesse asked.

"Just me."

But Jesse sensed Wendy had more to say.

"Wendy, if you have more to add, I need to hear it."

"But . . . I like—she's a friend, Jesse. We all like her."

Thinking of Gino Fish and Vinnie Morris, Jesse said, "I like people who've done bad things, too."

"There have been rumors about her . . . you know."

"Please don't make this harder for both of us, Wendy."

"Just this morning, at the Keurig machine, I heard people talking about how they'd seen her spending a lot of time with Chris Grimm and Petra North."

"People? What people?"

"I don't remember, people, the other teachers who were standing around the machine behind me," Wendy said. She was on the verge of tears.

Jesse didn't believe Wendy couldn't remember, but it was always the same. It didn't matter if it was the police department, a school faculty, or a baseball team. No one wants to be a rat. And while she could justify passing the note on to Jesse, it would be harder for Wendy to justify naming names not mentioned in the note.

"That's okay, Wendy."

Molly reentered the office. She held an evidence bag and two pairs of gloves. Both of them gloved up and placed the note inside the evidence bag. That done, Jesse removed his gloves, stood up, and took the note.

"Wendy," he said, "Molly will take a full statement from you about the note. We need that on the record. Thank you. I'm sorry if this has been stressful."

First, he had to get Principal Wester. Then he had to search the supply closet in the art room, where he was sure he would find drugs.

Seventy-seven

Maryglenn took the cuffs being clicked about her wrists by Molly without incident. They had escorted her outside and had moved the cruiser to a side entrance, out of sight of the students, before they cuffed her. There had been no protestations of innocence or of a setup, though she and Jesse knew that both of those things were true. Well, he was sure that Maryglenn had been set up. He was less certain of her innocence as a state of being. No one hiding their past is innocent, but of her innocence concerning the drugs, Jesse was sure. Jesse's certainty, however, would not stand up in court, not against what they had found in a box at the back of the art supply closet.

There they had found a vial containing both Oxycontin and Vicodin, three packets of powder that would prove to be heroin cut with fentanyl, and, most damning of all, a vial containing a powdery substance that, when analyzed, would prove identical to the powder found beside Petra North. The setup had been simultaneously amateurish and very effective.

"We won't find your fingerprints on any of it, will we?" Jesse said through the metal screen that separated the front of the cruiser from the rear.

"Unlikely, unless the person who did this found a way to transfer prints."

Molly glared at Jesse.

"Relax, Molly. She's been Mirandized." He turned back to Maryglenn. "Any ideas about who? Spot any other teachers in the art room nosing around?"

"No, but we don't keep the classrooms locked and lots of people have access to the art supplies."

"Anybody with a grudge?"

"Apparently."

Neither Maryglenn nor Jesse could help themselves from laughing.

Again, Molly glared at Jesse.

Jesse's cell buzzed. Abe Rosen's name flashed on the screen. Before he picked up, Jesse asked the women in the car to be quiet. When they both nodded, Jesse put the call on speaker.

"Abe."

"Stone."

"Got anything for me?"

"I've gotten warned off this woman's file by upper management. The minute I started looking, it set off all kinds of warnings."

"Witness Protection?"

"No. I have contacts at the Marshals Service and we can usually gain access to the files of those in the program because it's law enforcement. We often need to access those people for trial prep and debriefing. At the very least, I can find out if they are in the program or not and why. They've never heard of your subject and they weren't bullshitting me."

"What, then?"

"Best guess?"

Jesse said, "If that's all you've got."

"CIA, military intel, or State Department intel. I did some time in counterintelligence, so I'm familiar with this sort of thing. It's not detailed enough to be a cover story for infiltration. There are too many holes in it. Besides, who is she going to infiltrate up in Paradise, the Portuguese Fisherman's Association?"

"What is it, then?"

"Again, this is an educated guess. I think it's an exit cover for someone to leave an agency. A story that would pass muster if the scrutiny weren't too intense."

"They do this for everyone?"

"Not hardly," Abe said.

"Thanks, Abe."

"Stone."

"What?"

"Don't call again."

Jesse hung up, faced the metal grate, and said, "Well?"

Maryglenn sat back, refusing to speak for the remainder of the ride into the station. She didn't speak when she was booked or when Jesse attempted to interview her, didn't ask for a phone call or a lawyer. So they put her in a cell and left her there.

THE ONLY PEOPLE at Chris Grimm's burial were his mother, Jesse, Molly, and Rich Amitrano. Jesse looked at Rich and remembered how teenage crushes persisted and that sometimes not even death could interfere. Kathy Walters's husband, Joe, was nowhere to be seen. The sun was out, the wind blowing so strong the priest could not keep his place in the Bible. He recited the remainder of Psalm Twenty-three from memory. Molly mouthed the words with him.

Jesse kept his eye out for anyone who didn't belong. But they were alone except for the groundskeepers and the men hanging back to cover Chris Grimm's coffin in dirt.

When it was done, Jesse approached Kathy Walters. She wasn't crying. Hadn't cried through the service, and she didn't look about to break down. She looked resigned.

"I failed him. I was never no good, and my nonsense helped plant him there."

Jesse could see she was in no mood to be consoled or argued with. "Where's Joe?"

She snorted. "I moved out. If I want to atone for the wrong I done my boy, I can't stay with that man. Thank you and your lady officer there for coming. That was a kindness I didn't expect."

"Good luck."

As they walked away from the grave, Jesse noticed Rich Amitrano trailing behind them.

"Molly, I'll meet you at the car in a minute."

Molly went on, but Jesse stood his ground and waited for the boy to catch up.

"I felt like I should come because I knew no one else would," Rich said. "What he did was wrong, but you know how I felt about him."

"It was a good thing to do."

"Chief—Jesse—this may sound stupid, but I've been thinking."

"About what?"

"I think I'd like to be a policeman." He laughed a mocking laugh. "Stupid, right?"

"Why is it stupid?"

"You know, because I'm . . . You know, I'm gay."

"We are what we are, kid." Jesse tapped Rich on the temple and on the chest. "The only thing I care about is who you are in there and in there and whether or not you can do the job. The rest doesn't matter to me."

"You mean it?"

"Absolutely. When you graduate, come talk to me and we'll see about it."

The kid turned and headed to his car. Jesse did the same.

Seventy-eight

Before she opened her eyes or was awake, she became aware of the odd smells: the powerful tang of alcohol, of pine and chlorine and just beneath the chemicals, the sour and nauseating stink of human waste and decay. Then there were the sounds: the *whoosh whoosh* of machinery, the video game pinging, the hushed voices and distant groaning. When her eyes fluttered open, she was lost, disoriented. *God, where am I?* She jerked up. She tried to speak, but she couldn't. She was gagging, choking, a thing stuck down her throat. Instinctively, reflexively, she grabbed and clawed at the thing in her throat. Bells rang. Lights flashed. Strong arms grabbed her, hands pushed her back onto the bed. A soft hand stroked her cheek to calm her.

JESSE SAT ON A STOOL outside the bars of the cell. Maryglenn hadn't said a word since Jesse received Abe Rosen's phone call in the car. Hadn't asked for her phone call. Hadn't asked for a lawyer. Jesse, in turn, had asked her if she wanted an attorney. He suggested his friend Monty Bernstein, a slick and talented Boston lawyer. She hadn't even bothered shaking her head no. But Jesse was determined she was going to get a lawyer of some kind, whether she wanted one or not. When the legal aid lawyer showed up, she refused to talk to him. So Jesse sat with her. She lay on the bed in the cell, face to the wall, the silence between them loud and unceasing.

"I have to go see how my son is doing," he said, looking at his watch. "But I'll be back in the morning."

She didn't stir.

SHE HAD PULLED IT OFF, deflected attention from herself, but she wasn't sure how long it was going to stick. The other, more dangerous factor was the girl. As long as Petra was alive, she couldn't count on the girl. As silly and moony as Petra was for her, even she would have her limits. Once the police convinced Petra the powdery concoction mashed up for her by her lover was meant to kill her, the girl would give her up. The problem was eliminating one if from the equation and substituting another in its place. If the girl never woke up, she could then move on. But there was another problem, a more immediate one. In setting up Maryglenn, she had nearly exhausted her supply. If she didn't score soon, none of it would matter. She figured to fix both problems with one call.

ARAKEL WAS PLEASED to hear the news about the deflection, but not about the girl clinging to life.

"You should have made sure," he said, his anger obvious.

"I made the stuff so strong, it should have killed her."

"Yes, should have." He paused in order to take a gulp of vodka.

"There have been many should-haves that have not been where you are concerned. Have you read a Boston paper recently?"

She swallowed hard before answering. "Yes. I've read about the mur—the deaths."

"Then you understand. I will see about the girl, but you have to disappear . . . soon."

"But I need—"

"At the moment I care very little for what you need. What I need for you is to prepare to go away."

He was off the line, but she had already stopped listening to him. She was staring at the white plastic container on her dresser. The one that was nearly empty of everything but the silicate drying packets. It held the few pills she had left to her. She had no choice but to score.

COLE'S FACIAL BRUISES had darkened and he looked worse than he had the day of the accident. Even so, he claimed to feel better. Jesse had already explained that the car accident was no accident and that he, not Cole, was the intended target.

Cole had laughed it off and said, "Jeez, Dad, it was safer when I hated you."

It stung, but Jesse realized his son was in no shape to comprehend how that comment hurt. Two important women in Jesse's life had been murdered due simply to having a relationship with him: Abby and Diana. And there it was again, the thirst. So he was learning how important the meetings were, because there was no way to control what would trigger the thirst. With Maryglenn in a cell and the real suspect still out there, he had no time for a meeting. He excused himself and went into his bedroom to call his sponsor, but as he was scrolling for Bill's number, the cell vibrated in his hand. His landline rang as well. For once, the simultaneous calls were a good omen.

ARAKEL TURNED TO Stojan and Georgi. He despised these men for what they were and for what they had forced him to become.

"The time is here," he said. "Go to Paradise. The girl and the teacher. No torturing them, none of your twisted pleasures. Just kill them and be done with it."

Stojan screwed his ugly lips up into a sneer. "The teacher, yes. We are already told to do this. We know where she is. She is a threat."

"I said no torturing. Just kill her."

Stojan laughed. "We have instructions. We do not listen to weak fools." He pointed his thick, gnarled index finger at Arakel. "The girl, you. You, you do the girl."

Arakel thought he had not heard correctly. "What did you say to me?"

"You are hearing right, rug merchant." He stepped close, jabbed his big ugly finger into Sarkassian's chest. "You are wanting the girl dead, you do it. You have gun. You have killed. Is easier the next time. I know it. Right, Georgi?"

Silent, Georgi nodded.

"See, Georgi says so."

"The girl is in a hospital under police guard."

Stojan frowned and shrugged. "Too bad on you. You wanting the girl dead, is for you to make it so. Georgi, *neka trugnem*. Let's go!"

As the men walked away, Arakel grabbed Stojan by the shoulders. Stojan turned and slapped Arakel across the face, knocking him to the floor.

"We do not work for you, idiot. Yes, the teacher, she is a threat, maybe to all of us. The girl, she knows nothing of us, only of the teacher and maybe of you. Why should we kill this girl? Think of how you will enjoy prison when you are squeezing the trigger."

Arakel Sarkassian, the taste of his own blood in his mouth, was stunned and frightened. Frightened because the thug had confirmed for him what he always believed—that Stojan and Georgi were tools not of Mehdi and him, but of the people who had entrusted the franchise to them. Frightened, too, because the brute was right.

Seventy-nine

etra North's face went blank when she saw Jesse walk into the ICU. Her parents were on either side of her, and it was clear Annette had been crying. The shocking thing for Jesse was that Ambrose North's eyes were no less red. *Maybe,* Jesse thought, *it isn't so shocking after all.* He couldn't imagine how he would have reacted had the Explorer crash been worse and Cole's injuries more serious.

"Hi, Petra," he said. "Can I borrow your parents, just for a minute?"

She seemed relieved and a bit confused. "Sure."

The three of them stepped outside the unit, where Robbie Stanton was now stationed.

"Go get a cup of coffee, Robbie." Jesse tilted his head at the stairway door.

Before Jesse could speak, Ambrose said, "She's scared, Chief."

"Of what? We don't want to get her into trouble, we just want to get her help."

Ambrose turned to his wife. "Annette, go be with her. I'll be in momentarily."

Annette looked scared, opened her mouth to protest, but instead placed her hand on Jesse's forearm. "She was desperate, Jesse. Please remember that." Then she walked past him and back into the ICU.

"Jesse, I heard you have a teacher in custody. Is that correct?"

"Am I speaking to Ambrose North, Petra's father, or Ambrose North, attorney at law?"

"Both, I'm afraid."

"We have someone in custody."

North took Jesse by the left biceps and began walking down the hospital corridor. Jesse walked with him. "What if I told you I have it on good authority that you have the wrong woman in custody?"

"I know that already, but the evidence is damning. Until I can have someone or something to refute—"

"And what if I could give you the identity of the person you should have in custody? Would you be willing not to press charges of distribution of a controlled substance? Hypothetically speaking, of course."

"She dealt drugs, your hypothetical daughter?"

Ambrose flushed red, coughed. "This isn't easy for me to say, Jesse. This person, this other teacher, she . . . she seduced Pet— my hypothetical daughter. She promised to . . . God, this is difficult. She promised to continue their affair and to supply this daughter with drugs if she . . . did what she asked. It lasted for only a few days. Jesse, please. I'm begging you as a father not to imperil her future."

Jesse dropped the hypotheticals. "You know the charges are up to the prosecutor, but if you give me the name now and Petra is willing to testify, I will go to the wall for her with the prosecutor."

"That's not a guarantee, Jesse."

"Not mine to give, but I'll keep my word. I don't want to hurt any of these kids."

"I'm sorry," Ambrose North said, the strain evident on his face. "She's already been through so much and we didn't do the best for her in the past. Now we must. Call the DA's office and get someone over here."

"You're willing to let an innocent woman sit in jail?"

"I'm afraid so, if it means protecting Petra."

Jesse glared at the lawyer. "Then don't expect help from me, Mr. North. I was a professional baseball player. Trust me when I tell you, you don't know what hardball is. I walk out the front door of this hospital without that name and Petra's on her own with no backing from me."

Robbie Stanton returned, a white foam cup in hand, steam rising through a hole in the lid. The aroma cutting against the medicinal smells of the hospital.

"She's a target now," Jesse said to Robbie, loud enough for North to hear. "No one in but the parents, the doctors, and the nurses. Any of the visitors you don't recognize need approval from a nurse or a doctor. No excuses, no stories. I'll have Suit send someone down to help, but no bathroom breaks until your backup arrives."

"Okay, Jesse." Stanton took a sip of his coffee and put the cup on his chair. He stood outside the ICU entrance, arms folded across his chest.

Before leaving, Jesse turned to Ambrose North. "Remember what I said."

SHE HAD WHITTLED DOWN her essentials to two suitcases and a gym bag, but she knew her only real essentials were the dwindling tablets she rattled inside the white pharmaceutical container. She had just crushed up one of the few left to her and snorted it. It helped calm and focus her, but it removed some of the urgency from her packing.

Her plan, such as it was, was to head down to Boston. She still had some connections there that might help her out, at least enough to get her through for a few days. Then she was going to head west, call in to work from the road about a dying aunt or a sick uncle. Maybe if the girl died and things calmed down, she could come back and reclaim her job, but that was all too far ahead for her. At the moment, she was waiting for a call back from her old boyfriend from Boston, a doctor who had once professed love for her. If he allowed, she would put that faded love to the test. She was perfectly willing to prove herself to him. She hoped he would ask. She liked the idea of sleeping with an adult again, especially one who could write scripts and make her healthy.

The phone rang, and when she answered, she fairly purred into the mouthpiece.

Eighty

As the first set of automatic doors at the front entrance of Paradise General slid open, Jesse thought he spotted a vaguely familiar face coming toward him. The man, thirty yards away, illuminated by a pole lamp, seemed to spot Jesse at the same moment. The man stopped walking and turned away as Jesse came quickly through the second set of automatic doors. Approaching him, Jesse tried to put a name to the man's face. Then it came to him. *Arakel Sarkassian.* And when the name came to him, Jesse realized there was only one reason that made any sense for Sarkassian to be at the hospital.

"Mr. Sarkassian," Jesse said calmly, reaching for his nine-millimeter.

Sarkassian jumped to his left, taking cover behind a granite wall. But before he could go after Sarkassian, someone called to Jesse.

"Jesse! Jesse! Chief Stone!" Jesse looked over his shoulder to see Ambrose North coming at him in a full run. "I'll give you the name."

"Get down! Everybody get down!" Jesse was shouting. "North, get down!"

The few people around the hospital entrance at that hour of the evening fell to the ground, facedown, instinctively covering their heads with their hands. But Ambrose North was still coming toward Jesse. When he looked back to check on Sarkassian, Jesse saw Sarkassian's upper body was above the wall ledge, a pistol in his right hand aimed in his direction. Jesse had a choice to make and no time in which to make it. He turned, dived, and knocked Ambrose North to the ground, bullets whining over their heads. The glass of the hospital doors shattered. People screamed. Sarkassian ran.

North grabbed Jesse's collar, pulled him close. His voice was strained and cracking, his fight-or-flight reflex in high gear. "Brandy Lawton," he said. "It's Brandy Lawton."

Jesse pushed himself up, fished his cell phone out of his pocket, and took off after Sarkassian.

BRANDY LAWTON BROUGHT HER suitcases to the door. Foolishly and out of habit, she went back through the house, checking to make sure the lights were all out and that the stove was off. It was amazing how some routines persisted in the face of everything. Satisfied, she went back to retrieve her bags and take them out to her car.

ACROSS THE STREET, leaning on the side of the van, Georgi waited for Stojan to give him the signal. If he had had his way, Stojan would simply have broken into the apartment or rung the bell and killed the woman when she came to the door. His first preference would have been to use a Kalashnikov, to drive past, spraying the woman with bullets. Witnesses shocked and frightened, escape made easy because he would already be on the move. But their bosses had been explicit in their instructions. *Kill her quietly by her car. Put her in the car. Make her disappear.* Stojan once again saw the teacher's silhouette at the door. The door opening slightly. Stojan banged his hand against the van. Georgi made his way to the opposite sidewalk.

JESSE, PHONE BACK IN HIS POCKET, weapon drawn, took off in a sprint. Sarkassian was darting in and out between cars in the hospital parking lot. Jesse had a few clear shots but did not fire for fear of hitting a passerby. Arakel Sarkassian had no such worries. As he ran, he would half turn, fire blindly behind him in Jesse's direction—windshields spiderwebbing, side windows shattering, alarms shrieking. Above the din of the car alarms, Jesse heard sirens. He thought to pen Sarkassian in at a corner of the fence surrounding the lot until backup arrived. Until then, he would bait Sarkassian into exhausting his ammunition.

BRANDY LAWTON PUT HER suitcases on the front porch, the gym bag slung over her shoulder. She locked the door, pulled up the handles on both suitcases, and walked toward her car, wheeling the rollerbags behind her. She stopped, hearing sirens in the distance. She snickered at herself, realizing the sirens probably had nothing to do with her. She pressed the key fob and popped open the trunk of her car.

———

STOJAN AND GEORGI HEARD THE SIRENS, too. They were louder, coming closer, very close.

Stojan yelled to Georgi. "Hurry up. *Bürzam! Bürzam!*"

Instead, Georgi froze and stared across at Stojan. Then saw the cruiser coming down the street.

BRANDY HEARD THAT VOICE, recognized it. It was the voice of the man who had threatened her the night she had taken the stash bag back from the girl. She dropped her bags and ran back to the front door.

GEORGI SPRINTED, his .22 Ruger with sound suppressor held in front of him as he ran.

ONE PARADISE POLICE car and Suit's pickup skidded to a halt in front of Brandy Lawton's driveway. Neither Suit nor Peter Perkins looked at the white van, focusing instead on the man with the pistol in his hand turning into the driveway. A bullet smashed the passenger-side back window of Perkins's cruiser. He hit the floor. Suit dived out the passenger side of his pickup, grabbed his nine-millimeter.

BRANDY LAWTON, panicked, nauseated with fear, dropped her keys at the door, bent down to pick them up.

———

GEORGI TURNED THE CORNER of the driveway and rushed toward the teacher. He raised the .22, squeezed the trigger once, heard a moan, glass breaking, but also heard more than one shot. He fell forward, facedown in the gravel, unable to move, confused because he felt no pain. His confusion came to an end as his hand relaxed around the butt of the gun and his blood spilled out of his wrecked veins and arteries into the cavities in his body. He laughed a short bark of a laugh, a laugh wet and red. The last sound he would ever make.

STOJAN HIT THE GAS, firing out the window as he went, bullets flattening tires on the cruiser and pickup. Peter Perkins rolled out of the cruiser, took aim at the van, and fired. Two bullets hit the van's rear doors, the hole visible to him. But the van was quickly out of range for an effective shot and, like Jesse, Perkins feared ricochets or stray bullets hitting civilians. The taillights disappeared.

AFTER CALLING IT in, Perkins stopped by Georgi's body. He checked for a pulse, found none. Suit had already kicked the .22 far away from the dead man. Perkins found Suit hunched over Brandy Lawton. He was pressing his hand to her neck, blood spurting out between his fingers. She was clutching at him with one hand, clawing at her gym bag with the other. Her eyes were big with fear, her mouth open. Perkins ran to the car to put a rush on the ambulance and to get the first-aid kit. By the time he returned, the blood had stopped spurting between Suit's fingers. Brandy Lawton had stopped clutching and clawing forever.

Suit's hands and uniform were covered in blood. He fell back against the wall next to Lawton's body and hung his head. "What do you think she was clawing at in the gym bag, Pete?"

Perkins, hands now gloved to begin doing the forensics, knelt down beside the dead woman and unzipped her gym bag. He pulled out a white pharmaceutical bottle and shook it at Suit. "This, probably."

"But she was dying."

"These damn things are why she's dead, Heather Mackey is dead, and why he's dead," Perkins said, pointing at Georgi's body. "It's a plague, Suit, a goddamn plague."

Eighty-one

Jesse saw the light bars flashing a block away, and the sirens were deafeningly loud. It wouldn't be long now until Sarkassian would have no place to go. Jesse wasn't certain about the man's weapon, but it didn't seem to have an extended magazine, and he'd used a lot of ammo already. If he could only get Sarkassian to waste a few more bullets . . . But just as he was feeling confident, a yellow Camaro convertible backed out of a spot near the corner of the lot Jesse had worked so hard to herd Sarkassian into. Jesse understood Arakel Sarkassian was many things, but he didn't think stupid was one of them. It hadn't escaped his notice that Jesse almost had him penned in.

He ran toward the Camaro and jumped in just as the driver, a woman in blue nurse's scrubs, stopped to put the car into drive. Sarkassian pressed the muzzle of the gun to her neck. But instead of freezing, the woman screamed and flailed at him. He slapped her across the face with the side of the gun and pressed it once again to her throat.

"Shut up and do as I say or I shall surely blow a hole through your throat."

The nurse quieted just as the patrol cars stopped at the parking-lot gate, their sirens finally silenced.

"Sarkassian," Jesse said, "you can't get out of here."

"Oh, but I will, one way or the other, Chief Stone. The question is who I will take with me. That is in your hands. Now drop your weapon and order your people away from the exit."

"Take me," Jesse said, dropping his nine-millimeter. "Let the nurse go and take me. I'll toss my cell. My people won't shoot while I'm in the car."

"Do not take me for a fool, Chief. Go to the gate and order your people away. Now!" For emphasis, Sarkassian yanked on the nurse's hair and put the barrel of his weapon in her mouth.

Jesse didn't bother trying to retrieve his gun and walked to the parking-lot gate. Gabe Weathers and John Spellman met Jesse there.

Before Jesse could speak, Gabe said, "Two hit men killed Brandy Lawton. Suit got one of them."

"Dead?"

"Dead. The other got away. He was driving a white van. Word is out."

"Hurry, Chief," Sarkassian said. "I am not certain the nurse will live much longer."

"Deploy your spike strips on either side of the exit. We can't afford him seeing them as the car pulls out. When the spikes are out, move your cars away."

Jesse went back into the lot and walked toward the Camaro, hands raised above his head. As Jesse got within ten feet of the Camaro and the cruisers pulled away from the parking-lot gate, Sarkassian removed the gun from the nurse's mouth.

"That is sufficiently close, Chief Stone. Be assured no harm will befall this woman as long as you try nothing foolish. Now step away, please." When Jesse had walked back ten paces, Sarkassian turned to the nurse and said, "Drive, quickly."

She put the car into drive, the tires squealing when she stepped down hard on the gas. The black-and-yellow barrier arm smashed against the windshield as the car barreled through the exit. Turning left out of the lot, there were four barely distinct *pop-pop-pop-pop*s as spikes dug into the tires. The Camaro slowed, but skidded because of the speed and the severe angle of the turn. Sarkassian was thrown against the door. By the time the Camaro came to a stop and Sarkassian had reoriented himself, Gabe Weathers had his nine-millimeter pointed at his head. Officer Spellman had already gotten the nurse out of the vehicle.

Sarkassian dropped his weapon. He wept as he was laid face-down, frisked, and cuffed.

AT THE STATION, Jesse and DA Malmon sat across from Arakel Sarkassian. The digital video camera was pointed at the prisoner, a yellow legal pad was on the table in front of him, a pen atop the pad. For the time being, the camera was switched off. None of them said a word, but for this once, Jesse wasn't willing to let silence be his weapon of choice.

"I have Brandy Lawton in a holding cell, Sarkassian," Jesse lied. "DA Malmon is in a deal-offering mood today. Isn't that right, Mr. DA?"

"It must be the warm weather, but yes."

Jesse said, "You are the bigger fish, Mr. Sarkassian, so you get first crack. But if you don't supply us with a full confession and accounting of the mechanics of your operation, we'll march from here into Brandy's cell, and given the fact that she is willing to say just about anything for a Vicodin . . . She may not be able to give us much, but she can sure as hell give us you."

Sarkassian laughed. "You need not threaten me, Chief Stone. A man can only drown himself once. I believe I have already accomplished that feat. You may turn on your camera."

Jesse hesitated. "First, the name and location of the men in the white van."

"Gladly." Sarkassian smiled. "Sending them away will almost make my sins worth it."

After gleefully giving up Stojan and Georgi, Sarkassian explained as much of the network as he could. He explained how they used area doctors and the pill mills to find candidates like Brandy to use for their purposes. He explained how addicts like Brandy were eager volunteers and were willing to do anything to keep their drugs coming.

"She would find someone like Chris or this Petra, seduce them, and we would exploit their weakness for Brandy to distribute our products. Foolishly, I had let Brandy introduce me to Chris. I helped arrange for him to sell the goods he received in trade with Precious Pawn. I should never have done such things. It was inexperience on my behalf. And then I came to very much like the boy . . ." Sarkassian's voice faded away.

He remembered what he had witnessed Stojan and Georgi do to Chris and how they had turned him into a murderer. When he spoke again, any hint of gleefulness was gone from his voice.

Eighty-two

Maryglenn was standing on the tarmac at the foot of the small jet's door ladder. The engines were spinning in earnest, whining. The air stank of spent jet fuel and hot metal. The wind was whipping her hair into her face. Her face was lit on and off and on again by the strobing wingtip lights. Three black Suburbans were parked between the two of them and the hangar. There were six blank-faced special-ops types spread out around the jet. All of them seemed so uncomfortable in their civilian clothes. They looked much more at ease with the M4s held at their chests.

Jesse was surprised to get the call and had been reluctant to go to the little private airport in Marshfield. Still, one thing therapy and rehab had taught him was to not swallow as much pain as he always had. He'd always been so damn stoic about everything. What he had come to realize was that his Marlboro Man act was not only a defense but a means of intimidation. *You can't hurt me. You can't touch me.* But of course he could be hurt. He hurt a lot, and the tough-guy act only drove the hurt deeper and made it more persistent. Besides, he wanted answers. Jesse always wanted answers.

"Thank you for coming, Jesse. This is very *Casablanca*." She laughed. "The airport farewell, I mean. All we need is Claude Rains, Humphrey Bogart, and the usual suspects."

Westerns were usually the movies Jesse loved, but he got the reference. He had seen *Casablanca*. Can't be a cop in Hollywood and not pick up on movie history, no matter how hard you might try to avoid it.

"The end of a beautiful friendship," he said.

She bowed her head. "Maybe not the end, but at least a temporary halt to things."

"Why am I here, Marygl—wait, that's not your name, is it?"

She smiled. It was a sad smile. "No fooling you, Chief Jesse Stone." She held her right hand out to him. "Esther. I can't tell you my last name. Sorry. I'm sorry for the lies."

He took her hand and could not deny feeling the jolt of attraction. That hadn't simply evaporated. "Nice to meet you, Esther. Very Old Testament."

"It was meant to be. Obviously, almost nothing you know about me is true. Well, I have always loved art. Art is the only way I manage to hold on to who I was."

"Anything else?"

She leaned forward, kissing him hard on the mouth. "That is true. I am more than a little in love with you, I think. I don't even understand it." She pulled back and studied his face in the strobe light. "I think you may feel the same."

Jesse said nothing, but smiled.

"I do very dangerous work, Jesse," she said. "I *did* dangerous work. Important work, and there are some people looking for me."

"Bad people."

"The worst kind of people and the most dangerous kind. People with revenge on their minds and people with nothing to lose. People who would kill themselves and everyone in Paradise if it meant getting to me."

"A new name a new place for you?"

"There's a file on the plane and someone to teach me about who I am and will be."

Jesse looked past Esther at the jet. There was a man's head in one of the portholes. The man was staring back at Jesse. "I'm sorry," he said. "They probably aren't pleased about you talking to me this way."

"I don't care. They owe me and I owed it to you. I'm sorry, too, but I can't risk other people's lives, especially not yours." She reached out and stroked Jesse's face. "If I can ever get word to you, I will. But get on with your life, Jesse. You deserve happiness. I'll miss you."

"I already miss you," Jesse heard himself say without quite believing it. He really was making progress. "Be safe and take care of yourself."

"I promise I will. Enjoy Cole's party. I wish I could be there."

Before Jesse could say anything, one of the special-ops types came and stood between them. He turned to Esther and said she had to go.

She said, "Give me a second."

When Special Ops hesitated, she stepped around him and threw her arms around Jesse. Jesse hugged her tight. When they let go of each other, the special-ops guy told Jesse he had to leave before the jet took off. He did as he was told and didn't look back.

Eighty-three

Jesse had the party for Cole at Daisy's two nights before he was to enter the academy. It had taken a lot
of schedule rigging to allow Suit, Molly, Gabe, Peter Perkins, and
their spouses to attend. Still, they managed to do it without the
collapse of the Paradise PD. Healy and his wife were there, as
well as Lundquist and his girlfriend. Jesse's AA sponsor, Bill,
came. Tamara Elkin, the former ME and Jesse's friend, came up
from Austin to meet Cole and to visit. Jesse had invited Jenn and
Hale Hunsicker out of some strange sense of pride and loyalty.
He was relieved when they sent their regrets. Hunsicker, being
Hunsicker, sent a thousand-dollar gift card along with their regrets. Even Dix had broken protocol to come. But what made his
son happiest was that Jesse had flown in Cole's two best friends
from L.A.

Daisy, who had given Cole a job and welcomed him even before
his father had, waved Jesse over. "Nice party. You shocked we
pulled it off, Stone?"

"I guess."

"You didn't invite your girlfriend."

Jesse laughed. "She was never my girlfriend, and she's gone now anyway."

"I knew that woman was an idiot. Didn't she realize what she had in you?"

"She had her reasons, Daisy. Reasons I agreed with."

"She ever tell you why I wasn't a fan of hers?"

Jesse shook his head. "No."

Daisy didn't quite believe him. She left it at that.

It had been a quiet month since Arakel Sarkassian's capture, but the town was changed by the violence in the streets as it had been changed by the violence and destruction of the old meeting-house. Though Jesse was at a loss to explain why, he felt these recent events were worse somehow. Maybe, he thought, the trouble with the white supremacists was like a virus that had run its course and gone. Sure, there was damage in its wake, but a form of immunity as well. If that disease came around again, they would recognize it. This was different. There would be no immunity from drugs, only temporary respites. Even now, he knew, there were greedy people in a room somewhere, planning on how to get a supply chain back up and running in towns like his. And though he had a lot to thank Vinnie Morris for, Jesse damned him for being right about the crime that had come to Paradise.

It was good that all the kids they knew about were in treatment. Petra North as well. The DA had declined to prosecute her. Jesse had no issue with the girl but found it difficult to forgive her father. He couldn't help but think that if Ambrose North had spoken up five minutes earlier, he could have spared a woman's life and saved Suit the trauma of killing a man. No one was shedding any tears for the man Suit had killed. He was a murderer, after all. Nor was anyone wringing their hands over Brandy Lawton's demise, especially not the North family. Yet Jesse understood she was a victim as well as a victimizer. Only an alcoholic or another addict could understand the hunger, the thirst, the ache.

Jesse knew despair. This wasn't despair, but it was in the ballpark. Because, in the end, Heather Mackey's passing would have little meaning in the scheme of things. There would be no one to pay the price. Chris Grimm, Brandy Lawton, and Georgi Lubinov were dead. The one name Arakel Sarkassian had given to the police that might have gotten them to the upper levels of the drug trade led nowhere. A week after the events in Paradise, Mehdi Khora's bullet-riddled body was found in the trunk of a stolen car in Maine, five miles south of the Canadian border.

If he lived long enough to get there, Sarkassian himself would spend the rest of his life in prison without chance of parole. He had foolishly neglected to mention killing Chris Grimm. When the ballistics reports matched the slugs from the shooting at the hospital to those removed from the Grimm boy's body, Sarkassian's fate was sealed. His repeated explanations about having killed Chris Grimm to save the boy from further pain fell on deaf ears. Only Stojan had gotten clear. By the time Lundquist and the Staties got to the warehouse in Helton, the van was a burnt-out hulk and Stojan was nowhere to be found.

"Hey, Dad," Cole said, noticing Jesse had isolated himself at a corner of the restaurant. "Why the face?"

"Nothing. I'm good."

"Thanks for this. Thanks for everything. Whose idea was it to fly Paul and Alan in from Woodland Hills?"

"Doesn't matter. I'm just glad you're happy."

"Here, this is for you," Cole said, handing Jesse a gift-wrapped package. "Before this, I haven't given you much except a hard time. It's my way of saying thanks for not giving up on me, on us, even though I was a real prick to you when I got to town. Open it up."

Jesse tore off the wrapping and opened the box. Inside was a brand-new glove, the exact model he wore when he played ball. Inside the glove was a baseball signed by Ozzie Smith to Jesse. He hugged his son harder than he'd ever dared.

"They don't make these gloves anymore. How did you get Ozzie—"

"Just say 'thank you' and put them on your desk."

"Thank you. Now go enjoy the rest of the party. You have some long days ahead of you."

As Cole walked away, Suit came toward Jesse. As Molly could read Jesse's expressions, Jesse could read Suit's. And what he saw in Suit's face wasn't good.

"I just got a call, Jesse. There's been a shooting."

JESSE HAD TRIED to get Suit to stay at the party, but it was no good. Truth was that Jesse was glad to have Suit with him. The address was in the Swap, a small basement apartment in a rickety old house three doors to the left of the Rusty Scupper bar. As they pulled up, they saw the one thing they dreaded seeing: the meat wagon from the ME's office. This was no longer just a shooting, but murder.

John was at the tape doing crowd control. As he lifted the tape for Jesse and Suit, he said, "The husband's in custody. Robbie took him back to the station to book him. We've bagged the weapon." He tilted his head at the short flight of stairs at the side of the house. "She's down there with the ME."

Jesse and Suit gloved up and carefully made their way down the steps. The door was open, and there in the middle of the small living room was Kathy Walters's body. She was on her back, eyes open, pale, expressionless. Even from where they stood in the doorway, Suit and Jesse could see that she had been shot several times at close range. There were defensive wounds on her hands.

"The husband had to be in a rage," Suit said, "to keep shooting her like that."

Jesse had nothing to add. Suit was right. But Jesse took no comfort in the fact that this wasn't the type of crime that had migrated up from Boston. That this was a crime as old as humanity, or at least as old as when humans began confusing love and ownership.

The ME looked over at Jesse. "I'm almost done here, Chief Stone. Better get your forensics man here."

Upstairs, Jesse called Peter Perkins, explained what had happened, and told him he was back on duty.

"What do you want me to do, Jesse?" Suit asked.

"When you get back to the party, get my friend Bill, and have him meet me in there," Jesse said, pointing at the front door of the Rusty Scupper.

Suit clamped one of his big hands on Jesse's shoulder. Jesse brushed Suit's hand away, walked the few paces to the Scupper's door, and disappeared.

WHEN BILL GOT there fifteen minutes later, he found Jesse, hand around a tall glass of Johnnie Walker Black, staring into the beautiful amber liquid as if staring into a bottomless pit. Both of them understood that a bottomless pit is exactly what it was.

Acknowledgments

I'd like to thank the estate of Robert B. Parker, Esther Newberg, Sara Minnich, Katie McKee, and all the folks at Putnam for their support and for giving me this opportunity.

But none of this would mean anything without the love and support of my family. Without Rosanne, Kaitlin, and Dylan, without their willingness to sacrifice on my behalf, none of this would have been possible. Thank you. I love you all more than I can say.